Curtains

The third novel in my *Tales from Great Yarmouth* series

– TONY GARETH SMITH –

An environmentally friendly book printed and bound in England by
www.printondemand-worldwide.com

www.fast-print.net/store.php

CURTAINS
Copyright © Tony Gareth Smith 2015

A catalogue record for this book is available from the British Library

ISBN 978-178456-251-9

First published 2015 by
FASTPRINT PUBLISHING
Peterborough, England.

Dedicated to

Catherine, Donna, Juley, Mrs Anna, Pippa, Sandra, Sue and Tara O'Hara.

And with a special mention to: Jo, Chris, Joe and Dee.

Boarding Tonight

A Short Tale from Great Yarmouth

Author of the novel *Twice Nightly* and *To Catch a Falling Star*
set in the world of seaside variety entertainment.

Website - www.twicenightly.net

Dedicated to my favourite nephew-in-law — Ian

Tony Gareth Smith

The conclusion of the short story "The Landladies Convention" (well nearly)???

The music box played Edelweiss as Shirley Llewellyn held her pearl earring studs to her ears and admired her new outfit from Palmers in the long mirror. She turned sideways to get a better look. Replacing the pearl studs she decided to wear the emerald studs which to her mind complemented her two piece. Closing the music box, she picked up her clasp handbag tucked it under her arm, collected her light mac from the hallway and headed out of the door.

In the room at the Town Hall, which had been booked by Secretary, Fenella Wright, the other landladies of GAGGA were beginning to assemble. Treasurer Agnes Brown turned to Fenella and commented on the turn out. This was the first full committee meeting of 1970 since the Landladies Convention of the previous year and all were keen to hear Shirley's address concerning the changes that were going to take place with regard to the voting system that had seen Lettice Webb become a member. Both Fenella and Agnes had been of the opinion that the whole thing needed careful handling as rumblings from others had often been heard as to how certain members of GAGGA always won prizes. Shirley's announcement at the Convention had raised many an eyebrow.

Rarely seen about the town since the evening in question, it appeared to others that Miss Webb had not been at all comfortable with her nomination to The Great Yarmouth and

Gorleston Guest House Association. Lucinda Haines who had invited Lettice to attend the conventions as her guest was of the opinion that something fishy was going on, a thought shared by her rivals Muriel Evans and Freda Boggis. Petunia Danger who had come third and first prize winner for Landlady of the Year Ruby Hamilton had kept their own counsel on the subject fearing that their days of leading lights within GAGGA were numbered. Who was Lettice Webb to steal their thunder?

Surveying the gathering from their table on the stage of the small room, Fenella and Agnes awaited the arrival of Shirley. Glancing at the clock on the wall the time was drawing near to the allotted start time of 10.30. Knowing how their leader loved to make an entrance, Fenella and Agnes glanced towards the door and right on cue, Shirley Llewellyn came into the room, raising a gloved hand to the gathering and took her place on the stage. She acknowledged her fellow committee members with a smile and removed her gloves in the theatrical one finger at a time move she had seen many times on stage and film and dropped them onto the table and sat down. Freda nudged her companion Muriel. "Here we go, here comes that blessed toffee hammer" and as predicted Shirley raised her gavel and brought the meeting to order.

"Good morning ladies" she said as her eyes swept the room. "It is so lovely to see so many of you present. This is a record turnout". Shirley turned to gain the support of Agnes and Fenella who nodded in agreement.

"I bet she didn't get that outfit off the market" said Muriel eyeing her neighbour's latest creation. She could feel the electricity passing through her body every time Freda fidgeted which was something Freda did a lot of at such meetings. Lucinda who was sitting behind the pair was keeping a listening ear, there was always something afoot with those two.

"She has more money than sense that one" said Freda as she noisily rustled a sweet wrapper and popped a mint humbug in her mouth. Muriel refused the offer of one and focused on the stage where she could see Shirley was getting agitated as many more murmurings could be heard around the room.

Shirley banged her gavel again, making Fenella jump. "Ladies please a bit of hush; we have a lot to get through." Shirley looked around the room noting that Lettice Webb was not present. "Agnes dear, can you give us all a run-down on the balance sheet. This will be of particular interest to those of you that wanted to know the cost of hiring venues."

A few calls of "here, here" were heard and Shirley frowned as she sat down. Agnes gathered her papers and with the use of the microphone, that she secretly hated using, began addressing the audience. After fifteen minutes of Agnes droning on, several excused themselves to go to the ladies; others thought they should use the time productively and get on with some knitting. As Agnes drew to a close, several loud sighs were heard. Freda, who had nodded off, awoke suddenly at the sound of the gavel and snorted loudly. Muriel raised her eyebrows suddenly to the ceiling as she was once again attacked by the electricity caused by Freda's dress.

"Thank you Agnes dear, for that in depth detail of our finances. Are there any questions ladies" said Shirley, secretly hoping that none would be raised, she had a hair appointment with Mr Adrian at 12.30 and didn't want to be late. He was fitting her in as a favour. Several hands went up and Shirley doing her best to keep her cool, allowed the questions to be addressed to Agnes. Agnes got to her feet and taking the microphone and placing it too close to her mouth, boomed out the answers causing several present to drop stitches.

Moving on Fenella announced that several suppliers had been in touch and that another date had been set with

Crockett, Crockett and Crockett who would be showing some newly acquired lines in cutlery, crockery and kitchen wares.

Shirley glanced at the clock, this was the part of the meeting she was dreading; with any luck she could get this over quickly and escape leaving the others to the tea and biscuits which had been provided.

"Thank you Fenella dear, I am sure that everyone has made a note of the extra date in their diaries. Crocket, Crocket and Crocket certainly have the edge when it comes to items for us landladies."

"And a price tag to match" said Freda out loud before receiving a jab in the ribs from Muriel.

Lucinda who felt she had stayed quiet for too long and still had her heart set on sitting at that table on the stage stood up.

"Lady Chairman" she said addressing Shirley with a smile "I wonder if I might be permitted to say a few words." Shirley looked worriedly at Lucinda and then down at her agenda, such things were rarely permitted unless noted beforehand. Fearing some reprisal would follow if she didn't allow Lucinda to speak, she replied with a sickly smile. "Mrs Haines, Lucinda my dear. Time is of the essence but I am sure that I can forgo the usual protocol and allow you to take the floor."

Lucinda, who wasn't going to be put off her stride thanked Shirley and spoke. "Lady Chairman and fellow landladies, I have to say that I think Crocket, Crocket and Crocket provide us with an excellent service. Their wares are second to none and though some among us may be tempted by the market stall, it really is false economy as I have proven to myself on more than one occasion." Ruby Hamilton and Petunia Danger nodded in agreement as Lucinda continued. "Furthermore Lady Chairman I would like to see the committee procure a discount with Crocket, Crocket and Crocket for those of us that purchase from them on a regular basis."

"What a marvellous idea" said Ruby Hamilton loudly; "I am surprised our Chairman hasn't thought along those lines herself."

Her feathers clearly ruffled Shirley whispered to Fenella and Agnes to look into it and get back to her as she stood up. But Lucinda wasn't finished "And on another subject Lady Chairman I would like to know and I speak for many gathered here, how the rules were suddenly changed to allow special awards to be made at the convention."

Shirley blushed. "Lucinda that was the very thing we were going to talk about next and if you have finished I would like to address that subject now."

Lucinda nodded and sat down as a few murmurs of thanks were heard. Shirley rapped her gavel to bring order and just as she was about to speak, the fire alarm sounded bringing the meeting to an unexpected close. Shirley looked to the heavens "saved by the bell".

"There goes the free tea and biscuits" said Freda hauling herself up "I suppose it will have to be Matthes or Palmers and it's your turn to pay Muriel."

* * *

As she sat under the hairdryer, Shirley knew she would have to inform the landladies about the changes to the voting, but wasn't sure how best she could do it without it causing stir. It was obvious to her that Lucinda was out for blood and wouldn't rest until an explanation was given.

Shirley had often been pressed by others about how the voting for the Landlady of the Year was done and she had had to admit to herself that ensuring that her more favoured landladies had always walked away with top prizes had been rumbled long ago. She had thought that by making sure that Freda Boggis walked off with third prize it would put the rumours to rest and that by awarding Lettice Webb an honorary membership would also provide a further smokescreen. It had been clear to her that her trusted team of Agnes and Fenella were also getting a bit fed up with things and that maybe they should be made to stand for re-election. They hadn't been challenged for years as no one seemed the remote bit interested in serving on the committee.

As Shirley had set up GAGGA she had no intention of stepping down as Chairman, but times were changing. Lucinda Haines had found her voice and she feared that Lucinda's friendship with Lettice, which couldn't be described as buddy buddy, would also queer her pitch further.

Mr Adrian minced over to the dryer and turned it off and motioned Shirley to take a chair at his station. As he began to work his magic on her blonde hair Shirley relaxed. She had an evening out to look forward to, she was off to see Rick O'Shea and the Ramblers and the thought made her go gooey inside. If she played her cards right maybe she could entice Rick to join her on the dance floor again. The thought of his hands caressing her derriere made her giggle girlishly out loud. Mr Adrian gave Shirley one of his knowing looks in the mirror opposite and continued with the job in hand.

* * *

As Lucinda made her way home she walked by Gull House where she spotted Lettice Webb in her front garden. "Good morning Lettice I had hoped to see you at the meeting."

Lettice who was sure she would be safe for at least an hour or so looked at her watch, it must have finished early. She stood up from her kneeling position, trowel in hand and turned to face Lucinda with a smile. "I was feeling a bit off colour this morning so I thought I would give it a miss. I hope there was nothing of any importance?"

"Not much" said Lucinda planning to play her cards close to her chest. "The fire alarm went off and brought proceedings to a halt. I am sorry you haven't been feeling well, nothing too serous I trust?"

Lettice laid her hand on her chest. "I suffer with my chest and the North Sea breeze does nothing for it."

"You want to careful out here" said Lucinda mindfully "I think we have some bad weather on the way, the shipping forecast didn't sound too clever."

Lettice pulled her open cardigan tighter. "I probably ought to go back inside. I thought tinkering in the garden would help."

Lucinda wasn't fooled by her friend. "You best make yourself a nice hot toddy and relax my dear. If you need anything give me a call." And with a wave Lucinda went on her way.

"I really enjoyed that custard" said Freda taking a slurp of her tea. "One thing you can say about Matthes is they do know how to make a good tart."

Muriel pushed her empty coffee cup away. "Which is more than you can say about their coffee, I wish I had had tea now. Palmers are best for coffee, Matthes are best for tea."

"They use tea leaves" said Freda lifting the lid on the pot and peering in. "I could go another custard tart, but think I best not."

"Very wise" said Muriel looking at her friend's ever expanding waistline. "If you've finished we'll have a stroll round the market, I promised Barry I would get him some grapes."

"Is he over his cold yet" said Freda picking up her bag "My Dick is murder when he's not well, he has me running in circles. Men are such babies when it comes to illness."

"My Barry is as good as gold, the perfect patient."

"Fancy" said Freda following Muriel out of the shop and onto a very busy King Street. Wednesdays were murder.

"We better make this a quick trip Freda Boggis, those clouds don't look none to healthy and I forgot to bring my brolly."

Deciding that she needed to nip things in the bud, Shirley made a diversion on her way home and called in on Fenella, who as she found was having some lunch with Agnes.

"I am so sorry to barge in like this" she said dashing in out of the rain and loosening her chiffon headscarf.

"I was just clearing away the lunch things" said Fenella asking her guest to take a seat. "Will you join us in a cup of tea, I was just about to pour?"

Shirley refused gently. "I have just had a coffee in Mr Adrian's, such a thoughtful man when it comes to his regular clientele."

Agnes and Fenella were used to Shirley's swank and said nothing.

"It is lucky that I have you two ladies together" said Shirley crossing her legs. "I was wondering what best to do about the committee as a whole and how to make changes to the voting for Landlady of the Year. It did cause something of a stir last year and one doesn't like to see one's members unhappy."

"Ones like Lucinda Haines" said Agnes knowingly. "If you ask me Lucinda would like a slice of the action."

"And who can blame her" said Fenella pouring two cups of tea and handing one to Agnes. "I have been saying for many a year that we need to become more democratic. There really should be election processes in place especially where the Chairman is concerned."

"May I remind you both that it was me that set the whole thing up in the first place?"

But Fenella had kept quiet for too long. "That is all very well Shirley and I am sure that the members would agree you have done a sterling job but is it right that just because you set it up you should front it for your own gain."

Shirley was visibly shaken. "Fenella is right" said Agnes "it is time for a change at the top. I have considered stepping down and letting someone else have a crack at the finances."

Shirley saw this as an opening. "But Agnes dear, you keep those books beautifully and you always balance. And Fenella who else could I trust at my side."

Fenella gave a nervous giggle, but Agnes wasn't to be so easily bought.

"I have heard what the members say about us" she said, pinning an escaping lock of hair back into place. "They all think I don't pay much attention, but believe me if you heard half of what they said you'd be turning in your grave".

"But Agnes dear, we are not dead."

"That's as maybe but it doesn't change what people are thinking. I happen to know that Lucinda has come into some money and she is going to give that place of hers a much needed overhaul."

"You'll be telling us next that Freda and Muriel are going to do likewise, the former certainly needs some work done."

"I know for a fact that that is also true. How will they stand for winning "Landlady of the Year" when it rolls around at the end of the summer? You both know as well as I do that the whole thing is fixed."

"But" said Shirley "Freda Boggis won a raffle prize."

"Only because you doctored the winning tickets, Freda Boggis was no more worthy of winning that prize than

Lucinda being crowned Queen of the May. You changed it because you wanted to award Lettice Webb with a bottle of champagne because it made you feel good."

Silence fell and the three didn't look at each other for several minutes, it was left to Fenella to speak up. "Well I think that has bought everything out in the open, wouldn't you both agree?"

The other two nodded and Shirley for once was lost for words.

"I suggest we have a meeting tomorrow and draw up some plans about how we can best deal with this issue. Shirley you should stand down as Chairman at the end of the summer and become Honorary President. Agnes and I will surrender our roles and all three can then be elected by the members. It will take some working out, but I am sure if we all pull together we can do it. We can write to all the members telling them of our decision, that way it will resolve us having to answer any further questions."

Shirley still shaken said they could meet at hers the following afternoon.

As Shirley left Fenella's house, the heavens opened and her hair became sodden with rain before she managed to reach the safety of her car. As she looked in her wing mirror, a rather bedraggled Shirley looked back. She turned the key in the ignition and started the engine. Feeling totally deflated, an evening out to see the Rick, the keeper of her affections, seemed to be less attractive that it had a few hours before.

* * *

The summer season of 1970 was upon the landladies and they were all gearing themselves up for what they hoped would be a good one. Lucinda had made many alterations to her guest house which had impressed Muriel and rendered

Freda practically speechless when the two had been invited to take tea and view the changes. Muriel made her own changes with the help of Barry and some money left to them by Barry's sister and with a neighbourly helping hand Muriel had assisted Freda in some much needed sprucing up to her guest home.

Notifications about the changes to GAGGA were duly sent out much to the surprise of many. Lucinda quietly smiled to herself when she read hers.

The elections would take place during October and the winners would be announced at the Landladies Convention at a venue yet to be decided. But it was hope that the Cliff Hotel in Gorleston would come up trumps again. Shirley continued to swank when she bumped into any of the GAGGA members and dismissed any idea that she wasn't fully behind the changes. She emphasised that her role as Chairman had taken its toll and that she would be happy to take a back seat, but that didn't fool anyone.

Lettice Webb looked forward to her forthcoming season, many of the regulars that had been with the former proprietors of Gull House returned year after year. Lettice was unshaken by the GAGGA plans and put that at the back of her mind. Never one for socialising until Lucinda had coaxed her out to the Landladies Convention of the year before she had retreated to her domestic duties, busying herself in bedroom and food preparation.

The summer season shows had been announced with an unusual turn up for the Golden Sands, which this year would see Don Stevens presenting a twice nightly show starring Derinda Daniels and company. Peter Noone would star at the ABC with Leslie Crowther and company booked to appear at the Wellington. The Little Theatre had given its final performances the season before and was showing films.

Talk turned to the introduction of decimal currency the following year and most shops and business were displaying their prices in new and old money. Mrs Jary had got to grips with the changes in her convenience store but many of her customers like Freda Boggis were resisting the inevitable. The ladies at the popular wool shop in Gorleston were not coping so well and couldn't quite get their heads around how one hundred new pennies would equal one pound sterling and the problem was also causing concerns for other retailers many of whom believed that it would never catch on.

It was on a fine summer morning that Lettice was alerted by the sound of her door bell and wiping her hands on her apron she went to see who it was.

The man had his back to the door, but she would have known those broad shoulders and slim hips anywhere. He turned round and smiled.

"What are you doing here?" asked Lettice. "I thought I was well shot of you."

"Is that anyway to treat your brother?" His voice was gravelly just like Lettice's. He was handsome with what many women would have called "come to bed eyes". Clean shaven, his features were defined and his plump lips revealed white teeth. There was no doubt about it Tommy was indeed a good looking man.

Dressed in a smart pair of casual trousers, winkle picker shoes and open neck shirt, his dark hair was swept back in the style of a teddy boy, albeit an older one.

"Aren't you going to invite me in?"

Not wishing to leave her brother on the doorstep for fear of prying eyes, Lettice stepped aside and gestured for him to follow her through to the kitchen. She filled the kettle and set out two cups and saucers.

"Quite a nice little place you have here" said Tommy looking around him. "Why did you leave Cornwall? I thought you liked it there."

"I did" said Lettice as she put some tea in to the pot. "Things got awkward."

"But they always do my sweet" said Tommy pulling a chair from under the table and sitting himself down.

"I hope you haven't come here to cause trouble" said Lettice looking at her brother directly. "I've a good little business here and it should see me through to old age. I cannot bear to think of moving again."

Tommy laughed. "You should have got yourself a caravan. Never known anyone to move as many times as you have."

Lettice poured the water on to the tea leaves and covered the pot with a cosy. "You know why, so don't pretend otherwise. What it is you want, money?"

"My sweet you cut me to the quick. I came back from Canada hoping to catch up with you. I was quite upset when I found you had moved. It took me ages to track you down."

"So how did you find me" said Lettice "I didn't leave a trail, I never do."

"Let's just say I know people."

"Like Bruce Warrington I suppose" said Lettice spitting the words out. "He never was any good."

"But he was sweet on you my sweet" said Tommy. "Even if it was for all the wrong reasons, no account for taste I suppose."

Lettice poured the tea and sat down opposite her brother. "You can't stay here, the house is full. How much do you want?"

Tommy stirred his tea adding three sugars. "That depends on how much you want to retain your identity my sweet. A couple of hundred should do for now, you can settle up the rest at the end of the season, now I know where to find you."

"I don't keep that kind of money in the house. You will have to wait until I can get to the bank."

"I can meet you in town tomorrow."

"And then you'll go?"

"My sweet, don't worry. I have plans. I don't want to hang around this place. I've bigger fish to fry. Now, any chance of a sandwich?"

Lettice heaved a sigh of relief when she finally saw her brother to the door. She went upstairs to her bedroom and opened the dressing table drawer. At the very back, hidden under some scarves was a metal cash box. She took the key from behind the ornamental clock and opened it. There was sixty pounds inside. She took out the money and put the box back in its hiding place. As she turned to leave the room, her eyes looked up at the top of the wardrobe and she stared at the brown suitcase and felt a cold shiver go down her spine. She didn't want to go back, not to that again. She took a deep breath and closing the bedroom door, hurried down the stairs.

The summer season progressed and all the landladies were kept busy with their guests with one or two mishaps on the way, especially for Freda Boggis, as some of her guests left without paying. But as the season drew to a close several were heaving a sigh of relief, Lettice for one who was pleased that her brother hadn't darkened her doorstep again. Once he had the sniff of money under his nose, he often returned for more, but Lettice thought he must have landed on his feet somewhere as no further contact had been made and she could breathe easily again.

Shirley was getting quite nervous as she knew that the elections were fast approaching. Several landladies had put their names forward for the elections and one or two were more than familiar. Shirley hated the idea of handing over the reins to someone else as it had been her hard work that had launched GAGGA in the first place. She called a meeting with Agnes and Fenella inviting them to take tea with her.

"I have been looking over the plans for this election" she said cutting slices of Victoria sponge for each of her guests. "There really aren't many worthy to take over our positions. The application from Janice Brent for treasurer, I mean to say the woman has never to my mind been numerate, which is why her market stall went under all those years ago. She turned her attention to the boarding house game only because she inherited her late mother's guest house. Alice Warden, hardly the calibre one would expect for a position on the committee, she really is too old to undertake this kind of work and ought to get out more and her charity shop clothes do her no favours at all."

Agnes gave Fenella a knowing look. "Is there anyone in your opinion with any merit whatsoever?"

Shirley blushed. "Well I have to say that Lucinda Haines makes a strong case, she certainly has been a bit of a dark horse."

"Lucinda is a shrewd business woman" said Fenella. "I think she would make a great chairman, she certainly wouldn't stand for any nonsense."

Shirley reluctantly nodded her head in agreement, "I did hope that Lettice Webb would have thrown her hat in the ring."

"I wondered how long it would be before you mentioned Lettice" replied Agnes with feeling. "I don't understand your fascination with the woman, firstly you award her a prize for best newcomer and ever since you have courted her attention.

I don't think she is remotely a bit interested in GAGGA. She likes to keep herself to herself. Besides we really don't know enough about her."

"At this rate we will have Freda Boggis running things" said Fenella with a giggle "now that really would be something."

Shirley busied herself pouring out more tea raking her brains to think how best she could rig the election. The other two who were quite used to Shirley watched her like hawks as she handed them refreshed cups and sat back in her armchair. Placing her fingers to her temples she looked down at her lap and then slowly looked up again. "Ladies I think we need to let things lie for the time being."

Agnes felt her hair stand up on the back of her neck; she had seen this coming, before she could say anything Fenella put down her cup and saucer and addressed Shirley directly.

"On what grounds are you planning to call off this election Shirley? I know you are reluctant to step down but you know the feelings of the members, we need change and we will never have it while you remain in charge. You swan around in your posh outfits, looking down your nose at everyone. You always want everything your own way and it has got to stop. Are you seriously telling me we are going to go back to the members and tell them we have had a change of heart, because I assure I intend to step down and I think Agnes is beside me in that?" Agnes nodded.

Not put off her stride Shirley smiled. "No, no you have it all wrong. I was going to suggest we postpone the elections until next year. After all 1971 will see the introduction of decimal currency and the books will need to be updated. We cannot possible hand over management of our finances until we are all fully au fait with everything ourselves. Why you have heard many of our members struggling to get their heads round what 1/9 is in new money. It will make more sense to wait until after next summer season and have the elections then. It will also give some of the members more time to put their names forward."

Agnes looked at Fenella with a furrowed brow. "You may have a point" she said but the members won't like it."

"Look to make up for it, I will stomp up for this year's Convention. I will pay for the food and the venue" said Shirley realising she now had them on side.

"That is going to cost you a pretty penny" said Agnes remembering the cost of hiring the ballroom at the Cliff the year before.

"Not if we go for a different approach" said Shirley who had already been making enquiries of her own. "The Star will give us full use of their function room with a buffet, providing we agree to a cash bar. I am happy to put up the money for the room hire and buffet and put fifty pounds behind the bar as security."

"Have you come in to money?" asked Agnes in disbelief.

"As a matter of fact a maiden aunt has left me some money in her Will so it will be my pleasure to share it around a little."

There was a silence in the room as her two guests digested the news. "It would mean sending out letters to the members explaining the delay with the election and enclosing details of this year's Convention with an invitation to include one guest a piece. I have a date in mind."

"You really have been doing your homework" said Fenella, "no doubt you have drafted a letter for me as well?"

Shirley smiled and handed Fenella a sheet of paper from her handbag. "Indeed I have."

Freda Boggis banged on her neighbours door. Muriel opened it looking slightly annoyed. "Freda whatever is it and why didn't you ring the bell?"

"Sorry" said Freda barging past her friend and making her way through to the kitchen. "Have you seen this letter from Shirley Llewellyn?" Freda was frantically waving the letter in the air looking like she was about to explode.

"Freda for goodness sake calm yourself down and have a seat. Yes I have seen it and as I said to Mrs Jary in the shop this morning it was no more than I expected. Holding back the inevitable that's what she is doing and then trying to win us over with a few bridge rolls at the Star. I heard the Cliff Hotel was fully booked."

Freda plonked herself down in an armchair and pondered. She had forgotten about the free buffet. "Well I suppose it was nice of her to offer."

"Freda Boggis you come in here like a thing possessed and then you are won over on the promise of a sausage roll with a few cheese and pineapple on sticks, because that is all it is likely to be, I suppose she might throw in a few crisps and nuts."

"I am very partial to a sausage as my Dick will tell you, there is nothing I like better than a toad in the hole" said Freda folding her arms across her more than ample bosom. "At least it won't cost very much, not like last year when we had to pay."

"It isn't going to be a free bar and the way your Dick drinks you'll more than double what you spent last year and no mistake."

Freda huffed. "That's as may be but it will be nice to have my dancing frock out again."

"Well for goodness sake have it dry cleaned first, the way that dress goes it's a wonder it doesn't dance on its own."

Silence ruled for a few minutes and then Muriel continued. "It's a sprat to catch a macaroon. Shirley really does not want to stand down, I can't speak for Agnes and Fenella, but Lady Llewellyn is another story."

"I was never very fond of sprats or a macaroon for that matter. I don't mind tinned sardines, you know where you are with a sardine. Though I do think it is cruel putting the key on the outside of the tin" She paused and then continued "I know Lucinda would like to be Chairman" said Freda rubbing salt into the wound. "I heard her telling Mrs Jary."

"Well I might just pip her at the post" said Muriel because after this surprise turn of events I am going to put my name forward too. What do you mean it's cruel to put the key on the outside of the tin?"

"Well how would they get out if they wanted to?"

"Sometimes I don't believe what I am hearing" said Muriel

"I bet that Lettice Webb has her eye on it as well" said Freda finding a mint imperial in her apron pocket, picking off the fluff and popping it in her mouth. "Not to mention Petunia Danger and that Ruby Hamilton, they'll all be at it. Well I am not bothering; I have enough to do at home without taking on any of those other duties. I know I would be very good at it and they would be lucky to have me, but as I said to my Dick, they will just have to muddle through without me."

Muriel raised her eyes to the ceiling. "Well I will give them a run for their money" she said with look of determination and went out to the gas cooker before her potatoes boiled dry.

Freda chewed on her mint and had a think, there was no doubt in her mind that what GAGGA needed was her at the helm so maybe she should reconsider, then swallowing her sweet she put her hand back in her apron pocket and discovered an unwrapped sherbet lemon, as no tea and biscuits were on offer she would content herself with her meagre findings.

The word was well and truly out and landladies across the town were talking about the letter they had received. Lucinda Haines wasn't a bit surprised, but it made her all the more determined to ensure she became the Queen of GAGGA, even if it meant fighting Shirley to the death. On the strength of the free invitation to the Landladies Convention she decided to treat herself to another new outfit. The summer season had been a good one and her newly furbished home had won many admiring glances even though there had been a tinge of sadness mixed in with the passing of Ted Ricer. On her way in to town, she knocked on Lettice's front door and getting no reply continued on her way. Lettice had peeped out from the curtains of an upstairs window and decided that she couldn't face the likes of Lucinda today. She too had read the letter and wished that she had never agreed to go along the year before. She had done something that she had never done in the previous areas she had lived and that was become part of the community. Though it had seemed exciting at the time she realised that it may be her very undoing.

Ruby Hamilton bristled when she read her letter, but was not put off, she had plans to ensure that she would stand out as a worthy candidate given the fact that she had won Landlady of the Year previous! Petunia Danger on the other hand wasn't at all bothered and was looking forward to the free buffet and dance. She knew from Agnes and Fenella the hard work that went into keeping GAGGA on its feet and preferred to watch from the side lines. Extra work was something she didn't need.

Shirley decided it was best to keep a low profile for a few weeks and was rarely spotted out and about and then only in her car. She did her grocery shopping in Lowestoft which was inconvenient but necessary if she wasn't to encounter the wrath of her fellow landladies. Agnes and Fenella were happy to go about their business as usual and passed the time of day with anyone they happened to see. Both took the stance that they were more than ready to hand over the reins of treasurer and secretary respectfully and emphasised that delaying the voting until the end of the 1971 season made logical sense, because of the decimalisation.

Most landladies nodded in agreement after giving the matter some thought, one or two remained suspicious of the motives while others shrugged their shoulders as if they knew defeat was inevitable when it concerned Shirley.

The evening of the 1970 convention arrived and the good and the great made their way to the Star Hotel where a spread that would have kept Robin Hood and His Merry Men fed for days awaited the landladies and their guests' pleasure. A complimentary sherry had been laid on and word soon spread that the bar would be free until the money Shirley had deposited ran out. In good spirit Agnes and Fenella had pitched in with an extra twenty five pounds between them.

The three ladies greeted their guests and once more were treated to some very fetching gowns and outfits. Muriel arrived in a mauve dress with her husband Barry togged up in his dinner suit. It was left to Freda to once again provide the jaw dropping spectacle that only she could manage. Many remembered the outfit from the year before and were having bets on what it would be this year.

Freda wore a long green gown that trailed at the back; it had a very plunging neckline that left her bosom resting on her stomach as her brassiere appeared to have given up under the strain. Her hair had been teased into an afro style, much loved by the youngsters of the day, but which on Freda looked totally wrong. Her feet were adorned in a pair of fawn coloured heels that matched with nothing, a beaded bag swung from her black gloved hands and the jewellery around her expansive neck would have not looked out of place on Danny La Rue. Freda was not the best when it came to applying makeup. In her usual manner she had over rouged, put on too much eye shadow, applied eyelashes that appeared to have a life of their own and had used an orange lipstick she had picked up on a market stall. Her husband Dick fared no better in his ill-fitting blue suit that was two sizes too big, a dickey bow that Coco the clown may have once owned and a pair of brown shoes that needed a good polish. Totally unware of any attention they were drawing they made their way arm in arm to the bar where Dick downed two pints in quick succession and Freda sipped a half of bitter.

Shirley sparkled from head to toe in an orange and black gown she had picked up while shopping in Norwich. It had been the last on the rail and one the store in question had been trying to get shot of for some time. It was in her size and reduced to such a low price that Shirley felt she would have been a fool not to purchase it. As she left with her findings in the paper carrier bag, the two shop assistants clapped their hands together glad to see the back of it after six years on the sale rail out back.

Lettice was the last person to arrive at eight and was quite alone. She had told Lucinda that she would make her own way as she would not be ready at seven when Lucinda had planned to pick her up in a taxi. Lettice was wearing a high necked red top with a long black skirt and low heeled red shoes. Around her shoulders she wore an evening stole and carried a dainty handbag. Her jewellery was minimal but Shirley thought she looked very elegant and complimented her on her choice.

Ruby Hamilton spotted Shirley at the bar and went over to speak to her. "Well my dear where have you been hiding yourself, I haven't seen you for ages."

Shirley who had had three gin and tonics felt more than able to deal with her accuser. "Here and there, people to meet, places to be."

"I am assuming there will be the usual awards this evening" said Ruby sipping her port and lemon and keeping a close eye on her husband who appeared to be asking some waitress if she would care to dance, that's what came of allowing him to have a couple before leaving the house.

"Oh yes the awards will go ahead as usual" said Shirley "I must thank you for your interest in becoming one of the committee members next year. It is regrettably we had to delay but there we have it."

"Indeed we do" said Ruby. "I shall listen with great interest as to who will be awarded Landlady of the Year."

Shirley knocked back her gin. "I am sure you will Ruby dear. Now if you'll excuse me I believe the cabaret artiste has arrived."

Muriel made her way to the Ladies only to find Freda dousing herself in perfume. "What on earth is that" asked Muriel with a sniff.

"It's my new toilette water" said Freda squirting some more on her neck.

"Are you sure it wasn't meant for the toilet dear" quizzed Muriel as she reapplied some lipstick. "It has a bit of a hum to it, what it is called?"

"Whoosh" said Freda putting the bottle back in her bag "I got it off the bloke on the market."

Muriel groaned. "Not the man that sells everything out of a suitcase?"

"That's the one" said Freda trying to adjust her hair which seemed to have a life of its own."

"He's the one that sold Gloria that shoe spray; it took the straps clean off her sling backs."

"Fancy" said Freda wondering whether she ought to touch up her rouge.

"He wants locking up. Really Freda you shouldn't buy things from him."

"I can't afford the fancy prices you pay for Estee Laundry or that Max Factor you are so fond of."

"But Freda dear there are some reasonably priced perfumes about and they smell ten times nicer than that stuff you waste your money on."

Freda picked up her bag. "I am going back in are you coming?"

"I'll follow on in a minute."

"But you won't know where to find me and my Dick."

"Find you" said Muriel "I won't have any trouble finding you, I'll be able to smell your Whoosh."

Freda pulled open the door. "See I knew you liked it really."

The time was approaching nine when Shirley took to the stage that had been erected especially for the occasion. The band led by Maurice Beeney played the final refrain of There is nothing like a Dame as Shirley picked up the microphone.

"Ladies and Gentlemen I hope you are all enjoying yourselves I am sure you will agree that the Star has laid on an excellent buffet and Maurice and his boys have kept us on our feet with their marvellous dance tunes."

A roar of appreciation went up around the room. "Now ladies and gentlemen before we announce this year's winners it gives me great pleasure to introduce our cabaret for this evening Rhonda Valli accompanying herself on her harp bringing us some memorable songs from Wales.

Rhonda Valley walked on to the stage; she was in forties, dressed head to toe in figure hugging leather and straddled her harp as if her life depended on it. She plucked and plinked and her soaring Welsh voice filled the room.

"She's a dead ringer for that Honor Blackman in the Avengers" said Barry to Muriel. "She has a fine figure."

"You keep your ears on the singing and your eyes on your pint" said Muriel. "She has got a nerve coming on in that get up."

"I quite fancy a leather outfit" said Freda butting in and was enjoying her fifth drink of the evening.

"You'd look like a bag of liquorice allsorts" said Dick who was way over his quota and was swaying from side to side. "Bertie Bassett, that's who you'd look like,."

"You keep a civil tongue in your head Dick Boggis or it will be curtains for you when we get home" said Freda "Now make yourself useful and get me another drink."

"I'll go with him" said Barry.

"You will stay right there where I can keep an eye on you" said Muriel.

"Yes dear" said Barry and supped his pint.

"Do you think Rhonda is related to Frankie Valli?" asked Freda.

"From where I am standing, more likely to be Rudy Valli" replied Muriel with feeling.

As Rhonda Valli came to the end of her thirty minute set with "We'll Keep a Welcome in the Hillside", there were a few whispered comments that it had been at least twenty minutes too long. As Rhonda stood in her thin spike heeled black shoes to take her final bow, in true GAGGA style she received a loud round of applause. As she wheeled her harp off stage several of the audience wondered how on earth she had managed to get through the act in leather without working up a sweat. Just as the band were about to play Shirley back on to the stage there was a loud crash and a lot of swearing, Rhonda had toppled off the back of the stage into a trolley of dirty plates and cutlery. Quite a racket ensued as staff went to help Rhonda back to the ante room reserved for artistes. Shirley unperturbed by the commotion signalled Maurice to strike up the band and walked back on stage to I took my harp to a party.

"My God, she is milking this" said Lucinda to a lady sat beside her who she had never seen before. The lady in question, who appeared to be deaf, did not reply.

"Ladies and Gentleman" said Shirley taking command of the microphone "we now come to the part of the evening where it is my great pleasure to announce this year's Landlady of the Year award."

"Here we go" said Lucinda "There will be no prizes for guessing who will win this" as she looked in the direction of Ruby Hamilton who was smiling serenely.

"In third place we have Clara Waters. Clara has done much to improve her lovely home, Sandcastle."

Ruby Hamilton scowled as she watched Clara go forward to take her prize as applause rang out around the room, with chants of "well done."

"In second place" said Shirley pretending to struggle with the envelope in her hand. "I am pleased to announce that Muriel Evans is a worthy recipient."

Muriel who had just taken a sip of gin and tonic nearly choked, Freda who was seated nearby and had more than enough to drink started wolf whistling and she got so carried away she had to be restrained by Dick who had never seen his wife so animated. As Muriel received her prize, she blushed, "Well done my dear" said Shirley.

Agnes turned to Fenella "She has switched the prizes; Muriel was never in the running."

Fenella nodded at her friend. "She is playing to the gallery my dear. We will soon know when she announces the winner."

"It's Ruby" said Agnes in a whisper "that's what was agreed on."

Shirley waited for the applause to die down and then with a flourish she tore open the gold envelope and smiled, she paused for dramatic effect and then pulled out the enclosed card. "And the winner of this year's Landlady of the Year Award is......."

There was complete silence in the room and then a drum roll.

"What's with Ringo on the drums" said Agnes "we don't normally have that."

Shirley gazed around the room and continued "and the winner is....Lucinda Haines."

There was a gasp of surprise from the audience, Ruby Hamilton fainted and Agnes picked up her neighbours vodka and tonic and downed it in one.

Lucinda walked to the stage enjoying every moment of it; she had done it at last. She smiled at Muriel and Freda as she went by them and Freda who appeared to have lost all sense of occasion was clapping and shouting. Muriel was pleased with her own award and didn't grudge Lucinda her moment of glory. Accepting the silver cup and the sash of excellence Muriel shook Shirley by the hand. "Well done Lucinda" said Shirley "you so richly deserve this award."

Cheers and applause filled the room as Lucinda went back to her seat as Ruby was seen being escorted out by the St. John Ambulance.

Shirley bought the room to attention. "Ladies and Gentleman in the year of 1971 we will see some changes to GAGGA, I and my fellow committee members Agnes and Fenella will be stepping down from our roles. We would like you all to consider either nominating yourselves or a friend to be become our successors. Now if Agnes and Fenella would like to join me on stage I have a little something for them both."

Once more applause and cheers rang out as the two ladies were handed a bouquet of flowers and a Palmers gift voucher."

"Before I bring this ceremony to a close" said Shirley wiping an imaginary tear from her eye and pausing again as if to compose herself "I have one last award to make. I did it last year and Lettice Webb was the winner as newcomer. As this will be my last convention as Chairman I would like to give a special award to someone who always tries her best. Ladies and Gentleman to accept my special award I would like to ask Freda Boggis to please join me on stage."

"Now I know she has lost it" said Agnes her voice trembling "here goes another bottle of bubbly, flowers and a gift token no doubt."

Fenella grinned. "You have to admire her pluck; I had a feeling she was going to go out on a high. Three of her most disliked landladies have all been awarded prizes and she has left the usual candidates with nothing. She has played a blinder and no mistake."

Freda Boggis steadied herself as she clamoured up on to the stage to accept her award. For once she was rendered speechless and there were quite a few in the audience who were much the same.

"I have had enough of this" said Agnes feeling aggrieved and taking the microphone out of the hand of a very surprised Shirley she bought the room to attention.

"Agnes dear what are you doing, Fenella do you know anything about this?"

Fenella shook her head with an admiring smile that her colleague had finally bitten the bullet. "No I don't but I think we are both about to find out."

"Ladies and gentlemen" said Agnes trying to keep the anger in her voice under control "We have heard our Chairman talk about changes to GAGGA and as I see it we will have to wait until next year's convention. Well I am proposing that the convention is brought forward to the month of April and that the elections will take place in March, so that by the summer we will have a new committee in charge. All those in favour raise their hands."

Hands shot up around the room. "I will take that vote as carried unanimous" said Agnes, "we will be in touch to give you the dates before Christmas."

A cheer went up around the room as Maurice and his band began to play a dance number.

"I really think you should have discussed that with Fenella and me before you did that" said Shirley who was clearly shaken and began to head off to the bar.

"And what good would that have done" said Agnes in a very confident manner and not the bumbling way she usually addressed things. "You would have found a way to stall it again."

"Agnes is right" said Fenella catching up with the pair as Shirley ordered a large brandy. "We have pussy footed around this long enough."

Agnes acknowledged Fenella. "Thank you for that, now I think that calls for a bottle of Champagne, will you join us Lady Chairman?"

Shirley who had downed her brandy in one nodded, feeling her firm grip on things ebbing away.

A couple of weeks passed and Shirley decided to drop in unannounced on one or two of the members. Agnes and Fenella were not at all surprised to see her, Ruby Hamilton gave her the cold shoulder and said she was then on her way out. Petunia Danger was always pleased to see Shirley and they had a chat over a coffee.

Pulling up outside Lettice's house Shirley locked her car door and went to ring the doorbell. She tried it again but it appeared that the bell was not working, so she knocked on the glass pane. When there was no reply she decided to go round the back of the house. She could hear voices as she approached the open back door.

"I have told you Tommy, not a penny more, you have had your last hand out from me" the voice of Lettice could be heard slightly raised.

"But my dear you know the game, until I can get myself established again you will have to help me out."

"Why don't you go back to Canada, or Australia, you seem to do okay for yourself there" said Lettice with a sense of frustration in her voice. "Just leave me in peace, please."

Shirley who was concerned stepped over the threshold and walked through the back kitchen to the living room area, she could clearly see a handsome looking man but no sign of Lettice, she ventured inside the room "Excuse me I was looking for Lettice."

Tommy grinned. "Well hello, Lettice you have a visitor."

Shirley heard a cry "Not now Shirley please I am not properly dressed."

"Oh don't worry dear, we girls must stick together" said Shirley walking further into the room and turning to where she had heard Lettice's voice. She stood transfixed at the sight before her. A man half dressed in women's clothes was standing with a wig in his left hand.

Tommy laughed "Whoops. Oh dear brother, it seems like your secret is out again."

Shirley composed herself. "I am so sorry I shouldn't have come in unannounced."

Lettice let the wig fall to the floor and picked up a dressing gown from the chair nearby and put it on. "I don't know what to say to you."

Shirley was not stumped for words. "My dear, I think I guessed a long time ago that Lettice wasn't quite all she seemed."

"My real name is Henry Willis and this is my brother Tommy."

Shirley held her hand out. "I am pleased to meet you Tommy, I didn't realise that Lettice had family."

"You don't have to call me that now" said Henry falling in to an armchair. "I always get found out. At the last place some little boy wandered in to my room while I was getting changed and told his parents. I had to hot foot it out of there and change my name again. I have been Jean, Dolores and now Lettice."

"To me you will always be Lettice" said Shirley taking a seat "Tommy perhaps you could manage to make us all a cup of tea while I chat with your sister."

Tommy looked astounded. "I have to say you are taking this all very well."

Shirley smiled. "I am a woman of the world Tommy. I have met men like your brother before. I am not one to judge others on how they choose to lead their lives."

"I'll make that tea".

"This changes everything" said Henry looking at Shirley. "I cannot stay here in this town."

"Why ever not?" said Shirley "I won't tell anyone, your secret is safe with me."

Henry shook his head. "No I am sorry, once the secret is out, there is always the chance that a remark may slip or come out unintentionally. It has happened before and I cannot take that chance again."

"What will you do?" said Shirley who was genuinely concerned, she had grown very fond of Lettice Webb and she knew that Lucinda Haines for all her bluster had a soft spot for her too.

"I will sell the house, move away and find myself another identity."

"But my dear, wouldn't you be better to stay here and put some trust in me. You cannot keep running away, because that is what you are doing."

"Maybe I will try my luck in Ireland or move abroad. Besides I have to keep Tommy sweet or he will let the cat of the bag no problem."

"Your brother needs sorting out" said Shirley "he shouldn't be allowed to black mail you."

"Who's being blackmailed" asked Tommy coming into the room with a tea tray.

"You are blackmailing your brother and it really isn't fair" said Shirley addressing him. "You need to sort out your own life and not prevail on Henry here."

"Easy for you to say lady" said Tommy sitting down and lighting a cigarette. "Life didn't exactly deal me the top deck of cards."

"I heard you mention money" said Shirley. "How much do you need and if I give it to you will you promise to leave Henry well and truly alone for good?"

"Depends on what you are offering."

"It depends on what you are asking. Look here is my address" she said handing Tommy a card "come and see me at the end of the week and we will discuss the finer details. But I warn you I will not be messed with and I will have a document drawn up which you will sign in front of a witness that will state you will never bother Henry again."

"That's some friend you have got there Henry" said Tommy looking at Shirley worriedly.

"You don't have to do this" said Henry smiling at Shirley. "It isn't your problem."

"Don't worry about a thing, I will sort something out, I regard you as a friend and I want to help. Tommy pour some tea dear, I am spitting feathers."

Henry laughed through his tears. "That's the first time Tommy had taken an order from a woman."

"And it won't be the last" said Shirley taking the cup and saucer. "Now let's enjoy this tea, I had a coffee with Petunia and I cannot stand that Camp stuff."

And Henry allowed himself a little laugh.

A week later, unrobed of his Lettice persona, Henry took down the brown suitcase from the top of the wardrobe. He opened it and once more took out the brogue shoes, socks, underwear, dark suit, shirt and tie. Once dressed he greased down his hair and made his way downstairs where two larger suitcases stood near the front door. The doorbell rang and the taxi driver took the cases and placed them in the boot. Henry followed carrying the empty brown suitcase and got into the back of the car. "Vauxhall station please" he said as the driver pulled away from the kerb. He turned round to take one look back, the house for sale sign was in place. He righted himself and looked straight ahead wondering where his journey would take him this time.

The End

CURTAINS

The Mists of Time (Prologue)

T he summer warmth of September gave way to the cold, easterly winds that blew in off the North Sea making October one of the coldest for years. Marine Parade was deserted and only a few people in cars ventured along the seafront, keeping warm from the inclement weather.

Walking dogs became a park activity for the owners of those beloved pets; the dogs tugged on their leashes and longed to run freely along the sand in the hope of chasing a wave as it rippled onto the shore.

Even fishermen who normally dangled their rods from the jetty stayed away; this change in weather had taken everyone by surprise and there seemed no let-up from the forces of nature.

Amusement arcades stood empty and dark, the flower beds were barren and the hotel façades looked grey and unloved.

In the town centre, shoppers wrapped in their winter best struggled against the wind and rain, juggling their wares. The chip stalls on the market offered some warmth for those that queued eager for something hot in their tummies.

The doors of the department stores *Palmers* and *Arnolds* opened, welcoming their customers who were hit by blasts of hot air making them feel suddenly overdressed. Many headed for a hot beverage and a sit-down in the stores' restaurants or cafés and the chance to remove their heavy winter coats whilst bracing themselves to return outside to do further battle.

It was on a day such as this that a lone figure walked around the back of the theatre and stood by the railings at the end of the pier, looking out to the seascape beyond. Climbing onto the railings, the person sat gripping the sides of the barrier, stared into the waters of the North Sea below and smiled.

Chapter One: *When Opportunity Knocks*

"**M**um, there is a lady at the door says she wants to speak to you."

Bessie Reeve wiped her hands on her apron and looked at her only son Patrick, who would soon be off to join the Royal Navy.

"Did you ask what she wanted?" she asked, removing her apron. "I am very busy getting the food ready for the tea later."

Patrick shook his head. "No, sorry Mum. She just asked if you were in."

Putting a comb through her hair and straightening her dress, Bessie walked to the front door.

"Yes love, how can I help you? Only I am rather busy at the moment."

The lady beamed a smile and held out a copy of *Awake*, "Did you know that the Lord is on your doorstep?"

Bessie groaned inside, she had no problem with any one of the different religious beliefs to her own but why did Jehovah Witness followers always ring the doorbell around lunchtimes?

"I am sure the Lord is on my doorstep," she replied with a smile, "but I would be grateful if He would remove himself as I only scrubbed that step this morning. Now, if you'll excuse me…"

Patrick watched as his mother closed the front door gently and headed back down the hallway. "Mum, that wasn't very polite."

Bessie sighed. "Son, I am very busy. You will have all your friends arriving later and I really must get the sausage rolls baked, plus a hundred and one other things."

Patrick smiled at his mother; she had always done the best by him and since his father had taken off when he five years old, she had been both mother and father. He knew that his going into the Royal Navy would leave the big house empty and his mother would be left to rattle around the eight-bedroomed property on her own. The house had been left to Bessie by her great aunt, Alice. Bessie's sister Pamela hadn't wanted anything as she was well suited in Bury St. Edmunds with a rich husband and two strapping lads that were in the forces. Her brothers, William and Benjamin were married with families of their own, one in London, the other in Caister and were happy for Bessie to have the house. They all knew her good-for-nothing husband Denis would never provide properly and were mightily relieved when he did the decent thing and left her.

Bessie kept herself busy; she did a couple of shifts at the *Beach Croft Hotel*, helping out in the kitchen and was often called upon to help out at the theatre when Alfred Barton was short of staff, but it really wasn't enough to keep her busy. Bessie filled her time by making things for local charities to sell at their fêtes and, being something of a seamstress, would also take orders for wedding outfits locally.

"Patrick, go and clean your best shoes for this afternoon; I have laid out a clean shirt and trousers for you on the bed."

Patrick kissed his mother on the cheek. "Thanks Mum."

"And don't forget to wash behind your ears; Uncle Benny and Aunt Phyllis are coming over from Caister this afternoon special and you know how fussy Phyllis is."

Patrick mounted the stairs. "Yes Mum, will do."

Bessie put her apron back on, washed her hands and began to roll out the pastry for the sausage rolls. Just then the back door opened and in walked her best friends Nellie and Molly.

"The Cavalry has arrived," said Nellie taking off her coat and rolling up her sleeves. Molly did likewise and the two began to help their friend prepare for her son's going-away party.

Patrick looked around his bedroom and knew he would miss his own room once he had arrived at *HMS Ganges*. He hadn't wanted to find a trade and listening to his Uncles Benny and William he wanted to do his mother proud and follow in their footsteps by going to sea. The one thing he knew for certain was that his mother had the house as her security, but he knew the upkeep of it had sometimes been a problem. Aunt Alice's furniture had been replaced with more modern things in a few of the rooms, including his mother's bedroom, his own and the rooms downstairs. The remaining six bedrooms still housed the dark oak, sturdy furniture and brass beds. There was a bathroom and separate toilet on the first floor, the second floor had a toilet and wash basin. The large kitchen had an adjoining scullery at the back of the house. A middle room was where his mother and he watched television and the large lounge that fronted the ground floor with its vast bay window was a vista on to the seascape beyond.

The house bordered the end of Gorleston's Marine Parade and Brokencliff-on-Sea. There was a lane that ran down the side of the property leading to the main road and adjoining roads that went through Brokencliff, Hopton and onto to Corton. Patrick had been born in a very small house at the back of Gorleston High Street, two-up-two-down, which was his grandmother's on his father's side. Patrick had hated living there; his late grandmother had an abrupt manner and clearly did not like children including her own son Denis. His father had never been able to hold down a job for long, was wasteful with what money he did manage to earn and when his mother passed away suddenly, the house had to be sold to pay off the debts that had accumulated over the years and that neither his father or mother had been aware of. Patrick and his mother moved in with her brother Benny and his wife, and Denis did a flit never to be seen or heard of again. It was a year later that Great Aunt Alice came to the rescue from her deathbed.

Patrick's grandparents on his mother's side had both passed away and he could only remember them from the descriptions his mother gave him and from photographs stored in numerous shoeboxes. Bessie had been in her late forties when Patrick was born, something of a shock, as she had thought that she could not have children. His parents had married when they were both in their late thirties and had never had the best start to married life; in fact the marriage had been doomed to failure from the word go. His father was full of promises he couldn't or wouldn't keep, Bessie struggled to keep body and soul together under the roof of a mother-in-law she couldn't abide and then a baby had come along to add to the mix. At first his father had tried to do his best by his son and wife, but with a gambling and drinking habit he found hard to curtail and his roving eye for other women, he was never going to make the father-of-the-year award. When he had disappeared, leaving his wife and child to fend for themselves, Patrick was wetting the bed, nervous and afraid of what he saw going on around him.

Moving to Caister to be with Uncle Benny and Aunt Phyllis was a turning point for Patrick; Aunt Phyllis was kindness itself and Uncle Benny became the father Patrick had never had. Used to her sister-in-law's funny ways, his mother had found some peace at last.

He took down the last suitcase from the top of the wardrobe and began packing some of the things he would need for the off, on Monday. He looked at the photograph of his mother on his bedside cabinet and placed it between some shirts for protection. He sighed as he set about getting himself smartened up for the party his mother had been planning for weeks. As he went along to the bathroom, he could hear his mother chatting away happily to Nellie and Molly, their voices carrying through the open doors to the landing above. He wished he could come up with an idea for his mother to keep her hands occupied as he knew she disliked idleness for the sake of it. It was later that afternoon that the inspiration would come to him and would be the making of his mother for the rest of her life.

Aunt Phyllis and Uncle Benny were the first to arrive and Phyllis hugged her nephew with great affection. "You are a handsome looking brute," she said, wiping away a tear; Phyllis was prone to emotional displays, no matter what the occasion. She brushed some imaginary fluff from Patrick's jacket sleeve and stood back admiring him.

"Benny, doesn't he make you proud! He will soon be off joining all the other boys in naval uniform."

Benny shook his nephew's hand. "You'll do, me lad. You will make a good sailor, it is a wonderful life in the Navy as me and your Uncle William would tell you."

"And so he will," boomed the voice of Uncle William as he entered the room, accompanied by Daisy his wife, who had pulled out all the stops in the make-up and hair departments. Daisy had never done a hand's turn in her life and relied upon her husband for everything. She was a good cook, a good housewife, but the whys and wherefores of any kind of employment remained a mystery to her.

"Uncle William, Aunt Daisy," said Patrick, moving forward to greet them. "I had no idea you were coming. Mum will be thrilled to see you both. Mum, come and see who's here."

Bessie came through the lounge, carrying a plate of sausage rolls with Nellie and Molly following her with plates of sandwiches and cheese straws. Bessie put down the plates, hugged her brother and gave Daisy a kiss. "Why didn't you two let me know you were coming? I thought you said you were going away to Swansea for the week."

"We cancelled that, big sis. We couldn't let our Patrick go away without our blessing."

Bessie was visibly moved, but did her best to conceal the fact and barked orders to Molly and Nellie to organise some pots of tea.

"Come and sit down, Mum," said Patrick, leading his mother to the settee. "Have a chat, before the other guests arrive. You won't get another chance when that rowdy lot get here."

Bessie smiled and sat down. "Now come on," she said looking at William and Daisy. "Tell Benny, Phyllis and me all your news. How are Davy and Hugh getting on?"

With the conversation in full swing Patrick went through to the kitchen where Nellie and Molly were busy organising beverages.

"Thanks for doing all of this," he said gratefully. "Mum's very lucky to have two such good friends."

"Don't you worry love," said Nellie, pouring some milk in a jug. "We three are always there for each other. Why, when my Breda took queer with the baby on the way, your mother knew what to do. I was all over the place, wasn't I, Moll?"

Molly nodded. "Like a fish out of water. She seemed to forget she had had four of her own. Your mum has always helped out others; when my Albie died, God rest his soul, she organised the funeral, the service, everything. My kids were useless, never had to do anything for themselves as it were; when I needed them to be strong for me, where were they?"

"Don't be upset Moll," said Nellie. "It all worked out in the end."

Moll nodded. "Yeah, I suppose you're right, Nellie. Mind you, I never have found out where the old bugger put that set of screwdrivers."

Some half an hour later the guests began to arrive and Patrick was surrounded by friends he had grown up with. A few of the neighbours popped in for a sherry to wish him well and everyone was having a lovely time. Lilly Brockett was one of the last to arrive with her gardener friend in tow.

"Hello Patrick love. My goodness, your mother has done you proud," she said, looking at the spread before her, which had been topped up by Nellie and Molly at regular intervals. "I wonder Bessie doesn't think of taking in guests with a big house like this, and now you are going away, Patrick."

Patrick hugged Lilly. "Thanks, Mrs Brockett, you have given me an idea."

The following weekend Patrick was home on leave knowing it may be the only one for quite a while.

His mother sat down at the kitchen table, Molly and Nellie had made a pot of tea and Patrick sat quietly waiting for his mother's reaction to the idea that had just been put to her.

"How would I know what to charge these people?" asked Bessie, tapping her finger on the table. "What do I know about doing bed-and-breakfast?"

"Daft question, Mum," said Patrick, getting a nod from Nellie. "What do you see every week at the hotel when you help out? It would be no different. I told you when I went for my exams a lot of the boys were telling me that their families don't get away often, many of them are worrying about their sons and husbands going abroad. You could provide a home from home."

"This house is not exactly up to modern-day standards," said Bessie. "One bathroom, a couple of toilets…"

"That's where our Ray and Stan come in," said Molly with a smile. "They could install wash basins in all the rooms if you were of a mind."

"But what about the cost? I couldn't afford all of that."

Patrick took his mother's hand. "Yes you could, Mum. Uncles Benny and William said they would chip in and I have some savings."

"You have discussed this with your uncles?"

"Of course, the minute Lilly Brockett sowed the seed. They could see the potential. It would give you your own business. You wouldn't have to provide evening meals. Just offer them bed-and-breakfast."

"And we would help out," said Nellie getting, into her stride. "We make a good team and besides it would stop this one here going off to play bingo on the seafront at every free opportunity."

"But how would I pay you? there is a lot to think about."

"Look, Ray and Stan can lay their hands on some wash basins. Stan is a plumber by trade and gets things wholesale. After all you have done for our family he won't be charging you top whack."

"But the furniture in the other bedrooms – it is very old and perhaps not to everyone's taste."

"Mum, the beds are comfortable – the people we are talking about are not going to be spending all day in their rooms; they will be on holiday. As long as they have a clean bed and good food, they are not going to be worrying about dark oak wardrobes and brass bedsteads."

Bessie went silent for a few minutes; she couldn't quite get her head round everything. "I am going to go over and see Benny and Phyllis; they will know what to do."

Patrick smiled at Nellie and Molly, the idea was practically in the bag, he knew Uncle Benny wouldn't let him down.

Chapter Two: *Moving On*

Early February 1971

I n a bed-sit in London, Matthew Taylor was weighing up his options. He hated working at the nightclub in Earls Court and wanted out. He picked up his keys and headed out onto Earl's Court Road. Perhaps Susie had an idea. Susie was his on-and-off girlfriend and she lived nearer to the Fulham Road. He knew he would catch her at home because, like him, she worked at night.

He rang the doorbell and a sleepy voice came over the entrance alarm. She buzzed him into the building and he made his way up the four flights of stairs where he found Susie standing in the doorway in her dressing gown, yawning loudly.

"What the fuck do you want? Can't a girl have a lie-in?"

Used to her ways, Matthew pushed by her, went into the gloomy room and pulled open the curtains. "It's past two."

The room was a fog of stale smoke, the wallpaper was pealing and the carpet was so dirty that you couldn't tell where the pattern ended and the dirt started. There were unwashed cups and plates strewn across the small wooden table, the bed looked as if it hadn't been made in weeks and the ashtrays were so full they had overflowed onto the floor below. A horrid smell of milk that had soured hit Matthew's nostrils and he yanked open the sash window.

Susie yawned and closed the door behind her. "What's with the window? I didn't get in until four, had to stay behind and help the boys clear the place up. The boss has some potential buyers coming tonight; he wants to sell up which means Susie will be looking for a job, again!" She stomped over to the sink, filled the kettle and turned it on.

"For a kick-off, it stinks in here; you need to clean this room. It's worse than Steptoe's yard in here."

"You haven't come here to lecture me on housekeeping…"

Matthew sighed. "I have got to get out of that club," he said, clearing a space on the only armchair and sitting down. "I don't mind men fancying other men, but they keep coming on to me."

Susie laughed and lit her first cigarette of the morning. "You love the attention, all those pretty queens eyeing you up."

Matthew looked at Susie; her bleached blonde hair was a tangled mess., She had spots around her mouth; obviously she had come on and had what she termed as her "curse". Her scrawny body was undernourished, her legs looked as if they could barely support her and she stank of cigarettes. Susie was in her early twenties but her complexion told a different story. She walked over to him and sat on his knee. "Fancy a quickie?"

Matthew pushed her away and she fell on the floor. "No I don't. You need to clean yourself up and stop smoking so much."

Susie laughed again and pulled herself up from the floor. "Hark at Mr. Perfect. It wasn't so long ago that you and that sister of yours were doing all kinds of shit."

Matthew didn't like talking about his late sister. "Well, I have cleaned my act up since then and you should, too."

"Who are you, my fucking keeper? Get back to your nancyboys and leave me alone."

Matthew hauled himself out of the low armchair and grabbed hold of Susie's arm. "I have tried to help you, you crazy mare. Well, no more, do you hear me? Don't come looking for any more handouts. I am getting out of London and I am going to make something of myself."

Susie shook herself free of his grasp. "Yeah, you and a lot of others, you twat. Clear off out of it, you'll soon know where to come when you want a shag."

Matthew walked towards the door and turned to face her. "I am through with you Susie, once and for all, I am through with you."

"Yeah, whatever you say, big boy," Susie called after him, as he slammed the door behind him.

March 1971 Great Yarmouth

Rita Ricer looked up from her desk and greeted Jenny Benjamin who came in with a tray of coffee and biscuits. *Rita's Angels* was situated above an antiques shop in Northgate Street opposite the parish church. It also housed the *JB Dancing School* which was run by custodians Jill Sanderson and Doreen Turner respectively.

Rita, whose husband, comedian Ted Ricer had died the year before had sold her home in Hull, moved down to Great Yarmouth and set up her own theatrical agency. Jenny had been a stalwart friend and had found a house for Rita in Gorleston and the office they now occupied.

"Thought you could do with a drink," said Jenny putting the tray down on the side of the desk. "How are things shaping up for *The Sands* this season?"

Rita put down her pen and took the welcoming mug of coffee. "Don Stevens has been on the telephone making suggestions for a summer line up and, in a nutshell, he is putting the show firmly in my hands."

"Well you did make a great success of last season," said Jenny, brushing a stray biscuit crumb from her blouse and sitting down. "It was a difficult time for all kinds of reasons, but you stayed strong and pulled it off."

Rita looked at the photo of Ted that stood in a silver frame on her desk and smiled. "Old Ted would have loved all of this."

She stood up and walked over to the window in thought, hugging her coffee mug close to her chest. "The problem, as I see it, is who I can put on the top of the bill. I've no chance of getting a big star. I was thinking along the lines of a magic show and getting young Jonny Adams involved and there is a great act I saw while we were in Blackpool last year, *The Oswalds*, they were spellbinding." She turned away from the window and sat down again.

Opening the drawer at the side of the desk she took out a folder containing portfolios of artistes that were now signed to her agency. The back pages consisted of acts that Don and Elsie Stevens had sent details of and suggested Rita might be able to represent, following the collapse of the Audrey Audley Agency in Norwich.

"Have you ever seen Lauren Du Barrie work?"

"Can't say I have," said Jenny, "but I have heard she is very good. I believe she did a run at the Palladium once and has toured abroad. By all accounts a wonderful singer, I bet Maurice Beeney would know her."

"That's what I meant to tell you Jenny. Maurice has hung up his baton; says he and the boys are getting too long in the tooth now. I am going over to see him next week for a chat; I will ask him what he knows about Lauren. On this photograph she looks every inch a Hollywood star."

"Probably taken years ago, you know how these things work. It costs a lot of money for photo shoots. I wonder how old she is."

Rita turned the folder so that Jenny could see. "By the look of this, early thirties."

Jenny laughed. "Then you can bet she is a least sixty."

"Jenny Benjamin, I am surprised at you!" said Rita with a grin. "Well with Maurice off the scene we will need a new orchestra. I have been on to Freddie Fish; he used to play up north and Ted worked with him. He is much younger than Maurice and I think he will be available, comes with his own line-up of musicians."

"So who else are you considering for the line-up?"

"I am going to ask Tommy Trent to join us; he did a great job when he stepped in last year and I did promise Ted I would look after him. I trust I can rely on having the JB Showtime Dancers, I have also got Penny's Puppets - it's only a six minute act but Penny also dresses wigs and alters costumes so she would be a boon to have on board. I am also going to approach Rick O'Shea and the Ramblers, they will bring in the young ones."

Jenny laughed out loudly. "Well, that will please a certain landlady I know. By all accounts Shirley Llewellyn, chair of GAGGA, Great Yarmouth and Gorleston Guesthouse Association to you, is crazy about him. She will be on the front row every night."

Just then Julie Porter, the receptionist knocked and popped her head around the door. "Sorry to disturb you Mrs Ricer, I have just had Tessie on the phone, says she won't be coming back to work, she has found a full-time job at Docwra."

"She wasn't a very good cleaner anyway," said Rita with feeling. "See if you can find the address for Mona Buckle; she may be glad of some work. If you can't find her in the book, give Beverley a call at *The Golden Sands*, she will know it."

"Mona Buckle, now she really is a character," said Jenny.

"And for all her funny ways, a bloody good cleaner," said Rita, finishing her coffee.

* * *

Mona Buckle opened the envelope and read the letter.

Dear Mrs Buckle,

I am writing on the off-chance that you would consider being employed as a cleaner at my offices, which also incorporates the offices of the *JB Dancing School*.

I was most impressed with the way you kept abreast of your workload at *The Golden Sands Theatre* last summer season and reliable cleaners are hard to come by.

This would be a permanent post and I am sure it can be arranged to fit in with your theatre duties when the season starts again, providing Bob Scott has no objections. If you would like to call into my offices anytime within the next few days I would be happy to have a chat with you and see if we can come to a mutual agreement.

Yours sincerely
Rita Ricer
Director: *Rita's Angels*

Mona smiled to herself. She looked at the clock on the mantel and there, as usual, was yet another bill that needed paying. She had not been able to secure any other work since her contract at *The Golden Sands* had ended and this would be the answer to a prayer. She heaved herself out of her chair and went in search of her hat and coat; there was no time like the present.

Julie knocked and waited for Rita to reply. "I have a Mrs Buckle here to see you."

"Oh good, please show her in," said Rita standing up and moving around to the front of her desk. She held out her hand to Mona as she entered, carrying her galvanised bucket and mop. "Mrs Buckle please take a seat, thank you for coming in so promptly."

Mona missed the gesture of the handshake and sat down. "It is best to strike while the iron is hot," she said, making herself comfortable.

"Julie would you bring in some tea and biscuits for me and Mrs Buckle please."

Mona looked up at the wall clock, her eye watering, it was ten thirty. "I never have tea before the allotted hour of eleven," she said, "It upsets my aura. But as it is business you wish to discuss I will join you."

Julie tried to hide a snigger and a warning look from Rita sent her off to do her duty.

Sitting back behind her desk, Rita smiled at Mona. "Did you walk here Mrs Buckle?"

"I did Mrs Ricer. I said to myself, Mona Buckle forego the bus and walk over the bridge. It does you good to walk, raises the energy and the spirits." She looked around the office. "There are spirits here have no mistake."

Rita's eye flicked quickly to the cabinet at the side of the desk where she kept a bottle of brandy and sherry.

"The spirits never lie," continued Mona. "I feel a sense of great fortune here. You have found yourself a haven of tranquillity and the spirits will guide you."

"That is very comforting," said Rita. "I don't mind confessing that when Ted died last year I felt quite lost."

Mona leaned forward placing her hands firmly on her knees. "Ah yes, Mr Ricer. He was a nice gentleman, your husband. It was his spirits that pointed you in the right direction. They knew where you were needed. And it was the spirits that told me I was needed here. Those photograph frames on the wall need dusting and this carpet could go a good hovering."

Julie arrived with the tea tray. "I hope you used tealeaves," said Mona taking the cup and saucer.

"They are teabags from the Co-op," said Julie and scurried out of the office.

"I shall get you some tealeaves," Mona called after her. "When I come to work here."

Rita smiled to herself. "So I take it Mrs Buckle that my offer of employment has met with your approval?"

"It was the spirits, Mrs Ricer. They told me, 'Mona Buckle, Mrs Ricer needs you, so stir your stumps and get to it'."

"Perhaps we should discuss the hours and wages then," said Rita

Mona placed her cup and saucer on the desk and looked Rita firmly in the eye. "I am sure we will be able to come to an arrangement to suit everyone."

"I am not sure what the hourly rate was at *The Sands*, but in conversation with Jenny Benjamin, we thought that forty pence might be appropriate…"

Mona's eye watered "That is very generous. How many hours were you thinking of?"

"Well that depends on you, Mrs Buckle," said Rita, relieved that her offer had not been rejected. "When you start back at *The Sands* you may want to reschedule your hours here. I think if you were to come in three times a week for a couple of hours, say Monday, Wednesday and Friday… The offices are open from nine until five, Monday through Friday so it would be ideal if you could work either before or after those times, even if it meant an hour either side. The areas that would need your attention are the stairs and reception as you came in, this office and the office next door. There is also a small kitchen and bathroom that would need looking after."

Mona sat back in her chair and took up her cup and saucer. She drank the beverage and placed the cup and saucer down again. "I didn't realise that the stairs would be included and I would need to see the kitchen and bathroom."

"Yes of course," said Rita. "Perhaps we could do that now."

Mona got to her feet. "I will leave my bucket and mop there for the moment. I take it you have lino or tiles in the facilities?"

"Tiles in the kitchen and bathroom," said Rita, leading Mona back to the reception area.

"You know where you are with tiles," said Mona. "I don't hold with carpets in washing areas."

"The stairs would need mopping perhaps once a week?"

Mona stopped in her tracks. "If I am to do a job Mrs Ricer, I like it done properly. Those would need doing more than once a week, what with all the people going up and down."

Rita knocked on the door of the *JB Dancing School* and entered. "Sorry to interrupt, Jill, Doreen, I think you have both met Mrs Buckle. It is hoped she will be coming to work for us."

Jill and Doreen smiled and said hello; Mona nodded. "Quite a big office, Mrs Ricer," she said, "and thick shag if I am not mistaken. You'll need a powerful Hoover to get this clean."

Jill tried not to laugh and Doreen busied herself with something in her desk drawer.

"We have a Hoover Constellation," said Rita.

"Oh, one of those things that floats," said Mona looking disapprovingly. "I prefer an upright; you know where you are with an upright. I can't be doing with one of those floating contraptions, too much bending and me with my leg…"

Mona had a pained expression as she limped to the large window. "I shall need a step ladder if I am to clean these once a month; they have some nice ones in *Hammonds*."

Rita made herself a mental note to buy another Hoover and some sturdy stepladders.

When she was shown the kitchen, Mona tut-tutted. "A tidy kitchen is the sign of a tidy mind. That milk should be back in the fridge and those crumbs should have been wiped away."

"A few crumbs from an Eccles," said Rita feeling herself blush; she felt like she was back in school. "Julie likes a cake in the morning."

They returned to the office and sat down. "Well, Mrs Buckle, what do you think? Will you join the team?"

Mona leaned forward again. "I think you need my help, Mrs Ricer."

Rita wasn't sure quite where the conversation was going and suddenly found herself offering another five pence an hour to secure Mona Buckle's services.

Mona smiled. "Well, that is most generous of you, Mrs Ricer. I shall start tomorrow with it being a Wednesday. A week's trial to see if we like each other."

"I will give you a set of keys," said Rita, "so that you can let yourself in. I will ask Julie to show you the ropes. Would you like to leave your mop and bucket here?"

Mona nodded. "I will for the time being. I shall have to buy another for when I start back at *The Sands*. You know where you are with your own mop and bucket. I like a galvanised. I don't hold with those plastic things."

"Mrs Buckle, please allow me to buy you a new mop and bucket. Get yourself one that you like and Julie can give you some money from petty cash. I will arrange for an upright Hoover and a stepladder to be here first thing tomorrow morning."

Mona got to her feet. "I shall report for duty at seven sharp, you have the word of Mona Buckle."

Rita showed Mona out and left her in the hands of Julie; she closed the door heaving a sigh of relief. She looked at the cabinet where she kept the spirits and was very tempted to pour a large brandy.

Jenny came into the office smiling. "I've just seen Mona, she was humming the *Old Rugged Cross* going down the stairs, so I take it we have a cleaner on board?"

Rita let out another sigh. "Ask Julie to bring in two black coffees; I am having brandy in mine, care to join me?"

Jenny looked at Rita and laughed. "Something tells me I might need one."

One morning as the sun was trying desperately to make an appearance, Rita sat quietly opening the post. There were a couple of bills that she would pass to Julie for paying and a letter on gilt-headed notepaper. She stood by the window and read the content with interest. It was signed Alfred Barton of the *Beach Croft Hotel*.

Rita went into the reception area where Julie was just finishing a phone call.

"Have you seen Jenny this morning?"

Julie nodded. "She's with Jill and Doreen."

Rita knocked on the door and went in. "Sorry to barge in, Jenny, have you got a minute?"

"Yes of course. We were just going over some ideas for the male dancers."

Making themselves comfortable on the easy chairs in Rita's office, Rita handed the letter to Jenny. "Have you ever heard of Alfred Barton?"

Jenny read the letter and smiled. "Alfred owns the *Little Playhouse* at Brokencliff-on-Sea. It's between Gorleston and Hopton. You must have come across it on your visits here. There's a group calling themselves the *Clifftop Players* and they put on rep. productions. Though I have to say, since the demise of our own *Little Theatre* in Great Yarmouth, I think they have been struggling."

"Repertory theatre is not really my territory which is probably why I have never heard of them. Ted and I moved in variety circles and apart from going to the Little Theatre at Sheringham once we didn't see many plays."

"Well it is clear from this letter Rita that Alfred Barton wants your help. He is obviously thinking along the lines of some kind of variety show."

"How many does the theatre hold?" asked Rita, her mind setting to work.

"About three hundred or so I think," said Jenny "It's not that big, the backstage area is quite small. I did view it a long time ago when we were looking for somewhere to stage a competition. No orchestra pit. It used to be run as a cinema many years before and then the Bartons took it over. Alfred inherited it from his father."

"You seem to know an awful lot about it."

"I knew Alfred's Aunt Dolly; sadly she died a couple of years ago. Lilly Brockett bought Rose Cottage where Dolly used to live."

Lilly had been *The Golden Sands* theatre and general hospital cleaner until she had found fame as an author in 1969.

"I thought Lilly moved to Gorleston," said Rita recalling a conversation she had had.

"Well Brokencliff is adjacent to Gorleston, so it is easily confused. When people say they come from Great Yarmouth, it often turns out they live in Caister or Ormesby."

Rita smiled. "Do you think this theatre is worth a look?"

"No harm in it," said Jenny. "It will be more business for us."

"I'd like to know more about Brokencliff-on-Sea."

"Well," said Jenny, "that is another story…"

"You see, in 1967 Alfred ran into problems when the then-impresario Wally Warner told Alfred that repertory was dying on its feet and that he wanted to try and revamp the productions by introducing a new director for the *Clifftop Players*. Alfred was having none of it and said he wanted to stick with Ray Darnel. So for the season of '67 Ray directed the small company in four plays, none of which were really that good. Not on par with what the *Little Theatre* in Great Yarmouth was turning out."

"Where exactly was Wally Warner based?" said Rita, getting comfortable in one of the easy chairs reserved for clients and moving a cushion to one side.

"The Wally Warner offices were situated on the top floor of a shabby-looking building off the Earl's Court Road. The basement, ground and first floor were occupied by a record distributor who had been there longer than Wally himself. There was a black painted front door with a large lion's head knocker. I recall a tainted brass plaque with the words '*Wally Warner Theatricals*. Press Buzzer for Attention'.

I had to go there some years ago; Wally knew a lot of people in the business and although he didn't have a hand in variety as such, he proved a useful contact and helped me out a couple of times. I wouldn't say we were ever pally, but as business associates go he was okay. Don Stevens never understood why I had dealings with him."

"So Don knows him?"

"Knows of him, to be fair. The pair never moved in the same circles, but Wally's name came up from time to time."

Jenny moved herself towards the window in deep thought and Rita took the opportunity to order some tea.

Jenny had a good memory when it came to people and places and, as they sat and drank tea, she continued her description of the *Warner* empire.

"That black door was so imposing and when you stepped through it there were arrows on the fading wallpaper pointing up the bare, wooden stairs. You had to plan your ascent carefully for fear of stumbling on the piles of boxes full of records awaiting distribution on both sides of the stair treads leaving very little room for manoeuvre. I heard that many an actress had cursed as she caught her leg on the corner of a box laddering her newly purchased stockings. The staircase to the top floor was less hazardous if you allowed for the holes in the treads and the creaking of the wood."

Rita laughed. "It sounds awful."

Jenny nodded. "It was, Wally's office suite, as he liked to call it, would have not looked out of place in a Dickens novel. The furniture was old, the carpets threadbare and the wallpaper questionable. I remember there was a small kitchen area, a lavatory and this strange smell adding to its authenticity. Apart from his secretary, Miss Brown, a bird-like creature who sat behind a desk in the wide entrance hall, the only other person was Wally."

"I'm forming quite a picture," Rita interjected as Jenny continued.

"Wally's large antique desk was quite impressive; I remember thinking that it must be worth a lot of money and certainly an original. It stood in front of a large picture window. On one particular day that I visited the sun was beating through it and the only indication I had that Wally was even there was from the acrid smoke from his pipe."

"Jenny, have you ever thought of writing a book? You certainly have all the elements at your disposal."

Jenny laughed. "I will leave that to the Lilly Brocketts of this world. Now, where was I? There were one or two framed photographs hung on the yellowed wall; the curtains at the window, which may have been ruby red once upon a time, were more a rusty claret. Home comforts were few and far between, but Wally seemed quite at home."

"Why did you go there, surely Wally didn't have contacts in the dancing world?"

"Surprising enough he did. Although he mainly dealt with actors and actresses, through a previous business venture he had at one time found girls to audition for Miss Bluebell and as you know I was once a Bluebell myself. So that's where the connection lies."

"What of his secretary, did you get to know her well?"

"We chatted a few times," said Jenny. "She was a pleasant woman in her late fifties, slim with greying hair pulled tightly into a bun. She always had a surprised look about her. I remember her sharp nose and tiny hazel-coloured eyes which were adorned by some gold-rimmed spectacles. She never had a hint of makeup with the exception of some red lipstick on her thin lips. She was always neatly turned out in a black two-piece suit, white blouse and lace-up, black shoes; she was the model of professionalism and efficiency. She was always welcoming and had a rich honey-toned voice that belittled her years. She told me once that the four chairs that were lined up on the left-hand side wall were a job lot from a bistro that had closed years ago. The three leather armchairs in the office looked very uncomfortable and must have been longing for the rag-and-bone man to call. According to Miss Brown the lamp that sat on Wally's desk still housed the original bulb. Apparently when it got too dark in the winter months, Wally would gather his papers and head for home leaving Miss Brown to lock up."

"Was he married?"

"Wally! Oh no, no woman in her right mind would have entertained the likes of Wally. You see, at first glance, he looked well-heeled but on closer inspection, his three-piece suit had seen better days, however his shirt was always pristine and his various bow ties a conversation piece. His shoes, though old, were always glass-polished. Wally was slightly overweight and short into the bargain; what he lacked in height he made up for in his manner. I heard that he could reduce an actress to tears as soon as look at her and then charm her to within an inch of proposing marriage. Behind his gentle features there hid the ogre that reared its head from time to time. He had enough grease on his hair, black as I recall, that would have kept a chip shop in business for a week. His life was his business, putting on plays for those wanting to experience an evening at the theatre. To his credit he had several good actors and actresses on his books; but as with all good impresarios he was always on the lookout for new talent."

"And is he still in the business?" asked Rita, wondering whether she might ever get to meet this man.

"I believe he retired last year following a bout of ill health," said Jenny. "I read about it in the *Stage*, or maybe Don mentioned it to me."

"And what of Miss Brown?"

"Ah! Miss Brown! I am not sure what happened to her, but the offices are no longer operational, been brought by some commercial company to turn into flats, last I heard."

There was silence as Rita digested the information. Jenny really was savvier than she cared to let on. Her partnership was going to be one that would help Rita drive the business. It was funny how the two had become so close, when at first they had seemed poles apart. Rita counted her blessings.

"Do you think the theatre at Brokencliff would be a good venue for a variety show?"

"Well certainly not on the same scale as the one we present at *The Golden Sands*," said Jenny. "But I am sure we could come up with something."

"We had better make an appointment to meet Alfred Barton then," said Rita, getting up to stretch her legs. "And maybe we could call in on Lilly at the same time."

Chapter Three: *A Penny for Them*

M aud Bennett watched as her sister Enid was putting out some stock in her gift shop. Decimalisation had come in with a bang and Enid had struggled to get to grips with the new money, despite Maud prompting her at every given opportunity. The cash register had dual currency on the keys, which was only confusing the issue more.

"I am sure this price cannot be right," said Enid holding an ornament of a horse and carriage, bearing the 'A Gift from Great Yarmouth' logo, in her hand. "These were five shillings and now they are twenty five new pence. I don't understand it. I am sure that someone has got it all wrong."

Maud sighed as only Maud could and folded her arms. "Enid, for the last time I have been going on about this for ages and you haven't taken a blind bit of notice. It's the same for everyone not just you. When the theatre begins its season seats that cost ten and six will be fifty two and a half pence. You need to buck your ideas up my girl or you'll be robbed."

Enid put the ornament down and turned to face her sister. "The government is robbing all of us. All they have done is change the 'd' to a 'p'. I've heard Mrs Jary say that the kiddies that go into her shop for sweets complain that they are not getting as much for their pocket money."

"That may be a blessing in disguise. Kids eat far too many sweets in my opinion, they will be lucky if they have a tooth left in their mouth by the time they reach their teens."

Enid huffed. "I'll go and put the kettle on. At least the government haven't messed about with that."

"Give it time," her sister replied and picked up the pricing gun to continue where Enid had left off.

* * *

Landlady, Muriel Evans had just come out of her front door, when her neighbour, landlady Freda Boggis, came out of hers. Both were wearing their coats and holding a shopping bag.

"Good morning Freda," said Muriel with a smile, noting that Freda appeared to be wearing odd shoes; at least they were different colours. "You might want to change your shoes before we go up town."

Freda looked down at her feet and shook her head. "What's wrong with my shoes?"

Muriel pointed out the varying shades in colour.

"I got them in *Freeman, Hardy and Phyllis*," said Freda admiring the tan-coloured footwear. "One is slightly lighter than the other because it was out in the sun last summer on their rack. But they are the same pair. There's nothing wrong with them that I can see. I got them cheap and they had already been reduced in their sale."

Muriel raised her eyes to the heavens. "Perhaps you could take them into *Sampson's* and he could dye them for you."

"I am not wasting good money," said Freda. "Now, are new going up town or not?"

Noting that her neighbour was somewhat irritated for a Monday morning, Muriel nodded and the two set off.

"Did you see The Beverley Sisters on *Stars on Sunday* last night?" said Muriel trying to make polite conversation.

"No I didn't," said Freda swinging her shopping bag. "My Dick wanted to watch that Sunday serial on the BBC – the *Last of the Moccasins*; I went and turned the mattresses."

Muriel smiled; Freda did come out with some classics. "My Barry read the book when he was school. He still has a copy if Dick would like to borrow it."

"You wouldn't get my Dick reading a book! That will be the day; the only thing he's familiar with is the *Sporting Life* or the *Sun*."

They continued their walk in silence and on reaching the market, Freda headed for the fruit and veg stalls while Muriel engaged in conversation with an old school friend.

* * *

Lilly Brockett looked out of the window as she sat at her desk in the bay-fronted window. Rose Cottage had been an answer to a prayer; she was near enough to Gorleston-on-Sea and just far enough away from Great Yarmouth where she had left behind her working life as a cleaner. Now an established author, Lilly was putting the finishing touches to her latest story, a romantic thriller entitled *Julie's Keepsake*.

It wasn't a particularly good story, certainly not up to Brockett standards, but a magazine had invited her to write a short story they could serialise over six weeks and had given her an outline of what they expected. At first Lilly was reluctant to put her name to it and was trying to think of a nom de plume, but after writing down a few names she thought might be acceptable to hide her identity she had given up. She cast her eyes to the blotting paper where she had scribbled Gloria Turnstone, Penelope Reid and Breda Dermot. She chuckled to herself at such tomfoolery and wrote the final sentence of her mini serial and hoped the readers would enjoy it. The magazine in question had wanted to serialise Lilly's debut novel, but she had poo-pooed the idea. For the first time in years, Lilly was in charge of her own destiny and making decisions was getting easier as time went on. She put the top back on the fountain pen and placed it in the desk drawer. She just had time to change into something more befitting before her visitors arrived and she hurried upstairs.

Lilly opened the door of Rose Cottage and beamed. "Hello Rita, hello Jenny, oh please come in, it is so lovely to see you both. I don't get that many visitors."

Both Rita and Jenny were impressed by the décor of the cottage. It was plain and simple. It was carpeted throughout in a pale blue; the walls were covered in delicate floral prints of varying shades and the visible wood work was varnished to a high standard, matching the interior oak panelled doors. The furniture was modern and light and the soft furnishings enriched the colour scheme. Lilly showed them upstairs and the two bedrooms were quaint in keeping with the chocolate-box image that the exterior portrayed. There was a bathroom and a utility cupboard on the small landing, which Lilly explained she used to house a small Hoover and cleaning materials, so that she didn't have the trouble of bringing her larger Hoover from downstairs.

"Imagine me," said Lilly. "Two Hoovers!"

It was clear to her friends that Lilly was still stunned by her change of fortune.

The kitchen was homely and Lilly opened the back door to reveal her small but well-kept garden. "The man who looks after the vicarage grounds comes round and keeps things nice for me. I think his name is William or Ronald or something. He is very nice and only charges me for anything he buys to put in the beds. No labour costs at all, says he does it because it gives him something to do since he retired. The vicar put me on to him. I do make him a cup of tea and have a natter."

Rita and Jenny exchanged looks.

"Come into the lounge and make yourself comfortably and I will make us a nice pot of tea."

"Well," said Rita making herself comfy on the settee. "Lilly has certainly landed on her feet and no mistake."

Jenny nodded and sat down beside Rita. "I think she has an admirer too, though darling Lilly would never have even given it a thought."

"I love the idea of romance; it makes me go all gooey inside. It would be nice if Lilly did find love again."

"No doubt, time will tell on that one."

Rita gazed around the room and nodded her approval. "This really is a charming little cottage. I love the idea of it being double fronted; the room on the opposite side of the hallway is obviously where Lilly does her writing at that lovely desk in the bay window. I didn't notice a typewriter."

"I don't think Lilly can type," said Jenny

"But I am learning to," said Lilly as she came in carrying a tea tray. "I am going to evening college in Lowestoft. It is quite fascinating. Not to mention the people you meet: young, old, men and women. It is quite a humdrum of activity."

A smile was exchanged between Jenny and Rita who knew of Lilly's unique way with words only too well.

"Do you go on the bus?" asked Jenny.

"Oh no, I get a lift," said Lilly. "William or whatever his name is takes me over; he goes and visits his cousin in Oulton Broad and then collects me after."

Lilly poured the tea. "He says if I want to, he will teach me to drive."

Jenny choked on a mouthful of tea. "But Lilly, you can't even remember what this man's name is, you really should ask him to tell you."

"Yes," said Lilly settling herself down in her favourite armchair. "The thing is when I am writing I write about so many different characters that I find myself getting muddled. I think his name might be Bob, but I can't be sure. I will have to speak to the vicar and write it down. Perhaps I can get him to wear a badge, like we did at school."

Rita laughed. "Oh Lilly, you are funny."

The three chatted about this and that and then the subject of the theatre was broached.

"Oh it really is lovely in there," said Lilly. "I went to see a couple of plays way back when my friend Ellen was alive. She and I went to school together and she had an aunt that lived here in Brokencliff. Anyway Ellen loved to see a play and she treated me a couple of times. I think we saw *Murder at the Vicarage* and *It's a Boy*. Very good they were and as good as any I had seen at the *Little Theatre* in Great Yarmouth. It's a shame; I've heard that they won't be putting on any plays this year."

"That is one of the reasons I am over here," said Rita putting down her cup and saucer. "That and to come and visit you of course. I had a letter from Alfred Barton, he is hoping I may be able to come to his rescue and put on a small variety show."

"What a good idea," said Lilly, clasping her hands "It may be just what this place needs, something a bit different to stir the interests of the locals and holidaymakers alike. Many is the time I have heard of the holidaymakers going off to see *The Old Time Music Hall* at the *Gorleston Pavilion* or travelling in to Lowestoft for a show at *The Sparrow's Nest*. It's true that the bus service here isn't that great but the open-top holiday bus that runs from Great Yarmouth to Gorleston and terminates here is popular, they usually run hourly from about 10 in the morning until 10.30 at night from about early June until the end of September. Many get the Lowestoft bus and walk back to Brokencliff from the main road. It isn't that far really, but the lanes are a bit dark at night. Some of course arrive here in cars, but that's another problem and they end up having to park either in Gorleston or Hopton. I was speaking to Joe Dean the other day, he runs the caravan park and I was saying to him, they ought to make better use of the old railway station and make it into a car park; that would help business no end."

"We have an appointment to see Alfred Barton in an hour's time," said Jenny looking at her watch.

"Well why don't we finish our tea and go and sit in the garden," said Lilly. "I have some chairs that what's-his-name got for me, they collapse and everything. Not like deck chairs, I never liked sitting in deckchairs, I could never get the blessed things to stay upright."

The three retired to the garden to bask in the sunshine and enjoy the gaily coloured flower beds.

"Alfred is a nice man," said Lilly "not too keen on Jean, his wife. In fact I have heard one or two people around about who don't think too highly of her. I've only met her twice. Once when I was in the little shop down on the parade and another time when I was having afternoon tea in the hotel lounge with my publisher. She is always well dressed and always looks like she has just come out the hairdressers, but she lacks the charm of her husband. He is a bit like your late husband, Ted, Rita. He could charm the birds off the bushes."

"You are right there, me old lover," said Rita as the image of her much missed husband came to her mind. "My Ted was a charmer alright. I often think about Lucinda Haines who was besotted with him. She made us most welcome when we stayed with her, but her doe eyes when she came through with breakfast were something to be seen."

Jenny noted the catch in Rita's voice and changed the subject. "So Lilly, what are you working on at the moment?"

"Well, I have just put the finishing touches to a serial I was asked to write for a magazine. I am not too happy with it, but they seem to like it and the money is good. I have started work on my fourth novel *The Sand Dunes Are Calling*; the third is due out towards the end of the summer."

"What is the subject matter?" asked Jenny with interest and surprised that Lilly was writing more than she had imagined she would.

The Wooden Soldiers is loosely based on fact. I did some research; or rather my editor did, on men who went to war from Great Yarmouth. I have created my own four soldiers, Cedric and David are the two with families, and the other two are young boys. Eric is from a broken home and Samuel lives at home with his mother. It about their joining the forces and their experiences through writing letters home, Eric isn't very good at writing and gets one of his friends to write for him. I was given some books to read and by also looking at cuttings and papers from the library was able to piece together a story of my own."

"Why did you call it the *Wooden Soldiers?*" asked Jenny, intrigued that her friend had come so far.

"Because like so many of the men that went to war they come home in wooden boxes."

"So none of them have a happy ending?" said Jenny with a tear in her eye.

Lilly acknowledged the statement with a moment of silence. "I wrote the story to highlight the tragedy that war brings and the broken hearts it leaves behind. Films glamorise the war and make them seem like adventures. I didn't want to write of sentiment; I wanted to write of truth."

Jenny wiped her eyes and Rita sat in stunned silence which was only broken by the sound of gulls flying above.

"What is the fourth novel about?" asked Jenny composing herself.

"*The Sand Dunes Are Calling*," said Lilly with a smile. "A bit of romantic nonsense really. It's about a couple that meet on a summer holiday and picnic among the sand dunes. They each return to their own parts of the country with the plan to meet again the following summer."

"And do they?" asked Rita.

"I haven't decided yet," said Lilly. "That's the thing with writing; the characters often tell you which way the story should go. Now can I make some more tea? I am really enjoying our little chat, it is so lovely to see you both." And the present company acknowledged the sentiment.

Rita and Jenny went to the reception desk of the *Beach Croft Hotel* and were greeted by a surly looking character by the name of Angie according to the badge she wore on her left lapel. Her bleached blonde hair was piled on her head, she was overly made-up and with painted fingernails she clutched a pen as if poised to write. Her earrings, that would not have looked out of place hanging in a ballroom, were as garish as they were long. Her thin lips were outlined in a bright red lipstick and she looked as if she had never done a day's hard graft in her life. Angie was on the wrong side of fifty but trying to look on the right side of thirty with difficulty.

"Name please. Have you stayed with us before?" Angie asked with no hint of a smile. Her heavy false eyelashes were obviously causing her some concern as she struggled to keep her eyes open and appeared to be winking at the two ladies before her.

"Good afternoon, my name is Rita Ricer and this is my friend Jenny Benjamin. We have an appointment to see Mr Alfred Barton."

"Really," replied Angie, struggling to keep her left eye open. "The chambermaid jobs have all been taken. We are looking for a barmaid, if you are interested."

Jenny grimaced and Rita, who had dealt with far worse than the likes of the Angies of this world, continued. "I repeat we have a business appointment with Mr Alfred Barton. Now could I call upon you to tell Mr Barton we are here?"

Angie looked surprised. "He hasn't said anything to me about any appointment."

"I am not the slightly bit interested in what Mr Barton may or may not have told you. I repeat and for the very last time, we have an appointment so could you please alert Mr Barton to our arrival."

Angie picked up the telephone and dialled. "Mr Barton, its Angie, there are two old ladies in reception who say they have an appointment to see you. I have told them you haven't said anything to me about any appointment and I can't see anything written in the diary," she said, as she flicked open the book in front of her. "Oh wait a minute; it says here Rita Rising and Jennie Banjomen." She covered the mouthpiece. "Are you them?"

Rita snatched the receiver from Angie's hand and spoke directly to Alfred. "Hello Mr Barton, this is Rita Ricer, I am here to see you with my colleague Jenny Benjamin, and we will wait in your lounge area. Thank you." She handed the receiver back to Angie. "Thank you so much for your help Angie," she snarled. "And someone should show you how to apply false eyelashes correctly."

Jenny giggled and followed Rita to the lounge where they sat down at a table. "Oh that was harsh Rita, but very good, harsh but good."

Rita laughed. "Bloody incompetent bitch, how on earth did she get a job as a receptionist! She looks more like a lady of the night. Did you see that plunging neckline? My goodness, any lower and we could have seen Bristol."

Jenny looked around her. "It's like stepping back in time in here. I haven't seen legs like that on a chair since before the war and those drapes, it's like a Dickens novel. All we need is the wedding cake and the mice."

"It is pretty grim," agreed Rita. "And yet from the front it looks so lovely."

"Is that a pattern on that carpet? It is difficult to make out what the colour is supposed to be, it could do with a good shampoo."

"There is a sort of unloved feeling to the place," said Rita nodding her head and putting her handbag on the table. "I wonder what the rooms are like."

"Not a patch on the *Cliff Hotel* I'll be bound," said Jenny. "The Scotts keep that hotel beautifully. I stayed overnight there once when I was having some decorating done and fancied treating myself. I had a lovely evening meal and the bar staff were a delight. I always recommend it to friends."

Alfred Barton entered the lounge smartly turned out in a blue suit, collar and tie. He greeted Rita and Jenny with a smile and warm handshake.

"Hello Mrs Ricer, Miss Benjamin, thank you for agreeing to come and see me. Can I order you ladies some tea, coffee or something a little stronger?" asked Alfred sitting down at the table.

"No thank you," said Jenny. "We have just come from tea with a friend, Lilly Brockett, perhaps you know her."

"I do indeed," Alfred smiled. "She purchased my late aunt's cottage."

"Ah, yes, Aunt Dolly, is that right?"

Alfred nodded. "She is greatly missed, but she was a good age and she had a good life."

Rita sat back in her chair and looked Alfred straight in the eye. "Now Mr Barton - or do you prefer I call you Alfred? - you wrote to me asking for help, would you like to elaborate further?"

"Well it's like this," said Alfred. "I own the theatre here at Brokencliff and for many years we have run it with a season of repertory productions. Usually four plays every season alternating halfway through the week."

"Yes, I am familiar with how repertory works," said Rita "but I have never had anything to do with it in a professional sense."

"Well business hasn't been good the last couple of seasons and reluctantly we have had to pull the plug. Obviously having the theatre stand empty isn't good. I do run it as a cinema for a few months in winter and we also stage a Christmas pantomime put on by an amateur company. A few suggestions have been made to me about running it as a bingo hall, but that really isn't my cup of tea."

Jenny interrupted. "Well Rita and I are in the business of variety shows and cabaret, do you think that is the kind of thing you would be looking to present here?" She paused for a moment. "This location is not ideal, but not impossible providing certain things are put in place."

Rita smiled. "I concur with Jenny. Firstly I would like to look at the venue and then I can make some suggestions to you. You must realise that I couldn't bring top names here, but I do have an abundance of good variety artists that would be interested."

Alfred stood up. "Shall we go and look at the theatre now?"

"That would be most helpful," said Rita and with Jenny following they made their way out of the hotel and onto the parade below.

The foyer of the theatre was neatly laid out, with the box office central to two entrances that led the way in to the auditorium. The theatre had raked seating as was usual in most theatres and cinemas; there was a panelled barrier at the back of the auditorium with a centre aisle. The seating had been well maintained and Rita and Jenny tested a few to get an idea of how a member of the audience would feel and whether or not the sight lines were good.

A proscenium arch with heavy velvet drapes hid the stage beyond, with side steps leading up at either side. Albert operated the curtains from behind the scenes and Rita and Jenny watched as the curtain rose to the small but adequate fly tower above. The stage had a flat front which then raked gently to the back of the stage area. There were two sets of wings either side of the stage and a lighting gantry above, with room to fly about three flats but no more. The dressing rooms, two on each side of the stage and one larger, longer one at the back were small. There was no orchestra pit to speak of, but Alfred explained that two rows of seats could be removed to accommodate a small orchestra or band as required.

Looking out from the stage, the theatre had a warm and homely appeal that was often lost in larger venues and Rita could understand this had been the perfect place to stage plays.

Jenny inspected the stage floor with due care and attention and a surprised Alfred watched as she began to tap dance across it. Rita concentrated on the whole area and in particular the dressing room facilities; only two had washing facilities. She discovered that toilets were located beneath the small, cramped stage area where an array of props from past productions was housed.

She walked down the side steps of the stage and sat in the front row, never a good place to sit, especially if the stage, as was the case here, was quite high. Jenny joined her and Alfred stood centre stage as he watched the two ladies in deep discussion.

"Well, what's the verdict?" he asked as he came down the steps.

Rita and Jenny had been making some notes.

Rita smiled. "Well Alfred. It would be possible to stage a variety show here, but it would have to be small scale and play once nightly. In order to ensure that you could make some money on this venture you would have to look at the parking situation. Many holidaymakers drive to the resorts these days. I understand the local buses stop running at ten, but there is an open-top holiday bus service during the season."

"The buses come under the Great Yarmouth Corporation," said Alfred.

"Well then, that's one problem solved, but you must think about the parking situation,"

"The old railway station is often mentioned but I don't know how the corporation would feel about leasing the land," said Alfred feeling a bit out of his depth.

"Well you won't know unless you ask.," said Rita firmly "It will be a waste of our time to put together a programme only to have it scuppered by poor attendance."

"When we had a rail service, it was never a problem."

"I will let you think things through and you can come back to me with your decision," said Rita picking up her bag.

"How many weeks are you thinking of running the show for?"

"Well it couldn't be a long season. I would suggest no more than eight weeks, Monday to Saturday with a performance time of 7.30 and no more than two hours and fifteen minutes which would include the interval."

"What kind of prices would we be charging?"

"That depends on the calibre of the artists but I think we are looking at fifty five and forty five pence. It would be down to you to ensure that the programmes had plenty of local advertising as this will keep costs down. Jenny and I will provide the running order and page layout; we are both experts."

"You must also ensure that posters are distributed and displayed, anything at all that will attract people to the show.," said Jenny adding her own thoughts.

Alfred's face expressed some doubt.

"Look me old lover, we are not offering you the services Wally Warner was able to," said Rita getting to her feet and standing in front of him. "What have you to lose? If this doesn't work then you may have to consider other options.

You have asked for help and I am offering it, the rest is down to you."

"There's the hotel to think of," said Alfred imagining Jean's reaction to the news that he would need to spend more time arranging the theatre organisation.

"That is your problem," said Rita, motioning Jenny to join her. "You have always had the hotel. I suggest that you use it to your advantage. Perhaps advertise rooms to include a theatre ticket or a complimentary drink. You are a businessman Alfred, in much the same way that I am a businesswoman. Let me know how you would like to proceed, but your cooperation is vital if this project is to work."

And Jenny and Rita left Alfred with a lot to think about.

As they drove back to Great Yarmouth both ladies were deep in thought. "You know, he could actually make better use of that lounge area," said Rita.

"You are not thinking of branching into the hotel business are you?" asked Jenny, who had been writing some of her own thoughts down.

"Well when I see something that needs organising I cannot but help thinking of what could be done. For example that dining area is what it is, but the lounge I suspect is hardly used by residents. Let's face it, the décor is hardly enticing. I wonder he doesn't think of having a cabaret at weekends, nothing too much, a piano or even one of those dreadful electronic keyboards that many bands are so fond of and a resident singer. That would bring in more revenue to the bar."

"It may upset regular residents," said Jenny.

"What, on a Friday and Saturday evening!" exclaimed Rita making a sharp turn to avoid a pheasant. "Most people are packing on a Friday evening ready for the off on a Saturday. Besides it may attract a few of the locals. I am not sure what the population of Brokencliff is, but there are a fair few houses and cottages about. And of course it borders the end of Gorleston and Hopton either side."

Jenny put her pen and paper back in her bag. "Rita Ricer, you have the whole thing sewn up. You never fail to astound me. You have been in Alfred Barton's company for – what? - all of half an hour; you have viewed the surrounding area and obviously seen what was needed. Why is it that Alfred cannot see that?"

Rita laughed. "I rather think, and I may be wrong, that Alfred Barton is running scared of his wife. From what I have heard about him he does have a passion for that theatre that he lacks for the hotel. Perhaps his wife is holding him back, maybe she is the problem."

Jenny gazed at her friend in amazement. "Never mind Mona Buckle and her aura, I think she would agree with me, that you have the gift!"

And with that the two friends laughed.

Chapter Four: *All Change Please*

Late April 1971
OWLERTON HALL

Owlerton Hall had been quite an attraction in its heyday. It stood in its own walled grounds up a small hill to the south of Brokencliff. The hall still opened to the public during the season, but the number of visitors had dwindled over the years. A bank of volunteers played host to coach parties and conducted tours through the house and gardens. The ample car park had room for ten coaches and any number of cars, although it was now lucky to see one or two coaches a week and the odd influx of cars from visitors to the surrounding resorts. The price of parking was included in the entry fee and if all was well on the volunteer front, a small drawing room was used for refreshments at a minimal cost. If Mrs Yates the housekeeper, chief cook and bottle washer of the hall had time, she would bake fresh sausage rolls and serve scones with jam and cream.

"Would your ladyship prefer kedgeree or bloaters this morning?"

Lady Samantha looked up from her *Eastern Daily Press* and smiled. "Tell Mrs Yates kedgeree would be lovely Penge. Sir Harold will be down shortly and I am sure he would enjoy the bloaters with some brown bread."

Penge nodded. "Very well your ladyship."

A few minutes later Sir Harold Hunter walked into the dining room dressed in his shooting attire and took his place at the table.

"Morning Sammie," he boomed placing his monocle on his left eye.

"I do wish you wouldn't call me that, what if Penge should hear?"

Sir Harold snorted. "It's a damn funny business when a man cannot address his wife as he likes. He twiddled his moustache and stroked his beard, clearly agitated.

Lady Samantha folded her newspaper and laid it down gently on the table. She caught a wisp of hair and pushed it back on the top of her head. Her blonde hair was done in flicked ends; much in the style favoured by some of the female singers she had seen on the television, it was held by a diamanté clasp at the back. Her neck sported a chain with single dropped pearl and she wore matching earrings. Her make-up was minimal and gave her the appearance of a woman of much younger years. She had taken care of her figure and was the model of grace and elegance.

"Now Harold dear, don't go getting into one of bothers, you know it isn't good for your blood pressure."

Sir Harold grunted. "What's for breakfast?"

"Mrs Yates is preparing kedgeree, you are having bloaters."

Sir Harold mumbled something under his breath.

"What was that Harold?"

"Nothing my dear, just clearing my throat," he replied. He really fancied kedgeree this morning.

Bob Scott sat behind his desk in his office at *The Golden Sands Theatre*. He looked at the application forms in front of him and thought, not for the first time, that replacing Jim Donnell wasn't going to be easy. When Jim had been taken ill the previous season, Roger Norris, who had worked in Jim's team, had stepped up to the mantle. As the weeks had gone by, it soon became apparent that Roger was not in same league. Roger had since moved on to work at *Sparkles Nightclub*, stepping in to the vacant shoes of Dave Grant, Jim's best friend. Dave and Jim had worked for Dave's cousin during the winter months at the popular nightclub. Dave had now moved to pastures new in Blackpool after meeting the love of his life, Dan Forrester. Jim's death had been a bitter pill to swallow for all that knew and loved him, not least Jim's daughter Debbie who had had her first born with husband Peter and named the baby girl after her late mother Karen, much to everyone's delight.

Bob's trusted secretary, Beverley, came in carrying a cup of coffee and some letters for him to sign.

"Thanks Beverley, just what I need," he said with a smile. "I am having problems deciding who to invite for interview. Replacing Jim is not a task I relish."

"It is a pity that Roger didn't work out," she said placing the letters to be signed in Bob's in-tray. "I hear he is getting on okay at *Sparkles*, it's just a shame he didn't put as much time and effort in here."

Bob nodded. "Not one of these applicants is from our regular staff, which I find surprising, I thought young Nobby might have applied."

Beverley laughed. "Jim had a job keeping Nobby on side most of the time; a grafter, I will give him that, but his mind is always on girls, though how he expects to find any women worth their salt until he tidies himself up I don't know.," She paused for a moment as she caught sight of a group photograph that hung on the wall. There was Jim Donnell at the centre of things as he had been for many years. There was no doubt about it; the place was not the same without him.

"Why don't you invite all of the applicants for an interview?"

"Well," said Bob leaning back in his chair. "I don't think I have the stomach to interview seven."

"Would you like me to look through them for you?"

"Bev, you are a life saver. It needs another set of eyes."

"Look, I have some time now, give them here and I will whittle it down to three and send the others a 'keep you in mind' letter. Now while I am doing that you should go and see how the workmen are doing with the bar refurbishment. The sign has arrived '*Ted's Variety Bar*' and there is a brass plaque to commemorate Ted Ricer as agreed with Rita. Don't forget you will need to arrange a launch. I left you some catering details from *Matthes* with suggested dates. It will need to be before the summer season show starts and there is also a list of the people I thought you should invite."

Bob watched as Beverley left the office and acknowledged that every manager needed a Beverley.

The transformation of the theatre bar was going very well. New flooring and wall panels were now in place with mirrors etched with variety stars including Dora Bryan, Dickie Henderson, Charlie Drake and The Kaye Sisters. The bar itself had been stripped and a new one built to ensure that bar staff would have more room to manoeuvre during the busy season.

It had been agreed that *Lacon's* brewery would be the sole supplier with their *Encore*, *Legacy* and *Affinity* beers headlining. *Lacon's* would also supply all beer mats and glasses bearing their emblem. New seating and tables had been ordered and the walls were to be adorned by framed photographs of many of the artistes that had played *The Sands* over the years, with Ted taking pride of place. Bob was impressed with the work that had been carried out and couldn't wait to give Rita a sneak preview before the grand opening.

Changes were also being made to the theatre foyer, with new carpeting and much-needed paintwork. The box office at the front entrance to the pier was also getting a makeover which would mean having three windows available for bookings instead of the current two and a much larger back-room area instead of the cramped conditions that had had Maud Bennett cursing on more than one occasion. Knocking through to a storage area that had been used for cleaning and general maintenance materials had seen a proper kitchenette put in place and plenty of shelving on which to store the books of theatre tickets and receipts that were needed.

A third member of staff would be employed part-time to join Maud and her assistant Barbara.

As Bob Scott surveyed his kingdom he felt a sense of pride and achievement. Things were moving in the right direction.

* * *

The church clock at Brokencliff-on-Sea was just striking six am as Philippa Tidy closed the door of her cottage and set out on her morning constitutional with Dingle, her highland terrier in tow. Dingle, eager for his exercise, cocked his leg as he did every morning as they reached the gate and Philippa waited patiently for him to have a good sniff. Although it was not considered cold for the end of April, Philippa wore her tweed jacket and skirt, at the end of her dowdy, thick stockinged legs a pair of brown leather brogues completed the look. Around her neck she had a floral chiffon scarf, a birthday present from a cousin in Scotland some years before, and on her head a brown tweed hat that had become part of her signature wear. Whenever anyone spotted the hat, they were assured that Philippa's wrinkled complexion would be gently edging her radiant, sunny smile. Philippa was neither short nor tall, but somewhere in between, in fact perfectly formed for her age. With a loan from the bank she had secured the purchase of what was now known as *Tidy Stores*, a retail outlet. Philippa had purchased the convenience store from the Barton family when Dolly Barton had given it up due to her failing health.

Her walk took her along Sandy Road through the village and past St Paul's Church, where she turned onto Common Hill, the road leading down to Clifftop Parade.

On her right-hand side was the *Fisherman's* public house and next door *The Sea View* guest house. The wasteland on the opposite side had been bought ten years ago. Joe Dean, a charming Irishman who had been on holiday in the village made enquiries about the land and within a year had transformed it with thirty five gaily coloured caravans which now formed *Finnegan's Wake* caravan park. There was a communal wash house with facilities for both sexes. A small bungalow acted as a base and office.

At first the locals had been wary of Joe Dean, but with his dashing good looks, twinkling emerald eyes and his Irish blarney, he had soon won them over and was now considered a part of the village community. He ran a tight ship, would not entertain rowdy behaviour and any troublemakers were soon given their marching orders. Philippa liked Joe a lot, he was like the son she wished she had had, but romance had never featured greatly in her life and the odd times when a glimmer of hope shone, something would happen to extinguish it and the liaison went no further.

Philippa continued to walk down Common Hill, deciding to give her usual Cliff Way route a miss, she liked to alternate her walks for Dingle's sake. Turning right onto Clifftop Parade she passed the frontage of the *Sea View* guest house. The *Toasted Teacake* stood on the corner and her own store further along the parade on the corner of Beach Road. Sandwiched between the two establishments was *The Little Playhouse*. The impressive double-fronted *Beach Croft Hotel* stood at the end of the parade on the opposite corner to Philippa's shop. The bay-fronted windows stood akin to the stepped entrance leading to the small reception area. Either side of the reception were the dining room and lounge bar respectively, both with impressive views over the secluded beach area below. On the turreted fifth floor were the living quarters of Alfred and Jean. The hotel car park at the side of the hotel on Beach Road was the view Philippa could see from behind her counter.

The train that had run from Great Yarmouth through to Lowestoft and had serviced Brokencliff-on-Sea was now sadly no more thanks to the Beeching cuts. Philippa didn't drive very often and her red Mini stood idle most of the time, as she used the bus whenever possible. Her driving was renowned throughout Brokencliff and she had earned herself the title of "Second Gear Phil," by those that had shared a ride with her.

Her walk almost complete, Philippa stopped for a moment to drink in the sea view. You couldn't buy mornings like these and Philippa was ever grateful for the summer months ahead when fires would no longer need to be laid. Noticing the milkman dropping off her delivery at the shop, Philippa clicked her tongue and took a resilient Dingle home for his breakfast before she set out to open the shop. She was expecting to be busier this week as Joe had warned her that he had let six caravans and he always sent his guests Philippa's way for any provisions they might need.

"There goes Second Gear Phil, she takes the same route as Aunt Dolly used to," said Alfred Barton looking down from the turreted window of the bedroom. His wife Jean, seated at her dressing table, turned to look at him.

"No doubt she will have that shop open by six thirty," she replied. "You would think she would be grateful of a lie-in before the season kicks off".

Alfred knew only too well the luxury of a lie-in, but with the hotel open all year round, except for a couple of weeks in January, lie-ins were not top of the Barton priority list.

"Not Phil's way, she has carried on Auntie's tradition and will be out to catch the trade from Finnegan's. I hear Joe has a few in this week."

Jean groaned to herself, people who holidayed in caravans made her shudder, how could they possibly enjoy two weeks in a pokey caravan? She completed her make-up and put the finishing touches to her hair. She was tired of this ever-constant early rising and getting to bed late. She longed for a quieter life, preferably one that didn't involve guests, especially those that were a hangover from her in-laws' days.

"Oh, Alfred's father would never had done it that way." How many times had she heard that old chestnut? If you had to run a hotel, the least you could expect would be being able to put your own mark on it. But the Beach Croft was in a time warp, like a memorial to her late in-laws. The furnishings were clean but dated and the whole place needed a complete overhaul, but Alfred was less keen to spend money updating the hotel than he was to throw it at his beloved hobby, the theatre. Many was the time Jean had thought that if she encircled herself with a pair of red velvet curtains and drew them back occasionally reciting some words from Shakespeare she might well get more attention from her husband than she currently did.

Jean made for the bedroom door. "Well, breakfast won't cook itself," she said in her business-like manner "Chef has the day off. Are you coming down to give me a hand?"

"In a moment," Alfred replied, continuing to enjoy the view. Jean straightened her skirt and headed downstairs knowing full well that Alfred would appear the moment the last breakfast had been served. It was on days like these that she wished she had taken up her sister's offer to join her and her family in Australia. It would be nice to meet her sister's grandchildren that she had only ever seen on a photograph, not to mention her Australian husband. As she reached the bottom of the stairs she encountered Mrs Wilmington, a regular guest who, with her husband, came to the *Beach Croft* at least three times a year.

"Good morning Mrs Wilmington," said Jean as pleasantly as she could muster. "It looks like it is going to be a lovely day out there."

Mrs Wilmington, never the easiest when confronted by conversation of any kind grimaced. "It will be if the sun shines, but I don't hold out much hope on that."

"Of course not," Jean thought to herself. "It might just put a smile on your face, you miserable old sod."

Jean checked the reception desk and caught the night porter eating a sandwich. "I have told you before about eating at the desk Shaun and if I have to mention it to you again I will have no alternative but to let you go with a week's notice."

Shaun tugged on his peaked cap and felt himself blush. "Sorry Mrs Barton."

Alfred continued to look out of the window for some time; he had no wish to join his wife in the kitchen only to be told that he was getting in the way. At least when Chef was in he could be guaranteed a good man-to-man chat and a sneaky bacon buttie that Jean would disapprove of.

Reverend George entered *Tidy Stores* at seven precisely and was greeted by a queue of strangers all awaiting Philippa's attention. When the crowd had dispersed, he took a small brown loaf and a pint of milk and put it on the counter.

"Good morning Philippa. My, you have been busy this morning," he beamed.

Philippa liked Reverend George, a fine looking man in his late thirties. His jet-black hair always well-groomed and the dark shadow of a recent shave gave him a rugged look. His slight figure gave the impression of one who was undernourished, but with his many lady admirers, who were often rustling up a meat pie or cake for him, nothing could have been further from the truth.

"Good morning to you Reverend George," said Philippa with a smile. "They were the latest arrivals from Finnegan's. Joe always lets me know so I can get in extra provisions. There was a time when he had thought of opening a little shop on the site when Dolly gave up but when he got to know me, he decided against it. I look after his clientele and give him a discount on his groceries as a thank you, it is something that Dolly Barton started and I am happy to keep the arrangement".

"That is very Christian of you, Philippa. It is nice to know that there are still people looking out for each other".

Reverend George enjoyed his life at Brokencliff and couldn't believe that five years had passed since his arrival. He liked the locals and seeing all the new faces that came during the summer months for their holidays. He crossed the road to enjoy the view from the cliff wall over the sandy beach below. On the horizon he could see the large cargo ferries on their way to the Great Yarmouth port. He marvelled at the size of the vessels and having seen them close up on one of his trips into the town, wondered how they navigated the river mouth without hitting the Gorleston Pier or the banks of the South Deans on the opposite side of the river. Thinking about his day ahead, he made a mental note to visit Joe Dean at *Finnegan's Wake*. He hadn't seen Joe at Sunday service lately and hoped everything was well with him. Even though the vicarage was a stone's throw from the caravan park, his small office faced the rear of his home and apart from the odd person making their way along Railway Lane there was little people traffic to speak of, so he was rarely distracted from the job in hand.

He started his day with a prayer in the church and then, following his breakfast, he would get down to parish business and arrange time to visit the sick, catch up with any letters that needed his attention and make time for a morning coffee with his 'daily', Martha Tidwell. Martha had been employed by the previous vicar and he found her to be hard-working and reliable. She lived just outside the village and came to work on her bicycle complete with basket on the front. Often she would make him a cake or a pie for his lunch, believing him to be totally incapable of looking after himself, when in reality he liked nothing more than rolling up his sleeves and putting together a tasty meal, when time permitted. His female parishioners were of the same opinion and were forever dropping off little packages of food, using the excuse that they had had some pastry left over or had made too much for themselves. This always made him smile, but he was very grateful that they cared enough to think of him. In turn he took a great pride in his parish duties and ensured his door was always open to them when they needed his advice and guidance.

He breathed in the sea air, took one last look at the vista before him and crossed the road to make his way back to the vicarage, giving a wave to a couple of ladies who took care of the alter flowers every Sunday, who were out and about early walking their dogs.

* * *

Jean was not finding cooking breakfast a pleasurable task, especially as, yet again, Alfred had failed to materialise and Tim the commis chef had called in sick again. It was always the same when the chef had a day off, Alfred would make himself scarce, leaving her to do all the work. Once again she thought of the offers she had received to go to Australia and right then she felt like going upstairs and packing a bag. Remembering her duty to the paying guests, she took her second deep breath of the morning, looked at the clock and carried on.

Alfred appeared in the kitchen on cue just as Jean was clearing the work service. "Everything alright my sweet?" he smiled.

Jean looked at him in disbelief.

"Just off to see Phil and then I think I will take a walk before we get busy here."

Jean sighed. "We have the draymen at eleven so make sure you are here because I doubt that lazy barman will be on time; it is high time you had a word with him. I have already reprimanded Shaun this morning. So don't let me be the one to have a word with Danny or you will be a member of staff short. I have the laundry room to sort out, not to mention the accounts to do. Alfred Barton, are you listening to me?"

Alfred waved his hand and stepped out of the back door.

"Hello Phil," said Alfred. "Any chance of a cup of tea?"

Philippa smiled as she looked up from her newspaper accounts. "I am sure you have had your tea this morning, but I will pop the kettle on anyway".

Alfred picked up a packet of digestive biscuits from the shelf. "What about a biscuit?"

"Put those back this minute. I have my own back here in a tin. You will have to make do with a custard cream," said Philippa filling the kettle, "That's my profit you are tampering with. I wonder your poor Aunt didn't go bankrupt. How is Jean this morning?"

Alfred made himself comfortable on the chair near the counter, which was there for any customers who had trouble standing too long. "Jean is her usual self," replied Alfred.

Philippa hesitated before responding, Jean was a tricky one, no mistake, and not the happiest of people at the best of times but Alfred could do more to help her about the hotel. "I expect she is preparing for the summer season, the same as the rest of us. Young Joe is off to a flying start already – had quite a flurry of his early birds this morning, that till is looking quite healthy."

"I thought I saw a few of them across the road as I came over; he does seem to do quite well there."

"The man is a grafter. I remember your aunt telling me how he had transformed that piece of waste ground and made a go of it and although there was some around here not attuned to the idea at first, even they acknowledge that he has brought more visitors in."

"It's just a pity they are not theatre goers," said Alfred, strumming his fingers on the counter.

"You can't blame people for wanting to have a bit of fun, that's why they all go off to Great Yarmouth for the fun fair and the amusements. I wonder someone hasn't thought of putting something here."

"The reason people come here is to be free from the smell of candy floss, hotdogs and the noise of slot machines."

"But it that true now?" asked Philippa pouring milk into two cups, "I think we need to look at what the visitors want. There are no proper places to park cars here so that rules out using their own transport for those that have any. Why haven't they made use of the old railway station site? Coaches are somewhat restricted and buses stop running after ten, so unless people are actually staying here what chance are they offered? The area needs proper parking."

Alfred nodded in agreement. "I am hoping that the variety show planned for the *Playhouse* this season will pay. I haven't said anything to Jean, she really isn't interested, but I know you are."

Philippa handed Alfred tea and a barrel of biscuits. "It's a shame you had to lose the rep company," she said. "But by all accounts Rita Ricer will see you right. Lilly was telling me what a grand job she made at *The Golden Sands* back in '69."

Alfred helped himself to a custard cream. "I hope you are right. I would hate to see the theatre close."

"I am sure it won't come to that, have faith." And at that moment that was all Alfred had.

* * *

Lady Samantha was taking afternoon tea in the garden room; the sun had been shining through the glass panels making the room pleasantly warm without being stuffy. She opened the *Great Yarmouth Mercury* which she hadn't had time to look at earlier as she had had some bills to settle and without the aid of the secretary the Estate had once employed, she now had to do these chores herself.

An article concerning the theatre at Brokencliff caught her attention and she read it with great interest; it wasn't often that Brokencliff got a mention and the advertisements she had once placed for Owlerton Hall had long since been seen as unnecessary expenditure.

The article stated that a variety show would be staged instead of the usual repertory season, something that Lady Samantha frowned at. She had often taken in a play especially when his Lordship had had friends over for a few days to go out on one of his shoots. To be honest they never seemed to shoot anything much, but the brandy decanter was replenished more than she thought was strictly necessary. She rang the bell to summon Penge.

He dutifully arrived and bowed his head.

"I wonder Penge if one might trouble you for another pot of tea, I seem to have a thirst this afternoon, I do hope I am not coming down with a cold. The weather does play with one so and I never know quite what to wear."

"Will you be requiring anything else, another slice of cherry cake perhaps?"

"Oh dear me, no," said Lady Samantha with a smile. "As much as I adore Mrs Yates's cake, I would only spoil my dinner. No, another small pot of tea should suffice."

"Very well," said Penge picking up the tray.

"Before you go Penge, do you know anything about this new idea for our theatre this season?"

"Only what I heard in the *Fisherman's* one evening. Some of the locals were saying it was a great shame to be losing the little plays and I think it was the landlord who said that Alfred Barton was worrying about getting more people along to Brokencliff."

"Yes I see the problem. We really must do something about getting Brokencliff back on the tourist trail. You must remember when our car park was full with coach parties and afternoon teas on the lawns. Now everyone drives a motor car." She paused and looked about her. "If only there was some way of getting more of the public to visit the house. I know the old place needs sprucing up a bit, but I am reluctant to pour any more money into it if there is no guarantee that business will improve. Without the volunteers that do help us I don't know how we would open for the few weeks that we do."

Penge nodded. "Perhaps milady should have a word with Alfred Barton."

Lady Samantha looked quizzical. "About what, Penge?"

Penge smiled. "Oh I am sure that your ladyship can work that one out for herself," and with that he made his exit.

"Mmh," said Lady Samantha looking at the article again. "I wonder…"

Chapter Five:

I n Great Yarmouth Rita and Jenny had been busy putting together not one, but two summer season shows. Rita had decided against using her stage name Moira Clarence as the director of the show. She reflected that by using her married name, she would keep the name of Ricer alive and she was sure Ted would agree.

The line-up for *The Golden Sands Theatre* has been confirmed, with one exception; Freddie Fish had already accepted a summer season elsewhere and it was left to Rita with the help of some of Don Stevens's contacts to find a replacement.

The Vic Allen Orchestra was highly recommended and Rita and Jenny went to see them in action in Clacton where they were playing a week's engagement. Vic Allen, who had the looks of an Italian matinee idol, was more than interested. A summer engagement had fallen through and he was open to offers. His small orchestra consisted of male and female musicians, all about the same age as Vic, which was mid-forties. They had years of experience between them; they had played summer seasons around the country and performed many times in Europe. The orchestra's home base was Norwich, so it would mean that, like Maurice Beeney and his orchestra had done before, everyone would be able to go to their own homes after the show. Keen for Vic and his gang to meet the company, a date was arranged when all would be able to attend the London studios where Rita had met with the previous year's company; Jenny would be on hand to assist.

Though it would mean some acts travelling from Great Yarmouth, it made it fairer for the others on the bill who would be travelling in from various locations. Rick O'Shea and the Ramblers would be playing a gig in Earls Court that night so it was ideal for them. The title of the show would be *Summertime Magic*.

It had been decided that the JB Showtime Dancers would be a line-up of four girls and four boys. The introductory of two male dancers the year before had proved to be successful and the eight dancers would complement each other giving Jill and Doreen greater scope for routines.

The show at Brokencliff on the other hand would not open until July and the company would assemble at the Little Playhouse a week prior to opening. The acts had been selected with care and Rita was happy that she had the right mix in place.

The acts would include top of the bill Pearl and Sidney Arbour (Sweethearts of Song); a letter would be on its way to them but Rita had it on good authority that the pair had no bookings for the coming summer. It was confirmed that comedian Hughie Dixon and Ukulele Una would appear and that Phil Yovell would provide the music from his baby grand. There was also Jimmy Joe with Tiny Tom (a ventriloquist act) and, as a special attraction to boost the programme, Mystic Brian had agreed to be a 'Special Guest Star' with his Turtle Doves. The Clifftop Gaiety Girl's would consist of four female dancers and they would be choreographed with some routines that Jenny Benjamin had used in many shows. Jill and Doreen intended to make a few changes but still in keeping with Jenny's original work. As the show was on a much smaller scale it was imperative to keep the balance just right. Rita had her eye on another act she had recently seen if Pearl and Sidney Arbour were unavailable.

* * *

Joe Dean busied himself at his desk, looking at the bookings for the forthcoming season. They were slightly down on last year. Situated on The Parade he was a magnet for passing trade, so he wasn't unduly worried, but a few more bookings would be a Godsend. Viewing his accounts he wondered if he was charging enough for his vans. Most stays were for a week or a fortnight and he had to supply a change of bed linen once a week. The laundry he used in Lowestoft had recently put up its prices and, with the cost of electricity and the wages for two part-time staff to find, he sometimes doubted whether he had done the right thing in moving away from his home. Brokencliff was a far cry from his life back in Ireland, where everything had seemed more laid back. Making *Finnegan's* pay during the winter months was sometimes a struggle. The vans had minimal heating but the wash facilities were a main concern. People didn't want to venture across the park to take a shower if a cold wind was blowing off the North Sea.

It was mainly manual workers away from their home towns who would take up residence in the winter or long-distance lorry drivers needing a bed for a couple of nights. But these bought their own problems – all Joe needed was a couple of blokes who had over indulged at the *Fisherman's* public house and all hell let loose, usually over a disagreement about football or, worse still, politics. He wanted to make the park a residential one with permanent mobile homes, each with their own wash facilities. He feared this idea might cause resentment within the local community not to mention the council. He closed the accounts book and grabbed his bunch of keys. He headed off to do his daily inspection to ensure everything was as it should be. If his watch was right, one of the staff should be in by now, cleaning out vans seven and eight. He breathed in the morning air and set forth.

Deanna Williams, landlady of the *Fisherman's*, who was checking that the barrels were ready for collection, watched him as he strode purposefully across the park and, not for the first time, did she think what a dashingly handsome man he was. Her thoughts were soon disturbed by her husband Tom calling from inside that breakfast was ready.

Deanne and Tom Williams had been managing the *Fisherman's Arms* for fifteen years. It had never been their intention to stay long at Brokencliff. When the tenancy had been advertised, they were both getting itchy feet at a pub they were running in Ipswich and thought the change of air would do them both good. Both in their late forties, they had been childhood sweethearts who had married at sixteen and, through thick and thin, had stayed together. Tom had originally been in the Army and Deanne had worked behind the counter at a local newsagent. When Tom came out of the Army at 25 and was looking for a career, he had taken work in the public house he would later find himself managing on a temporary basis. It was an interim arrangement until he decided what else he might do, but then Deanne decided to do a couple of shifts to supplement their income and the rest was history. They had no children, which was more to do with fertility problems than their desire to have them. Deanne was of the opinion that some things were not meant to be.

As Tom handed Deanne a cup of tea, her thoughts drifted once more to those of Joe Dean. She looked at Tom who was busy dishing up their late breakfast. He was still quite good looking, he kept himself neat and tidy, but the lean muscle he had during his Army days was no more. His beer belly had ruined his once perfect physique and the full head of hair had long since gone, leaving a shiny dome. Deanne, on the other hand, had maintained her figure and ensured her hair, make-up and nails were immaculate. She dressed in clothes that flattered her figure and had been known to turn many a head in her stiletto heels and fishnet stockinged legs. She liked to keep an orderly house and was the more likely of the two to deal with any trouble makers.

Tom put a plate of breakfast in front of her and sat down to join her. "You look miles away," he observed buttering some bread. "Are you going anywhere nice?"

Deanne smiled. "Nowhere you would want to go," she replied.

"No doubt," thought Tom, "she has spotted a new outfit."

Tuesday 4 May

As the company for *The Golden Sands* summer season show gathered at the *Studio 4* in Earls Court, the headliner was still missing. Checking her watch, Rita whispered to Jenny that she hoped that this wasn't a sign of things to come.

Vic Allen had assembled his small orchestra of eight at one end of the studio and with the dancers keen to try out their new routines was accompanying them as Jill and Doreen kept a watchful eye on the proceedings.

Jonny Adams was setting up his tricks and was a slightly more confident young man than he had been the previous season when his stammer had been a problem. It had been down to the careful nurturing of the late Ted Ricer that he had progressed so well.

The comedian Tommy Trent was looking over some new material that Rita had given him. It was what Ted would have used had he been alive. She had promised to look after Tommy as it had been one of Ted's dying wishes. His old friend had fallen on hard times and had had a difficult few years; now with Rita taking command of his bookings she planned to improve his lot.

The Oswalds magic act consisted of husband and wife Salvador and Carmen with their 20 year-old daughter Conchetta. From what Rita had witnessed at a previous venue, this act could well stop the show. The act moved at such a fast pace and was so slick, that it seemed impossible for them to pack so much into a relatively small time frame.

Rick O'Shea and the Ramblers were in a corner discussing their chosen set. Rick ran by the group some ideas and impersonations he thought would add to their appeal with a family audience and Miss Penny (Vickers) was sorting out her large marionette puppets and talking to herself.

When Rita had just about given up all hope, the studio double doors opened with a crash and a woman dressed in more furs than Davy Crocket had ever shot entered wearing dark glasses and a Russian Cossack hat followed by a mousey looking lady, who looked downtrodden as she carried what appeared to be the whole scores of every Rodger and Hammerstein musical written and more besides. The lady, who was short with a mop of mousey curly hair, no make-up to speak of and a pair of glasses that magnified her eyes making them look like saucers, tried to keep up with her companion's pace.

The first lady stood centre studio and removed her sunglasses in a theatrical gesture and surveyed the assembled company by sweeping round full circle. Looking straight ahead she flung her arms wide and spoke in a loud booming voice. "Rita Ricer I presume. Lauren Du Barrie. I am delighted to be here".

She turned to the mousey woman with another theatrical gesture. "And this is my personal assistant Millie. Millie darling put the scores down and shake hands with Rita. I am sorry we are a little late, but we had problems with the Rolls and had to hop in to a cab. Such a bore darling don't you know."

Rita and Jenny shared a knowing smile. "I am pleased to make your acquaintance," said Rita moving forward to shake Lauren's hand but not before doing likewise with Millie and giving her a warm smile. Rita then proceeded to introduce everyone in the room. It turned into something of a royal exercise; Lauren Du Barrie certainly considered herself to be every inch the Grand Dame of theatre.

Jenny looked at the publicity shot she had of her. Lauren had certainly been much younger when that had been taken. Sixty plus, she was shorter than her photograph suggested, she was however slightly taller than her assistant who would have not have looked out of place as one of the munchkins in *The Wizard of Oz*. Lauren was heavier too as the removal of her furs revealed. Her carefully applied make-up hid a multitude of aging flaws; her eyes were made-up for a stage performance with eyelashes that could have swept the ceiling. Her outfit, a loose-fitting, three-quarter length dress in black covered her obviously expanding waistline, her legs were encased in American tan tights and on her rather out-of-kilter dainty feet she wore three inch black stiletto heels that were adorned with ornamental bows. With the gesture of a Bette Davis hand minus the cigarette and a Judy Garland strut she commanded attention from everyone. It was going to be another interesting summer season, no mistake!

Back at *The Golden Sands* Bob Scott was showing Matthew Taylor around the theatre and left him in the capable hands of the back-stage staff so that he could be brought up to speed with what to expect. Matthew had had glowing references from previous employers and his experience managing back-stage areas, especially abroad, was second to none. He was 32, tall, with a mane of shoulder-length blonde hair, broad shoulders, tapered waist and had a chiselled, rugged face with generous, marshmallow lips. Smartly dressed, even in Levi's and a checked shirt, he was sure to become every girl's dream date. Bob had every confidence that Matthew would be able to fill the shoes of the late Jim Donnell.

Matthew surveyed the team he was going to be working with and felt that things were going to be relatively quiet. These men and boys had worked alongside Jim for some years and were seasoned professionals; Matthew felt he was going to have no problems getting the boys on side.

Bob had briefed Matthew on director Rita Ricer and what she would expect and he mentioned producer Don Stevens, who Matthew would meet in due course. Matthew acknowledged the information and made notes as he went along. Don Stevens, yes, he was looking forward to meeting the great man of whom he had heard so much about.

Matthew had taken a room over in Southtown and so he was a 15- minute walk from the town centre and the seafront. The rooms were let by an agency and as such there was no landlord on the premises. He had his own front door key and one to his room and wasn't duly bothered by the other tenants who he only passed on the stairs sometimes. They all had various jobs and no one in the house appeared to live a nine-to-five existence. He was able to make tea and coffee in his room and had a small oven with two hotplates so he could make something to eat. But he took most of his meals outside as *The Golden Sands* provided luncheon vouchers as part of the deal for the unsocial hours of the business. He came and went as he pleased which suited him fine and, as he didn't socialise with the others in the house, he managed to keep a low profile.

Chapter Six: *Faces from the Past*

Thursday 6 May

Plans were being made to launch *Ted's Variety Bar* and Beverley had come up with several dates, checking that the mayor and local dignitaries would be able to attend. Beverley who had good working relationships with secretaries and personal assistants ensured that the dates would be held until one was confirmed. Debating on whether it should be a lunch or an evening opening, Beverley had put the idea to Rita. Rita thought that an evening event would be more fitting and the date was finally agreed as Friday, 28 May. An announcement would be made in the local press and invitations sent out accordingly. The bar would be open to the public the following day and remain open until the end of September. Plans were afoot to recruit some new staff for the venue and Bob was pleased that everything was at last beginning to fall into place.

Maud and Barbara had been along to inspect their newly furbished box office and both were much surprised with what had been achieved. A part-time member of staff was due to start at the beginning of June when the box office would open for bookings.

Rita had arranged interviews with various members of the company and the *Great Yarmouth Mercury* would lead on several stories throughout the season. Lauren Du Barrie was lined up to appear on the local *Anglia* television news and also BBC radio interviews. Lauren who had for many years worked mainly abroad had once been a great star in the United

Kingdom, but rumours of retirement and ill-health over some time had marred the artiste's reign. Lauren was determined to turn those stories on their head and was looking forward to topping the bill at *The Golden Sands Theatre* in the hope that it would lead to being offered more lucrative work. Though unaccustomed to performing in a twice-nightly show, she had been rehearsing with her singing coach in London to ensure that she was ready. Deciding to sing songs from various musicals seemed to be the safest bet, but since the initial get-together in Earls Court she had also sourced some more popular tunes from the charts and hoped that she would be able to carry them off without embarrassing herself; she felt it was important to connect with younger members of the audience as well. Her personal assistant Millie, who had heard Lauren sing more times than she cared to remember, wasn't so sure about the choice of material; *My Sweet Lord* and *Knock Three Times* mixed with *Band of Gold* seemed like a recipe for disaster. She couldn't wait to find out what Rita Ricer would make of it all when rehearsals got underway proper.

Posters for the forthcoming summer show had been approved and were being pasted on billboards around the town.

The Golden Sands Theatre — Great Yarmouth

Don Stevens in association with Rita Ricer
proudly presents for the summer season

Lauren Du Barrie
The Voice of an Angel

in

"Summertime Magic"

Opening Friday 18th June at 8pm
And thereafter Twice Nightly at 6.10 & 8.45
(except Sundays)

With the Magic of local talent **Jonny Adams** Returning for his second season at *The Sands*	**The JB Showtime Dancers** with choreography by Jill Sanderson and Doreen Turner	The incredibly funny **TOMMY TRENT** Norfolk's best kept secret

The Fabulous
Rick O'Shea and the Ramblers
"Rockin' and a Rollin'"

Vic Allen and his Orchestra	Miss Penny's Puppets

The Spell Binding Magic Act
THE OSWALDS
Direct from their sell-out season in Belgium

Produced by Don Stevens and Directed by Rita Ricer

Seats Bookable in Advance from the Box Office
65p, 55p and 45p

Thursday 27 May

It was the day before *Ted's Variety Bar's* grand opening when Mona Buckle reported to *The Golden Sands* for her first day back of the season. She had sat down in the front row of the auditorium to await the arrival of her new boss, Matthew Taylor.

Jack, the stage-door keeper, looked anxiously at the clock; he hoped that Matthew would arrive on time as he knew that Mona Buckle did not like bad timekeeping. Jack had arrived for duty at eight that morning and Mona had followed half an hour later dressed in her usual attire - coat and hat - and carrying her beloved galvanised bucket and mop.

At five minutes to nine, Jack heard a familiar whistle and Matthew came through the stage door smiling. "Morning Jack, a bit sharp out there this morning."

Jack nodded. "They say it will rain later according to the wireless. Mrs Buckle has arrived and you will find her in the front row."

Matthew smiled. "I have heard a lot about Mona."

"You best address her as Mrs Buckle, lad. She doesn't do first names and for goodness sake, don't ask her to take off her hat. I think it is moulded to her head. And another thing, she doesn't entertain tea until eleven on the dot and she will expect you to join her."

"Thanks for the warning," said Matthew with a grin. "I shall tread carefully."

Jack watched as Matthew headed for the door. "Good luck lad, by God you are going to need it."

"Mrs Buckle, good morning, I am very pleased to meet you. I am Matthew Taylor, the new backstage manager." He held out his hand which Mona totally ignored. She eyed him up and down as her eye watered.

"I am pleased to meet you Mr Taylor. Do you always wear plimsolls?"

Matthew looked down at his feet. "I find them comfortable."

Mona shook her head. "You would be wise to wear boots like Mr Donnell and that Mr Norris after him. All kinds of things can happen in a theatre you know. Lots of heavy things to move, you don't want to go dropping anything on your feet."

Matthew felt his face flush. "I will change them, promise. I have some boots in my locker."

Mona heaved her bulk out of the seat and stood and faced Matthew. "You won't need to show me the ropes. I know what I have to do and where to put my things." She paused for a few moments making Matthew feel uncomfortable. "You have had sadness in your life Mr Taylor, I can feel it. I have the gift you know, I see things." Matthew began to feel even more uncomfortable but his feet remained rooted to the spot. Mona picked up her bucket and mop; she eyed him up and down again as she began to move away. "I will see you at the allotted hour of eleven, Mr Taylor and we will chat over a cup of tea. Do you like bourbons? Mr Donnell liked bourbons, very partial to a bourbon biscuit he was, and that Mr Norris…" Matthew nodded in reply unable to move. "That's good because I have a packet of bourbons in my bag. Now I must away to my business, I have brasses to clean and floors to mop." With that, Mona Buckle waddled slowly up the theatre aisle leaving a very unsettled Matthew in her wake.

At *Rita's Angels*, Jenny picked up her handbag and folder. "Right Rita I will go over and speak to Alfred Barton. I think we have agreed the opening date and I thought it would be an idea to give him a run-down on how we see the show shaping up. Is there anything you wanted me to add?"

Rita put down her pen. "You could ask him if he is coming tomorrow night. I know he has been sent an invitation. It would give him a chance to meet some of the company. Mystic Brian is coming along and Pearl and Sidney are going to put in an appearance; they are looking for somewhere to stay near Brokencliff, perhaps Alfred will be able to help them."

"Are you okay Rita? You look a bit pensive this morning."

Rita smiled. "There is a lot to think about with two shows to run. I will be glad when we get *The Sands* up and running. I am a bit concerned about our top-of-the-bill. I really didn't think her voice was all that good when we met up in London."

"Yes, she did sound a bit on the baritone side," said Jenny. "Probably age, possibly drink?"

"Oh don't say that," said Rita. "We had enough of that the other season. I have to say I am slightly concerned about letting Mystic Brian loose in Brokencliff; you know he likes a drop or two, I hope I have made the right decision."

"Stop worrying," said Jenny reassuringly. "As the saying goes, it will be all right on the night; besides Brian has never missed a performance and he really will be a draw for the show. He is well loved in the profession."

Rita sighed. "Yes, you are right. I expect I am worrying for nothing. I think it's the opening of *Ted's* bar tomorrow evening that is getting to me. Bob wanted me to see the finished article last week, but I said I wanted it to be a surprise."

"And it will be," said Jenny, heading for the door. "Now finish your coffee and get yourself up town and buy yourself a new frock for tomorrow evening, you deserve it."

"Thanks me old lover," Rita replied. "I think I will do just that."

Friday 28 May

Walking across the market place, Freda and Muriel were heading towards *Palmers* to have a coffee and a cake. As they were going to take the stairs they spotted Lucinda in the ladies' department, looking at dresses.

"Now what do you think she is up to?" said Freda, folding her arms. "It is not like Lucinda Haines to be buying a new dress."

Muriel agreed. "Well, maybe she is going to a wedding."

Freda huffed. "Whose wedding might that be, I wonder, she doesn't know anyone. Come on, let's go over and say hello."

And before Muriel had a chance to stop her, Freda had marched across the shop floor, catching her shoulder bag strap on a rail of garments and was pulling it along behind her.

"Freda, you've hooked up to a dress rail," Muriel called after her, which caused Lucinda to stop what she was doing and turn around. A sales assistant had disentangled Freda's bag from the rail and was wheeling it back to its rightful position.

Lucinda smiled to herself. She was going to have some fun with these two.

"Why Freda and Muriel, hello to you both. Fancy seeing you in here."

Muriel grabbed hold of a nearby coat. "I was thinking of buying a new coat for the summer."

"Really," replied Lucinda, eyeing the garment Muriel was holding. "I wouldn't have thought a heavy coat like that would be suitable. You should look in the Windsmoor section. They have some lovely light macs there."

Muriel put the coat back on the rack, noting that it had been reduced from last season's winter stock.

"And are you looking for a new coat Freda?"

Freda huffed. "No, I am just keeping Muriel company."

"Well I mustn't stop you ladies from your shopping," said Lucinda with a smile.

"We are in no rush," said Freda, not wishing to be fobbed off. "Are you buying anything?"

"As a matter of fact I am," Lucinda replied enjoying herself. The face on Freda was a picture and Muriel seemed lost for words.

"Is it a special occasion, a wedding perhaps?"

"Not a wedding, but a special occasion yes," said Lucinda. "Now if you'll excuse me, the young lady is holding some things for me to try on and I am rather pushed for time as I am having my hair done and I don't wish to keep Mr Adrian waiting."

Muriel looked dumfounded. Mr Adrian was where the head of GAGGA, Shirley Llewellyn had her hair done.

Lucinda turned back and smiled. "I expect I will see you ladies later?"

Freda huffed again. "Later? What do you mean, later?"

"Well surely you have both been invited to the opening of the new bar at *The Golden Sands*, in memory of Ted Ricer?"

Muriel steadied herself on a nearby rail of clothes feeling slightly faint.

"Muriel dear, are you okay? Only you don't look very well," said Lucinda showing mock concern.

Freda grabbed hold of Muriel's arm. "You take hold of me Muriel, I best get you upstairs for a strong cup of coffee."

Lucinda watched as the two left the section and chuckled to herself.

By the time Freda had returned with a tray of coffee and cakes, Muriel had managed to pull herself together.

"Lucinda Haines going to Mr Adrian!" she exclaimed "it doesn't sound right."

"Fancy," said Freda helping herself to a large jam puff and leaving the smaller one for her friend. "Well you know what she has been like since she had all that work done last year on that guest house of hers. She is moving up in the world."

"You needn't remind me," said Muriel stirring her coffee rather too vigorously and spilling some in the saucer.

"Fancy," said Freda through a mouthful of jam puff. "You rather thought of yourself up there on that top table at GAGGA didn't you?"

Muriel scowled. "If Lucinda Haines becomes the chairman of GAGGA I will eat my hat."

Freda finished her jam puff and stirred her coffee with two sugars. "Well you best make sure it's one with fruit on, that's all I can say. After all, we will know the results of the outcome at Thursday morning's meeting."

Muriel glared at her neighbour and scowled even more.

* * *

Mona had done one final check to make sure that everything was pristine for the arrival of the guests to the opening of *Ted's Variety Bar* and had been surprised when Matthew had handed her an envelope containing an invitation to attend the event at the request of Rita Ricer. She hurried off home to find something suitable to wear and thought she would wear her hat with the feathers on; that always set off any outfit, she thought.

Matthew and the backstage boys were suitably attired in evening dress and bow ties, hired from *John Collier* at the theatre's expense. Bob Scott wanted to make sure that it was an evening to remember.

Beverley had arrived wearing a black evening gown and looked every part the hostess. Standing beside Bob she brushed some fluff off his jacket and smiled. "I think Rita is going to be remarkably impressed when she sees the turn out.

I have told everyone to be here by seven thirty and Rita is to arrive with Jenny at eight."

"Thanks Beverley," said Bob, "for sorting everything out so efficiently. Shall we have a quick drink before the others arrive?"

"Why not!" said Beverley feeling she had earned a Babycham. Bob motioned to one of the bar staff and with Beverley's perry poured, he joined her with a pint of *Affinity*.

Matthew and the boys ordered half a beer each and then prepared themselves to act as waiters for the evening to ensure that everyone was offered something from the buffet which had been laid on by Matthes catering.

Maud and Barbara were the first to arrive, followed by a rather glamorous-looking Lucinda, whose hair was in a bouffant carefully crafted by Mr Adrian who had also agreed to do her make-up. Her three-quarter length dress sparkled in red and gold and her elegant shoes from *Freeman, Hardy and Willis* set it off a treat.

The arrival of some of the show-business crowd brought a hub of activity as old friends said hello to each other. The mayor and several councillors arrived in force along with one or two staff from local businesses including Stella from *Henry's* bar who was accompanied by Mr Adrian himself.

Everyone admired the décor and there were gasps of wonder at the etched mirrors and the wonderful memorabilia from shows past. The photographs and engraved plate surrounding the late Ted Ricer drew the most attention.

Vic Allen had assembled his small orchestra at the side of the room and they were playing show tunes quietly in the background.

Then Matthew gave the signal from the door to the crowd that Rita and Jenny had arrived. As Rita entered the bar, the orchestra struck up *Hello Young Lovers*, which had been Rita and Ted's song to each other.

Visibly moved by what she saw, Rita found herself shaking hands with people from her past and acknowledging the good wishes from those members of her two new companies who had been able to attend.

Bob Scott brought the proceedings to order and from a small raised platform he asked Rita to join him. With words written for him by Beverley he looked back at the career of Ted Ricer and his connections with Great Yarmouth. The assembled crowd applauded and then it was Rita's turn to say a few words before cutting the ribbon that had been placed over a large portrait of Ted on the wall behind her.

When she declared that *Ted's Variety Bar* was officially open, the orchestra played *For He's a Jolly Good Fellow* and everyone sang along.

"Ted would have loved this," said Rita to Lucinda as they stood at the bar together. "He loved crowds; he loved people."

Lucinda laid her hand on Rita's. "And he loved you."

Rita smiled, acknowledging the fact. "Oh look, a latecomer".

All eyes turned to the entrance and there stood Mona Buckle in a very fetching red velvet two-piece, sporting the largest red hat flowing with peacock feathers. She limped in. Her leg was bandaged as always and she made her way to towards Rita.

"Mrs Ricer, good evening," she said as her peacock feathers caught several people in the eye. "I am sorry I am late. Not like me to be late, but my aura must have been off side today. Most unusual I know, but I lost track of the time and confused eight with nine o' clock."

"Please don't apologies Mrs Buckle I am just so happy you came along. Can I offer you something to drink, a sherry perhaps?"

Mona's eye watered. "I won't partake of anything stronger than a pineapple juice Mrs Ricer, if you'd be so kind. I have a busy day ahead of me tomorrow. I've the offices to attend to as I couldn't get in there this morning due to having to be here."

"I am sure that leaving the offices until Monday won't hurt," said Rita handing Mona her drink.

"That won't do," said Mona taking the glass of juice. "When Mona Buckle gives her word that a job will be done, then a job will be done. You pay me a wage to look after your offices and I won't let you down."

Rita smiled. There was no one quite like Mona Buckle, she felt sure.

Later in the evening Rita was engaged in conversation with Don Stevens and his wife Elsie. Elsie and she had become firm friends the year before and it was thanks to the support of Elsie and Jenny Benjamin that Rita had come through what many considered to be her darkest hours.

"They have really done Ted proud," said Don. "The work this must have taken. Those mirrors alone must have taken hours of labour and that painting of Ted is quite magnificent."

Elsie nodded, agreeing with her husband. "Rita, it really is quite wonderful. How are you getting on with everything? Is there anything you need a hand with?"

"Everything is coming together just fine," said Rita enjoying her third gin-and-tonic of the evening. "I will be pleased when this show is up and running and then I can turn my attention to the theatre at Brokencliff, Jenny will be able to take care of things here for a bit. Though I have to say Lauren Du Barrie is a bit of a worry, I don't know what it is about this theatre but we always seem to end up with a top-of-the-bill that comes with problems."

Don looked surprised. "Problems with Lauren? I wouldn't have thought so, she is a seasoned pro and has never once missed a performance, at least that's the information I have on her."

"I am a bit concerned about her voice," said Rita not speaking too loudly in case of being overheard. "Let's put it this way, at the run through in Earl's Court she did a good imitation of Paul Robeson."

"What did she sing?," asked Elsie with concern.

"*Climb Every Mountain, You'll Never Walk Alone* and *Something Wonderful*," were among those I remember."

"Maybe she was having an off-day."

"I hope so for the audience's sake," said Rita, with some feeling. "Anyway, we have a good line-up and I am really looking forward to seeing the audience's reaction to Rick and the boys. They really know how to belt out a tune, I felt like dancing when we were in Earls Court, they are going to look and sound great up there. The designs I have seen for the sets are first class and when Rick is on, there will a large juke box centre back and the dancers are going to jive."

"Who is that over there?," asked Don, looking towards Matthew.

"I believe that is Jim's replacement, though I haven't met him yet. Matthew Taylor, I believe his name is. Jack, the doorman says he seems to be the business from what he has seen."

"Taylor," said Elsie, "Where do I know a Taylor from?"

"You and your names," said Don, ordering another round of drinks. "We must have come across loads of people with that name. You are probably thinking of Elizabeth Taylor, she was on the television the other day in *National Velvet*, you always cry when you watch that. Let's have another drink and then I really must go and say hello to Brian, just hope he hasn't got those pesky birds with him."

Rita was pleased to see that Maurice Beeney and some of his boys had turned up and she exchanged pleasantries with them, emphasising again that she was sorry they wouldn't be in the orchestra pit that year. But as Maurice explained once more, they had all felt that they were getting past it and had welcomed retirement. In the normal course of events, Maurice and his All Rounders' Orchestra would have retired years before, but their services had often been called upon and they had felt obliged to accept. Maurice was happy to see his old pal Vic Allen now in charge of the musical direction and told Rita that she was in very safe hands.

Matthew surveyed the scene and especially took note of Don Stevens. He put down the tray he had been carrying and went over and interrupted Don's chat with Brian.

"Hello Mr Stevens, I am Matthew Taylor, the new lead here," he said holding out his hand and accepting a warm handshake in return.

"I am very pleased to meet you," said Don. "How are you finding things here at *The Sands*?"

Matthew grinned. "Fine, the management and staff are a very fine bunch and I am used to working in theatres."

"Bob was telling me you had extensive experience abroad."

"Oh yes, I have," replied Matthew helping himself to a handful of nuts. "I worked in several of the large cabaret venues including the Moulin Rouge in Paris."

"Really," said Don, impressed. "You might have come across our Jenny Benjamin at some point, though it may have been before your time."

Just at that moment Rita came over to say hello to Mystic Brian.

"Rita, have you met Matthew Taylor yet?," asked Don "He has taken Jim and Roger's role here."

Rita smiled at Matthew and the two shook hands. "I am sure Matthew and I will become properly acquainted when we kick off the rehearsals."

"I shall look forward to it "said Matthew. "Now if you will excuse me, I have neglected my duties long enough."

"He seems very pleasant," said Don.

"He looks familiar," said Mystic Brian butting in before Rita had a chance to reply. "I am sure I have seen his face somewhere before."

"What with you and Elsie over there," said Rita with a laugh "Are you sure you haven't had too much to drink, me old lover?"

Brian feigned a look of hurt. "Oh Rita, you cut me to the quick, as if old Brian would have had too much sherbet... Seriously, I could swear I know his face."

Rita excused herself and went around the room, saying hello to familiar faces and generally thanking all of those who had attended.

Alfred Barton, without his wife, was in attendance and was smartly turned out. Rita was pleased to see him and asked him to come along and meet Don and Elsie Stevens.

"So you are the man keeping our Rita busy," said Don with a smile. "I hear you have had to stop doing your usually repertory productions, that must have been a blow."

Alfred nodded. "Yes, I can't say it was welcome news and it was something I wasn't expecting. That is why I am so glad that Rita here has been able to help me."

"You are in good hands there," said Elsie. "If Rita cannot sort you out, then nobody can."

"Steady on me old lover," said Rita. "We don't know how successful this venture will be yet. I've managed to bring together some variety of talent and with some persuasion Don has got Brian on board."

"Well Brian will attract an audience," Elsie added. "His reputation goes before him."

"Not to mention those bloody birds of his," said Don remembering his encounters with the little darlings.

Alfred grinned. "I have heard all about Mystic Brian from several quarters. My main concern is that Brokencliff really doesn't have car parking in place and many holidaymakers, I am reliably informed, use their own transport these days. I only have twelve bays available at the hotel and guests book those in advance."

"I can see your problem," said Don knocking back the remains of his whiskey. "But surely when you had rep productions the problem was the same?"

"Well, yes and no," said Alfred "You see the plays attracted a lot of parties from local communities and they arrived by coach. They were dropped off and then the coach driver would park up either in Gorleston or as far off as Lowestoft where there were adequate facilities to do so. Now, this being a variety show and with no matinee performances it may not appeal. The locals may as well come to Great Yarmouth and catch a show here."

"I hadn't thought of it like that," said Rita with some concern.

"Then you need to be able to advertise," said Don, "and promote the show. I am sure we can line up some BBC radio and newspaper interviews. Rita, we could place a whole page advertisement in our *Golden Sands* programme and have fliers available. I wonder if we might be able to sell tickets for Brokencliff at our own box office as well."

"Steady on me old lover, we have Maud and Barbara to consider. Anyway how would we be able to issue tickets? The seating plans would be at the theatre in Brokencliff along with the tickets."

Alfred looked puzzled. "I don't see how that would work."

"Let me explain," Don continued. "Our box office would call the *Playhouse* box office and ask what seats were available for a certain performance. Maud would issue the date and seat numbers on special triplicate dockets. One for the customer, one to be sent to the theatre and one copy to held at our box office. The docket would be exchanged at the *Playhouse* box office for the actual theatre tickets. The money and duplicate dockets at our box office would be sent over on a weekly basis so that the books tallied."

"What if Maud or whoever takes down the wrong seat numbers or writes down the wrong date?," Elsie asked.

"Well we would have to allow for human error," said Don. "But if it helped we could offer some kind of discount if they booked the two shows together."

"Now you are complicating things," said Elsie looking at her husband in disbelief. "I can see old Maud pulling her hair out and sighing more often than not."

"Well, a free programme then," said Don.

"That's our profits you are talking about," said Rita.

"I think I have the answer," Alfred broke in. "Something that Rita mentioned the other afternoon, perhaps a complimentary drink at the hotel bar after the show."

"You are forgetting you already have a transport problem. If the show comes out at ten, the last bus leaves at 10.30 so people won't have time to go to your hotel bar."

"Perhaps we could offer them a drink before the show," said Alfred.

"I've got it," said Rita. "We could supply them with tickets to travel there and back on the open top bus."

Elsie had had enough. "You are all making this far too complicated. Okay, I see the advantage of Maud and Barbara selling tickets for the *Playhouse*. I cannot see any of your other suggestions working without it creating more paperwork in the form of yet another voucher. On the *Playhouse* ticket voucher, why not have a line saying, 'This voucher also entitles you to a free programme'? I suggest we negotiate for both programmes with our regular printers and keep the cost of the *Playhouse* programme down by getting as much advertising as possible – do a deal – advertise in the *Sands* brochure and get another advert free in the *Playhouse*, except the cost of advertising will be slightly more than last year."

"Isn't that dishonest?," asked Alfred, worried he might end up with a lawsuit.

"Of course it isn't. We are going to be giving them something that other theatres cannot offer, double the advertising."

"And who is going to put these wheels in motion?," said Rita "I have enough to keep me busy through next summer season, let alone this one."

"Well, if bug-a-lugs here will release me from my duties in London, now that we have managed to find a suitable replacement for Gwen who is starting next week, then I will move down here and get the ball rolling."

"And where will you stay?," asked Don thinking of the cost of putting his wife up in lodgings.

"Elsie can stay with me," said Rita. "I could do with the company and besides it would be nice to have Elsie here."

"Well that looks to be settled then," said Don. "Now, Alfred, come with me to the bar and we will get some more drinks in. I would like to offer you some advice about working alongside my wife and Rita..."

* * *

It was the following day that Alfred Barton received an unexpected visit from Lady Samantha Hunter. Alfred found her waiting in the lounge, seated in one of the more comfortable armchairs. She was wearing a very elegant outfit with matching shoes and handbag. Her blonde hair was swept up in a roll on her head and she wore the minimum of make-up. She stood up and held out her hand as Alfred approached her.

"Lady Hunter, this is an unexpected pleasure."

Lady Samantha sat down and crossed her legs. "I remember when I and His Lordship came in here quite often. I believe your late parents were often guests at the Hall when my in-laws still held the reins there. I am sure I met your parents once, but that may be just a fanciful thought on my part. We have so many photograph albums of what we term 'The Good Old Days'."

Alfred seated himself. "Yes, I remember them talking about the Hall. I did come there once when I was about 10."

"Things have changed a lot since then," said Lady Samantha smiling.

"I say, where are my manners? Can I offer you a drink, tea perhaps or a sherry?"

"That is very kind you Mr Barton, but I will pass. I really came to talk business with you."

Alfred sat back in the armchair "What kind of business?"

Her ladyship smiled broadly. "Nothing to worry about I assure you, but something that I believe may well benefit both of us in the long run."

Monday 31 May

"That was a call from Alfred Barton," said Rita, replacing the receiver and looking at Jenny and Elsie in turn. "He has found a solution to the parking problem at Brokencliff."

"Really," said Jenny. "Pray tell."

"It appears that Lady Hunter at Owlerton Hall has struck a deal to allow cars and coaches to use their car park at an agreed price. In return, Lady Hunter would like us to promote the Hall as a visitor attraction by advertising it in our programmes, free of charge."

"I say, steady on," said Elsie. "How will that balance the books?"

"We have to look at the whole picture: we get an audience, and they get punters. Besides the advert needn't be that big, and I am sure we can swallow the cost; we already have a deal with *Palmers* and some of the local traders."

"I see your point," said Elsie.

"Well I think it is a great idea," said Jenny.

"The best of it is that she approached him after reading that article about the theatre in the *Mercury*," said Rita moving to look out of the office window. "I say girls, we may be in business after all. Now all we have to do is get the acts in shape to ensure that Brokencliff is the place to see variety."

Elsie tapped her pencil on the desk gaining the attention of Rita. "I am never one to rain on anyone's parade," she said, "but it might be an idea for one of us to go and meet with Lady Hunter and discuss this idea further. I don't doubt it has merit but surely some kind of contract needs to be drawn up between the agreed parties."

Jenny thought for a moment and looked at Rita. "Elsie's right Rita. What is to stop this agreement stalling at some point? If Brokencliff is to become part of the variety scene for future seasons then we must have some legally binding document drawn up."

"I do agree," said Rita "but we have to think of this coming season as a trial run. Lady Hunter may decide that after one season the cons outweigh the pros. Elsie, why don't you go and have a word with Alfred and Her Ladyship, I expect they have come to some agreement between them. We can look at the longer term once the season is up and running. I appreciate we are taking a risk, but let's give things time to settle down. Let's face it, Alfred Barton will not be going into this arrangement blindfolded and if Lady Hunter is as astute as rumour would have it, she won't be either."

Chapter Seven:

The Chairman
of the Board

Thursday 3 June

T here had been a lot of mutterings of discontent that this meeting had been called at what was regarded as the beginning of the summer season. After all the stalling many did agree that at least they would see a new chairman at the helm and not before time. Some landladies had called in favours from friends to take care of their guest houses while they attended this very important landmark in the history of GAGGA.

The main hall meeting room of the Town Hall had been decked out in flowers at some considerable cost by the instructions of Shirley Llewellyn. *White's* the florist in Gorleston High Street was very happy to take on the work and had sent four members of their experienced staff to ensure that that everything was done to specification. Shirley had spent countless days and nights going over the proceedings in her head.

She had not involved the secretary or treasurer in her plans, wanting to put on a show in the hope of changing the landladies' minds about who they wanted as their chairman, even though she and her committee had agreed to stand down and let others take the reins. But again Shirley was reminded of the fact that it was she who had set up GAGGA (Great Yarmouth and Gorleston Guesthouse Association) and it was she who had arranged the initial meetings, setting up a committee and leading those that joined the association in what she had described as a uniformed excellence among the guest houses of the popular seaside resort so that every guest could be assured of getting a good service.

Competing with the large hotels was never an easy task, but under her leadership, things had changed. There were of course exceptions, the likes of Freda Boggis had fallen behind but even Freda had begun to make changes to her décor with help from her neighbour Muriel Evans who now found herself in competition with her arch-rival Lucinda Haines. Lucinda had changed her modest guest house to a standard that even Shirley had thought impossible.

Letting go of GAGGA would be a wrench and she knew it. She enjoyed the power that had become part of her role; she enjoyed making an entrance to the gatherings and playing to the assembled throng. How would she be able to continue with this once she was replaced by someone else and she took on the mantle of honorary president? She felt she would not have any clout, unable to get her own way and that, with time, would eventually fade into the background as the new committee became proactive.

She looked again at the plans for the hall and was pleased. She was going to pull out all the stops to let members of GAGGA know what they would be missing if they let her go.

The hall had been booked for the day. The proceedings would start at ten thirty with tea and coffee, to make sure that those with guests had time to leave their homes. A formal meeting would take place at eleven with a luncheon served at twelve followed by the voting and counting at one thirty. Some landladies had already cast their votes, but it was hoped that some might change their mind after Shirley had addressed them all.

To make the voting sequence easier there were separate ballot boxes for chairman, treasurer and secretary. The voting form had the names of the people standing for election on each with a simple tick box. Some candidates were standing for more than one role, for example in the case of Muriel, she was hoping for either chairman or treasurer while Ruby Hamilton was standing for chairman only.

The personnel of four local businesses had agreed to give up their time to do the counting, none of whom were associated with anyone connected with GAGGA.

The results would be announced by local MP Arthur Winstanley who, on the promise of a free lunch, had agreed to come along; this was to be followed by tea and cake to congratulate the winners.

Shirley had been to her wardrobe earlier that morning and laid out her finest skirt, blouse and jacket; across town others had done likewise, all hoping to come away with the prize. With her hand trembling Shirley turned the ignition key and started the car. It was going to be an emotional and very trying day.

Arriving at the Town Hall shortly after nine thirty Shirley checked that everything was going to plan. She nodded her approval and left by the back entrance of the Town Hall where she had discreetly parked her car. She drove off along the quayside, turned off the road before reaching the power station and parked her car in the Masonic car park. She walked across Marine Parade and onto the Wellington Pier. The day was pleasantly warm and as the sounds of the gulls and waves hit her ears she strolled along taking in the view that she had enjoyed on many occasions before. Her stomach felt knotted and her throat was dry. Never had she felt so nervous, never had she felt so anxious and afraid. GAGGA was all she had. Her relationships with members of the opposite sex had never amounted to much. Friendships were built on weak and shifting sand; there was no one that she could call a true friend. Her hope of finding such a person had vanished when Lettice

Webb had left town in a hurry after her secret had been revealed.

Even her associations with Fenella and Agnes had never been more than business. Like the breeze that was gently blowing, she realised she had been surrounded by fair-weather friends. She took a handkerchief from her handbag and dabbed her eyes. Taking a deep breath, she calmed herself as best she could and continued her walk to the end of the pier.

"My goodness it looks like that scene from *My Fair Lady*," said Freda Boggis as she walked beside Muriel into the hall. "You know when she was selling flowers outside Convent Garden. I always thought that was a bit strange as you never saw any nuns."

Muriel, whose mind was elsewhere, looked at her companion in disbelief. "Come on Freda, let's get you settled with some tea and biscuits. I want to be down the front."

Freda sighed. "Well it looks like it is filling up nicely. Oh look here comes Laurel and Hardy."

"Freda, that is no way to refer to Agnes and Fenella, they might say the same about us," said Muriel.

Freda looked down at her rotund figure and then at Muriel's slender one and shook her head. "I can't see any resemblance at all."

Petunia Danger arrived with Ruby Hamilton; both were wearing their Sunday best. Ruby gazed at the floral arrangements and the trail of flora that lead up the steps to the stage.

"This must have cost a fortune," said Petunia just stopping herself from whistling, something she was in the habit of doing when something surprised her, it was a trait that had attracted the attention of her husband-to-be during their courting days.

Ruby grunted "And no guesses for who paid for it."

"Who is that over there in the peacock blue hat?" asked Petunia not wishing to engage in the whys and the wherefores.

"I have no idea," said Ruby her attention now honed in on the lady in question. "She is not familiar to me at all."

"I see Freda and Muriel are here," said Petunia watching the pair help themselves to beverages.

But Ruby had left her side and headed towards the peacock blue hat. Holding out a gloved hand she smiled. "Hello I am Ruby Hamilton; I don't believe I have had the pleasure."

The lady smiled in return "Erica Warren, pleased to meet you."

"And what brings you to our little gathering?" asked Ruby retaining the smile. "Are you a friend of someone here?"

"I moved to the area a couple of months ago. I am the new owner of the *Gull* guest house."

"Really," replied Ruby feeling ruffled, no such news had reached her ears. "I hadn't realised that it had become occupied again. I don't live too far from there. Of course one goes everywhere by car and the last owner of *Gull House* very much kept herself to herself. Did you ever meet Lettice Webb?"

Erica shook her head. "No we never met, but I saw the house for sale in my estate agents' window and thought a move to Great Yarmouth might be just the ticket."

"And where were you before?"

"I co-owned the *Richards Hotel* in Bournemouth."

Ruby recoiled; the *Richards Hotel* was a large sixty-bedroomed property with a sea view and advertisements were often seen in *The Lady* and other publications. Clearly Erica Warren was a woman of means. "One has heard of *Richards Hotel* of course. I have to say that my trips seldom took me to

Bournemouth but I have visited once or twice, staying with friends in the area, out of season of course."

Erica smiled, observing that there was coldness in Ruby's clipped responses; the smile was obviously one that had been used many times, but Erica was not fooled. Ruby Hamilton was never going to be a friend.

"If you'll excuse me, I think I will go and get myself a coffee before the proceedings start".

Ruby followed Erica "Am I to understand you have given up *Richards*?"

Erica turned and smiled. "Yes I have. When my husband Robert died a year ago I decided to hand the business over to our son and daughter. Now if you'll excuse me…"

It was clear to Ruby that no more information would be forthcoming so she smiled and returned to Petunia who had seated herself in the second row, a cup of tea in hand.

"So did you solve the mystery?," asked Petunia moving along the row to allow Ruby to sit down.

Ruby removed her gloves. "Oh no mystery dear, she is the wife of the late Robert Richards who owned one of the largest hotels in Bournemouth. I thought I vaguely recognised her, I must have bumped into her when I have been down that way on business."

Petunia wisely sipped her tea and said nothing.

Shirley Llewellyn brought the meeting to a close and everyone went to the adjoining ante room where luncheon was being served.

"Quite a hand you played there," said Fenella who was walking beside her, closely followed by Agnes who was having trouble with her spectacles. "I hope you are not planning on trying to go back on what we all agreed."

Shirley felt a cold shiver go down her back, she had found it difficult to conduct the meeting knowing in her heart of hearts that this would be the last time she would be standing before everyone, addressing them as their chairman. Her walk along the pier earlier had cleared her head and had given her food for thought.

She stopped and touched Fenella's arm. "Come along Agnes we can't possibly go in without you, after all this will be our last formal luncheon together as the committee."

And with that reply, Fenella was more than satisfied.

Arthur Winstanley thanked Shirley for his welcome and took the microphone in his hand. Beside him was a young gentleman holding three envelopes. Each was marked appropriately.

Arthur was handed the first envelope. "Well ladies, the votes have been counted and checked and in these three envelopes which my assistant is holding are the results.," He tore open the envelope. "Taking over the reins of treasurer… I am pleased to announce that Muriel Evans is the all-out winner."

A murmur went round the room, followed by applause and several whoops of approval from Freda. Muriel stood up and made her way to the stage, feeling all eyes were on her. Shirley, Agnes and Fenella greeted her with smiles.

"Well done my dear," said Shirley taking her hand. "You are a worthy successor to Agnes, who I am sure will help you get to grips with the task ahead."

"Indeed I will," said Agnes who was secretly relieved to be handing over the accounts.

"Congratulations," said Fenella. "Well done."

Muriel acknowledged the applause from the floor and stood beside Agnes smiling, not quite believing what had just happened.

Arthur then tore open the second envelope. "Now we come to the vacancy of secretary. And the winner is…"

There was added tension in the air. Lucinda Haines who was seated at the back craned her neck to see who it was going to be: Ruby, Petunia, or heaven forbid Freda, or maybe one of the ladies off Wellesley Road.

Arthur coughed, taking what he considered to be a theatrical pause. "The new secretary of GAGGA will be Erica Warren. Where is Erica? Please come forward to the stage. Applause began to fill the room. Ruby looked as if she was about to explode; Petunia, who could feel her neighbour's anger, smiled to herself.

Erica, who had removed her hat to show off her blonde hair, walked slowly to the stage. Dressed in a two-piece that could have come out of Shirley's wardrobe she was the vision of elegance. Shirley took her hand and gave her hug. "I am so pleased Erica, sorry it wasn't treasurer, I know you had your heart set on it, but maybe next time. Robert would have been delighted and I am sure that Penny and Charles will be too."

Ruby was seething with rage; who was this newcomer to walk in here and become secretary! She did her best to compose herself as the real prize was about to be announced and she was counting on being successful. Erica Warren had best watch her step; she wouldn't be secretary for long.

"And finally, I announce the position of chairman," said Arthur looking around the room. "It is with great thanks to Shirley Llewellyn that GAGGA came in to being and, before I announce her successor, I call upon Agnes to present a gift on behalf of everyone assembled to Shirley with grateful thanks."

Agnes came forward with a basket of flowers and a *Palmers* gift voucher. Agnes and Fenella had collected money from the members of GAGGA and added some more to make sure that the gift token was twenty pounds. Shirley smiled and accepted the gifts with a wave of her hand and a few blown kisses, refusing the opportunity to address the audience.

The applause died down and Arthur tore open the envelope. Ruby had prepared a speech earlier, took it from her handbag and waited eagerly. It was all she could do to remain seated.

Arthur looked at the card and held the microphone firmly "And the Chairman of GAGGA is to be…"

Shirley remained calm and continued to smile, Fenella grabbed Agnes by the arm and Muriel and Erica waited with bated breath.

"Lucinda Haines!"

Ruby collapsed in her chair causing Petunia to fan her, Lucinda rose from her seat and walked sedately and proudly down the centre aisle to the stage. Dressed in black and white, with matching handbag, shoes and hat she went on to the stage and smiled broadly at Shirley.

"My dear," said Shirley "I couldn't be more pleased.," And Lucinda knew that the words spoken to her were genuinely meant.

Freda stared at the ensemble on the stage, took a bite from a digestive she had saved from earlier and all she could manage in response was, "Fancy."

In the ante-room following the announcement, Shirley had arranged for a photographer and journalist from the *Great Yarmouth Mercury* to be present. Ushering the three newly elected committee members to the fore she spoke of her delight that she, Agnes and Fenella were delighted to handing over the duties of GAGGA to such a talented trio. Shirley went on to express that for some years she had found the chairman's role to be something of a burden, which caused Fenella and Agnes to nudge each other and exchange glances which the photographer managed to capture, intending to add it to the mix of the article.

Ruby Hamilton had been taken off to A&E with a suspected stomach complaint and had been accompanied by Petunia Danger who had had enough excitement for one day.

Muriel found the attention she was getting overwhelming, but Lucinda stood by her side with a comforting arm around Muriel's shoulders, taking charge of things.

Erica Warren smiled for the photographer standing beside Lucinda and Muriel for a group shot and said to Lucinda afterwards that she felt very honoured to be working alongside her. Lucinda responded politely, but wasn't easily fooled by the sudden camaraderie being shown from someone she hardly knew. Shirley worked the gathering taking the time to speak to members that she hadn't spoken to in a long while. Agnes and Fenella followed her lead and enjoyed themselves to the full, both secretly relieved that things had gone to plan and had not been scuppered at the last minute as they had both feared. In a quiet corner enjoying a glass of sherry that had been supplied courtesy of Shirley they spoke about Erica, a lady that neither were that familiar with and they tried to work out how a relatively unknown had been elected. Again exchanging knowing glances they both turned to look at Shirley who was at that moment approaching them.

"Well, Agnes dear," said Shirley, schooner of sherry in hand. "That seemed to go off quite well I thought. Fenella, I know I can rely on you to make sure that the new committee settles in well."

"With your assistance of course," said Fenella sipping her drink.

Shirley responded with a shake of the head. "No I have given the matter some serious thought. I believe it would be wrong of me to interfere with the running of things from now on. The members have had their say and it is only right that the new chairman, treasurer and secretary put their own mark on the future of GAGGA. Of course as honorary chairman I will try to be on hand for the odd piece of advice. No ladies, I have given enough of my toil, sweat and tears to GAGGA and it is time for me to look at my own life. I have a guest house to run first and foremost but in the quieter months I will be able to join outside activities that I have been unable to do in the past. I might even join the amateur dramatics, I am sure that Derek Marshall would welcome me as an extra person to call upon should he be in need of a principal boy or musical lead. I am also considering setting up a fan club for Ricky O'Shea and the Ramblers, the fun I could have organising that and I could steer Ricky in the right direction. I think he should be grabbing his career by the balls."

Fenella coughed loudly. "Shirley, language please!"

Shirley waved her hand in dismissal. "I think I might have another sherry, would you both care to join me?"

Agnes was quite stunned as she watched Shirley walk over to the drinks table; she couldn't help but wonder exactly how many sherries her exiting chairman had had!

Chapter Eight:

The Song – The Set –
The Show

Monday 14 June

The sets were being put in place at *The Golden Sands Theatre* under the supervision of Matthew Taylor. The backstage crew had taken to him, but each had privately agreed that he was no Jim Donnell. However he was pleasant enough, had a good sense of humour and seemed to know what he was doing. Matthew kept himself to himself and didn't enter into idle gossip. All that anyone knew about him was that he was living in digs in Southtown and had worked abroad extensively. There was no hint of a relationship of any kind, no talk about his parents and no indication as to where his birth place had been. Rita had watched the way he managed the staff and had expressed her satisfaction to Bob Scott, who was also pleased with his new member of staff.

Maud, on the other hand, wasn't so sure. Matthew checked the box office every day to make sure things were okay, never accepted the offer of a brew and didn't exchange any pleasantries the way old Jim had. Still, he seemed to be doing the job he was paid to do and that was all that was needed. Maud knew there would never be another one like her old friend Jim.

With their new part-time member of staff, a young woman called Dixie, Barbara and Maud had sorted out a workable rota between them and was also coming to grips with having to book the *Playhouse* at Brokencliff. The problem was that the box office at the *Playhouse* wouldn't open until the beginning of July so the only way they could book advance tickets was to call the *Beach Croft Hotel* and wait to be put through to Alfred who was looking at the seating plans. This proved something of a challenge but the three persevered in the hope that it would improve the business for their neighbouring resort.

Doreen and Jill had been putting the dancers through their paces with some new and exciting routines. Having four male dancers on board was proving to be a success and it meant that the routines were more modern and in keeping with the changing times. They were also going over the routines that would be used for the *Playhouse* that Jenny had given them and were planning on making a few tweaks to them once they began rehearsing the four "gaiety," girls.

Jenny put her face around the door of the dance studios once or twice a week and was pleased with what she had seen.

Mona was settling into her routine of cleaning the offices of *Rita's Angels* and the theatre and seemed to be enjoying herself if the sound of her singing was anything to go by. Matthew let her get on with the job in hand at the theatre, made sure she was kept stocked with the things she needed and at the offices she was often gone before anyone had arrived, which seemed to suit everyone. Mona, first thing in the morning, wasn't a force everyone felt completely comfortable with.

Ted's Variety Bar was doing a steady lunchtime and evening trade but was hardly busy. However this would change once the show had opened. Locals popped in to see what all the fuss had been about and were pleasantly surprised. The once tired-looking venue was now sparkling and they had no doubt that when word got around it would become a popular watering hole for locals and holidaymakers alike.

Bob Scott was pleased with the way things were shaping up, but as he had said to Beverley on more than one occasion, there was still something missing and neither of them needed to speak the name, they both knew the answer all too well.

The seafront had begun to liven up with day trippers from other resorts and holidaymakers; several of the guest houses were showing 'No Vacancies' with their regular guests booked in while several others would be busier from the month of July. Once the shops along Marine Parade and Regent Road had taken down their winter shutters and the beach balls, buckets and spades and beach sundries were displayed, summer felt as if it had finally arrived. The pony rides were back in business after a brief airing during Whitsun, the open landaus lined the parade. The ice-cream parlours were offering new flavours and the smell of candy floss and freshly made doughnuts filled the air.

The *Winter Gardens* were offering lunchtime kiddie shows one or two days a week, and the amateur roller skaters could be seen rehearsing on the rink adjacent to the Wellington Pier for their summer show every Monday.

Posters around the town advertised the many summer shows that were on offer with stars of stage and screen playing twice nightly along with the lesser known artistes of *The Old Time Music Hall* at Gorleston Pavilion. The circus which had opened in May was giving twice daily performances with an array of spectacular acts from around the globe and the animal acts were sure to prove a hit with the younger audiences and grannies and granddads alike.

The restaurants along Regent Road had display boards tempting those eager for a reasonably priced roast dinner and dessert with the opportunity to eat out while they were in B&B accommodation.

The amusement arcades were alive with pop music and the sound of new money tinkling as people tried their luck on one-arm bandits and penny cascades but all feeling slightly cautious that the new money was not offering them the same value as the old pounds, shillings and pence.

The river boats and broadland cruisers were once again ready to set sail and their gaily coloured canopies and flags swayed gently in the breeze.

The town centre was full of holidaymakers eager to explore the department stores and Wednesday and Saturday market stalls to find a bargain and that all-elusive present for Aunt or Uncle back home.

There was no doubt in many shopkeepers' minds that the new decimal currency would prove unpopular with prices being displayed for the time-being in both currencies. The older generation were of the opinion they were being ripped off while the younger ones argued they were not getting the same amount of sweets for their hard come-by pocket money.

Tuesday 15 June

It was the first day of rehearsals at *The Golden Sands* and the acts had started to arrive, making their way down the pier and entering the stage door where they were greeted by Jack, the stage doorkeeper, who told them which dressing room they had been allocated. Matthew and his boys were on hand to help carry any costumes and props, of which there seemed an abundance.

Maud and Barbara watched the arrivals from their box office window with interest.

"Nice to see young Jonny Adams back," said Maud, and Barbara agreed.

The four male dancers caused quite a stir with the two ladies. They were well-built, broad shouldered and looked super-fit into the bargain.

"My goodness!" Barbra exclaimed. "They are going to set one or two pulses racing. I wonder where Jill and Doreen found those four."

A large black Rolls Royce drew up at the roadside and a driver wearing a smart blue suit and matching peaked cap got out of the driver's seat and walked round to the pavement side of the car. He opened the back door and in a swathe of furs and a Russian cossack hat, Lauren Du Barrie alighted as gracefully as she could.

"Who on earth is that?" asked Barbara nudging Rita.

"I'll give you one guess."

The pair looked at each other, said in unison, "Lauren Du Barrie," and burst out laughing.

"She doesn't look anything like her photograph on the posters," said Barbara. "How old do you think she is, Maud?"

"I should say somewhere between late-fifties and mid-sixties. What on earth has she got on her feet? She will never walk up the pier on those, and she will get them caught in the slats."

"And pray who is that little thing?"

Coming around from the other side of the car was Millie, dressed from head to foot in slate grey with stockings to match.

"If I didn't know better I'd say Esma Cannon had blown into town," said Maud. "Must be madam's assistant."

Lauren Du Barrie walked forward with Millie trailing behind. She went straight to the box office window.

"Hello, I am Lauren Du Barrie. I am expected."

Maud smiled, while Barbara went and busied herself in the back, stifling a laugh.

"You will find the theatre at the end of the pier, the stage door is to the left," said Maud in reply.

"Is one expected to walk?"

Maud sighed "That's what most of the artistes do, yes."

"Dear, dear, this will never do. Don't you have one those trailer contraptions with seats?"

Maud shook her head. "I am afraid not and you have just missed the last of the delivery trucks for the bar or you may have been able to have cadged a lift on one of those."

Lauren Du Barrie looked none-too-pleased. "Millicent dear, did you hear that, we shall have to walk."

Millie appeared beside Lauren, looked up at Maud through her magnified spectacles and smiled. "Hello, I am Millie."

Maud returned the smile. "It really isn't that far."

"Oh well, I suppose there is nothing for it. Shanks's Pony it will have to be. Thank you dear. Millie, quick sticks or we shall be late and I don't think that Mrs Ricer likes late arrivals."

Maud and Barbara came out of the box office and watched as Lauren and Millie walked up the pier. Dixie arrived and looked to see who her colleagues were observing. "Who is that?" she asked.

"That, Dixie dear is our top-of-the-bill who has a voice that Al Jolson would have been proud of and beside her is her assistant. Thank goodness we have Rick and the boys on the bill, that's all I can say."

Lauren swept through the stage door totally ignoring Jack, the stage door keeper. Millie, who had been running along behind her in an attempt to keep up, stopped, slightly out of breath and smiled at Jack.

"Hello I'm Millie. Sorry about Miss Du Barrie, she is in rather a hurry to have a word with the orchestra."

Jack smiled. "Well, she will find Vic Allen and the boys in the pit tuning up. Look, if you ever need anything Jack's the name, just let me know."

Millie nodded her thanks and hurried away to find Lauren.

When Millie finally caught up, she found Lauren in conversation with Vic.

"Darling, you understand how it is; it's the voice you know."

Vic Allen nodded sagely. "Yes I do understand, but just run that by me again. It's green for a top C."

"No darling man, let me explain again," she replied, flinging off her furs which Millie expertly managed to catch. "It's red for a top C, blue for a couple of semi-tones lower and green for an A natural."

"My boys and I have been together for some years so will be able to adapt accordingly."

"One is so used to singing opera. I have never done much 'twice nightly', La Scala is more my thing."

"The Manchester Opera House," Millie chimed in, receiving a glare from Lauren.

"Millie dear, run along and find my dressing room and organise some honey and lemon, it's the voice you know."

Millie disentangled herself from the furs and, carrying them as best she could, scurried up the stage steps.

"Such a treasure," said Lauren waving her gloved hands in the theatrical manner she had seen many times during Shakespearian productions. "I will send Millie along with my sheet music presently and Vic, darling, you must call me Lauren."

As Vic watched her go on to the stage he thought that 'Call me madam' might be more apt.

"I say," called Lauren, looking into the wings. "Yes, the handsome-looking one with a tool in his hand, be a dear and help me find my dressing room; I am Lauren Du Barrie."

Vic tapped his baton and the boys looked up from the music stands. "What was it Bette Davis said in *All About Eve?* 'Fasten your seat belts, it's going to be a bumpy night'."

Lauren marched into the dressing room where Millie stood looking around her.

"Is this the best they can do?" Lauren stated, following Millie's gaze. "Well, I suppose one must be grateful we are only here for the summer, imagine being cooped up in here during the winter months, it would do my voice no good at all. Have you organised the honey and lemon Millie? I must prepare to run through a couple of numbers with Vic.," And with that, Lauren began her scales as she walked around while Millie tried to dodge her arm waving. She eventually escaped and went to Jack at the stage door.

"Hello again," said Jack looking up from his *Racing Post*. "Everything okay?"

"I need to prepare Miss Du Barrie some honey and lemon, I have got everything here in this bag," she said, waving a small carrier bag that had seen better days, "but I don't know where to find a kettle."

Jack looked over his spectacles, he was quite taken with this little waif. "Look, I can boil some water here for you if you like, can I make you a cup of tea while I am at it?"

Millie blushed and lowered her head. "That would be very kind of you, Jack".

Jack busied himself with the kettle "You will find a kettle in the green room for usual use. Some acts bring their own and have them in the dressing room."

"Oh Miss Du Barrie wouldn't like that, she says the steam would ruin her make-up."

Jack smiled to himself, some of these artistes had some funny ideas and he had seen enough of them over the years to form his own thoughts on the show business world.

"Have you got your lemon and honey there?" said Jack. "Look, come in here and you can prepare it if you like." He opened his side door and invited Millie into his small office where the kettle and tea-making things were laid out on a small table at the back.

Millie took out of the bag a lemon squeezer, a jar of honey, a spoon and a cup. "This is very kind of you Jack," she said, blushing again.

"Pleased to help," said Jack standing to one side, placing a cup of tea in front of her. "Look, I have an idea. It is a bit of walk from that dressing room you're in to the green room beneath the stage. What if I prepared a flask of hot water before each show and you collected it from me? That way you would be able to prepare this in the dressing room. Besides, going up and down those stairs with hot water isn't a good idea, the dancers will be up and down all the time and you could have an accident."

This was quite a speech for the usually quiet Jack, who was more interested in anything on four legs that he could have a bet on. In Millie he had been reminded of someone he had known many years ago and he felt comforted by the thought.

Millie prepared the lemon and honey, finished her tea, thanked Jack again and hurried off to find Lauren. "And the flask would be just perfect," she called out. "A great help, thank you Jack."

Millie found Lauren on the stage giving further instructions to Vic and his boys. "You see darling, the opening number should be soft and warm, which is why I have chosen *Shout*."

Vic looked at the sheet music. "This is the Lulu hit, *Shout*."

"Is it darling?" said Lauren, gazing out in to the auditorium "I picked it up in a music shop in town along with the others I have given to you."

Vic quickly looked through the sheet music and laid them to one side. "Forgive me, Miss Du Barrie, but the songs you have selected are hardly suited to an artiste of your calibre."

Several of the boys in the pit looked down at their shoes as if they had all suddenly decided they might need polishing.

Lauren waved her hand theatrically and smiled. "Well darling boy, when in Rome... I don't think a seaside audience would appreciate my Carmen."

"Miss Du Barrie, I wonder if you might allow me to suggest some more suitable material for you..."

"My dear boy, I am totally in your hands, what do you suggest?"

Vic coughed. "Well if you will permit me to have a look in my archives I am positive I can come up with something more suitable than *Shout*."

At that moment Millie walked forward with the lemon and honey. "You see Millie, I knew I would be in safe hands with this dear boy here. Let us retire to the dressing room and look at the costumes. I might want to make a few changes to some of them and I understand they have a marvellous seamstress in the town." And with a rather out-of-tune version of *Shout* which she began to sing, Lauren walked off the stage followed by her assistant.

Muriel was welcoming some regulars to her guest house and had just given them tea and biscuits when the doorbell rang. Freda was standing on the doorstep looking upset.

"Whatever is the matter?," said Muriel. "Are you unwell? You had better come in; we'll go through to the kitchen. Mr and Mrs James have just arrived and they are having tea in the front."

Freda sat herself down and began to cry. "Oh Muriel I don't know what I am going to do."

Muriel put her hand on her neighbour's shoulder. "Come on Freda love, tell me what is wrong. Maybe I can help."

Pulling a hanky from her apron pocket Freda blew her nose loudly and wiped her eyes. "I've lost my purse and I've nothing in for the people's breakfast tomorrow. Dick has been out all day and you know Mrs Jary won't give me tick. I am sure I put it in my bag like I always do."

"You have probably just mislaid it," said Muriel trying to use words of comfort. "I can give you some bacon and eggs for the morning and I've plenty of milk and bread, so your guests won't starve."

Freda sniffed. "You are a pal Muriel, thank you."

"Look, let me just show the Jameses up to their room and then I will come in with you and we can look for your purse together.

Freda and Muriel searched high and low, checking coat pockets, drawers and down the sides of the chairs, but they found nothing. True to her word Muriel fetched some provisions in for Freda to tide her over for the morning and just as she was heading out, a very drunk Dick came through the back door singing.

"Look at the state of you," said Freda. "Where have you been all day and where did you get the money to go drinking? You haven't been paid from the legion this week."

Dick Boggis, who was swaying from side to side, grinned and fell onto the sofa. "Been and put some money on the gee-gees and won. I treated the boys to a few bevvies."

Muriel watched in disgust, thank goodness her Barry never came home worse for drink.

"You haven't answered my question," said Freda, hands on hips and looking at Dick with daggers. "Where did you get the money from to go gambling on the horses?"

Dick fell to one side and as he did so something fell with a thud on the floor.

Picking up the purse, Muriel handed it to Freda "I think you'll find the answer there my love," she said and left before World War III broke out. She could hear Freda shouting at the top of her voice as she closed her own front door and hoped that the Jameses had gone out for a walk before their evening meal.

* * *

"Get down here now, Sidney Arbour and clean up this mess."

The raised voice of his wife Pearl rang in Sidney's ears like a never-ending alarm that someone had forgotten to switch off.

"Now, what is bothering her?" he thought, as he pulled on his favourite jumper he wore around the house.

"Coming right now my sweet!" he called through gritted teeth and went down the stairs as fast as his seventy year-old legs would allow. One of his knees had been giving him terrible pain but his doctor had told him it was down to natural wear-and-tear for a man of his age. Sidney was a tall man, who kept his body in trim. His face had very few lines and his moustache had often been likened to that of Clark Gable. Throughout his career he had always been nimble on his feet and could tap and dance with the flair of Fred Astaire. Likewise, his wife Pearl didn't look her age; like Sidney she had kept herself in trim. Despite having had two children she could still get in to costumes that had been made for her over thirty years earlier. Pearl was shorter than her husband and her neatly curled, short, dark hair wouldn't have looked out of place on a young Katherine Hepburn. Pearl had been a trained dancer when she had met Sidney who, like her, was coming out of a dance class. They had fallen in love, married and toured the world with their song-and-dance act. Pearl had a fiery temper and would go off at the slightest provocation. Sidney was no shrinking violet when it came to dealing with the likes of his wife, although it took him a little longer to lose his cool, but when he did, fireworks were guaranteed.

Their children, John and Jane, now in their forties had both emigrated to Australia in their twenties in search of a better life. Both were married to successful partners and each had two children and, as seemed to be the family trait, both had one of each. In Jane's case her daughter was the eldest and in John's his son was the eldest. Pearl and Sidney had visited their family as many times as their work would allow. Fortunately they did have a following in Australia and had been there seven times playing various theatres and clubs.

When Sidney walked in the lounge he found Pearl in her housecoat, a scarf tied loosely around her head, a pair of pompom slippers and a duster in her hand. She was just about to move some papers from the coffee table when Sidney intervened.

"Let me do that my sweet, you carry on with your dusting and then I will make you a nice cup of coffee."

Pearl looked at her husband with a scowl. "Coffee! When do I have time for coffee? If you tided your things away properly it would make housework a doddle; this house will not clean itself and you could get yourself out the front and trim that hedge. The neighbours must think we live in Sherwood Forest."

Sidney was about to remind his wife that they had only been home a week after a tour of the Scottish provinces in a dire production of *The Lilac Domino*. Under his breath he cursed. He had often wondered how they had managed fifty years of marriage. It was true that Sidney had a roving eye where the ladies were concerned, but whether she cared or was upset by his dalliances, Pearl had always turned a blind eye. There was no doubt about it, on stage they were the sweethearts of song and as the old adage went – the show must go on.

Sidney went through to the kitchen and as he did so spotted some mail. He had heard the postman whistling earlier. He picked up several envelopes, two were bills, and there was a postcard from Jane who was on holiday in Melbourne visiting friends. There was also an envelope containing a Christmas card that had obviously not arrived on time and a larger envelope bearing the postmark of Great Yarmouth.

Sidney tore open the envelope as he switched on the kettle. He smiled, the answer to a prayer, being in the terraced house with Pearl longer than a fortnight was more than his body could bear.

"Pearl, my sweet," he said, walking back in to the lounge. "How do you fancy a summer season at Brokencliff-on-Sea?"

* * *

Matthew watched with interest the comings and goings of the company as he went about his business at *The Golden Sand*s. He had never seen anything quite like this before and got the other stage hands on side to guide him through some of the things that were not making sense. The sets for the show were causing one or two problems and in the hands of the late Jim Donnell would have been dealt with swiftly. Matthew felt a little out of his depth, something that didn't go unnoticed by the watchful eyes of Mona Buckle. Bob Scott who was passing through the theatre stopped to speak to Mona and she mentioned what she had seen.

"It isn't my business to pry," she said her eye watering "but that Mr Taylor doesn't seem to know what he is doing. Twice I have watched him trying to haul that piece of scenery to its rightful place and twice he has failed, he doesn't seem to know his left from his right. Even I know that stage right is stage left if you are looking at it from where we are standing in the auditorium. Oh yes Mr Scott, I learned a lot from Mr Donnell when he was with us, God Rest His Soul," she continued, her eyes looking up to the theatre ceiling. "You see

Mr Scott I get these feelings about people, I see things, it's a talent I have and if you ask me Mr Taylor, he needs watching carefully otherwise, and you mark my words, there will be a dreadful accident."

Quite used to the ramblings of Mona, Bob acknowledged what had been said, assured Mona he would keep an eye out for anything of concern and went back to the sanctuary of his office where a pile of unsigned invoices awaited his attention in order to catch the last post before Beverley left for the day.

* * *

The rehearsals continued in full swing, dance routines were altered and magic tricks went wrong and had to be reset. Lauren couldn't make up her mind whether or not to sing popular hits or ones she was more familiar with. Vic began to pull his hair out as he tried to coax the singer back onto the right path. It was Rita who finally succeeded by walking up on to the stage and stopping Lauren who was in the first verse of a swooping version of *Knock Three Times*.

"Stop right there," she shouted as she stormed across the stage. "Lauren this really will not do. I have stood out front and listened to you sing songs that are clearly not your style and I cannot see an audience warming to them, even if they have recently been in the charts. Now where are the scores for some of the songs you performed back in Earls Court?"

"But darling..." said Lauren, flinging her arms out and nearly knocking Rita over. "I don't think a seaside audience would appreciate my *Salome*."

"They will appreciate even less your *My Sweet Lord*," said Rita dodging to one side. "Vic. what is Lauren doing as her opening number?"

Vic looked up from the pit. "Well I keep trying to persuade Lauren to do *Another Op'nin', Another Show* from *Kiss Me Kate*, but she seems set on doing *Shout*."

Rita turned back to Lauren and spoke firmly. "Lauren, I am sure that you have performed to worldwide audiences, but this is a summer season in Great Yarmouth. Now if I had wanted someone to sing *Shout* I would have booked Lulu, as it happens I booked you and I implore you to sing what you sing best and forget this chart nonsense or I will have to step in myself and let you go. It isn't too late for me to make changes to the bill."

"But darling…" said Lauren raising her left hand to her forehead in another theatrical gesture she had picked up from Vanessa Redgrave "I want to experience the songs of today and give them meaning; I want to try new things."

"Then I suggest you join the *Black and White Minstrel Show* my old lover, because you are not singing popular music. Now Vic, please will you take Miss Du Barrie aside and get some kind of semblance and order to her act. The opening number when she comes down at the beginning of the show can be *It's a long way to Fucking Tipperary* for all I care, but not bloody *Shout!*" And with that Rita walked purposely off stage right and bumped into Matthew who was standing in the wings watching. "And you, young man, get about your business, there is a show opening here in the next few days or had you forgotten? And for goodness sake get those bloody spotlights sorted out, they are all over the place."

"Well," said Jenny who was standing at the back of the auditorium "I have never seen Rita loose her temper like that before." And Mona who was polishing the brass rail nodded in agreement.

The Oswalds consisted of a mother, father and daughter. They had been performing their magical illusions around the world in circus and on the theatre circuit to great acclaim. Of Spanish origin they all spoke English well. Salvador and his wife Carmen had trained their daughter Conchetta well and despite her wanting to make another life for herself and fall in love, she did enjoy the act. Having a relationship of any kind proved difficult as they were never in places long enough to get one established. Now here they were for a lengthy summer season at the end of a pier, which would be a new experience for all of them. Maybe she would be lucky this time around. At twenty three she had become concerned about being left on the shelf.

The act was so well rehearsed that it really didn't warrant further work. Salvador would saw his wife in half while Conchetta paraded around the stage in her glittery refinery. He would also swallow swords, throw knives at his daughter and juggle with fire. The climax of the act was placing Conchetta in a cabinet, spinning it three times and opening the door to reveal his wife in her place. Conchetta would then walk down the aisle of the auditorium and join her mother and father back on stage wearing a totally different outfit and no one in the company had yet worked out how it was done.

Rita had been greatly impressed by the professionalism of the trio, who were always ready and never overran their running time. In fact Rita could set her watch on the act from beginning to end.

Rick O'Shea and the Ramblers had introduced new materiel to their act with Rick doing an impersonation of Elvis Presley and other rock stars of the day. New outfits had been made so that when they came down for the final curtain at the end of the show, they stood out from the crowd with trousers and jackets being made up of sequinned material which, if they had had to have endure them for longer than the two minute finale, they would have all been scarred for life. Putting cost before comfort the trousers had been made with no lining. As the season progressed the boys would invest in some long johns before permanent damage to their nether regions would surely put them out of action on the pulling front.

Tommy Trent had taken some good advice from Rita and had moved his act along a couple of notches and Rita was assured that he was a very good substitute for her late husband Ted.

Miss Penny's puppets were delightful and also being a wardrobe mistress meant that Miss Penny's six-minute act was more than compensated by the needlework and help backstage that ensued as the season progressed.

The JB Showtime Dancers were a great asset to the line-up and with Jonny Adams, who had worked on a whole new act, *The Golden Sands* was assured of having a great variety bill for the season.

* * *

Wednesday 16 June
Henry's Bar

Since the departure of barman Dan, *Henry's Bar* had seen many staff come and go. Stella however, though often being offered jobs elsewhere had stuck with her job. She knew her boss only too well and she also understood her customers. Stella had become one of the attractions, locals and holidaymakers alike enjoyed visiting the venue because Stella was always there with a smile and a listening ear, often hiding her own worries.

Stella had already seen two barmen come and go, the first tried to run off with some of the takings and the second failed to be on time. Stella was managing as best she could with little help from Ken, her boss. Stella's mate Katie had been in to help out at the busiest times but wasn't looking for a full-time job and certainly not one behind a bar. Ken had been placing advertisements in the local papers but those that bothered to turn up to be interviewed had no experience to speak of and he needed someone who he could rely on.

It was on the Wednesday lunchtime when things were winding down that Stella looked up and saw a face she hadn't seen in a while.

"Dave, David Grant what the hell are you doing here in town? You never let me know you were coming."

Dave beamed a big smile at Stella and she went round the other side of the bar to give him a big hug. "Where's Dan, is he with you?"

Dave shook his head. "No, he couldn't get any time off, but I needed to get down here to collect the last of my belongings, a mate has been keeping them for me."

"It is so lovely to see you, let me pour you a beer. Ken, come see who is here, it's Dave."

Ken came into the bar area and held out his hand to Dave. "Nice to see you again, are you back here long? Don't fancy a couple of stints behind the bar do you? Stella could do with a hand."

"Leave the man alone," said Stella handing Dave a pint of *Infinity*. "He is only down here to collect some stuff."

Ken laughed. "Worth a try. Where are you staying?"

"I only got here an hour ago I was going to see if Lucinda Haines had a room for a couple of nights."

"No need," said Ken "There is a room upstairs you can have if you want it. Very basic, but there is a bathroom up there. I use it for live-in staff but since the departure of your Dan, the room has stood empty."

"That's really good of you. Dan will be tickled pink when he knows I have been staying in his old room."

"What are you up to, you old rascal?" said Stella. "I know you too well."

"Ken wants me to do a couple of shifts behind the bar, is that right," Dave asked with a grin.

"Only if you are agreeable, I can then give Stella an evening off, she hasn't had one for ages."

"Okay then," said Dave. "Stella can have tonight off and I will cover. How much do you want for the room?"

Ken must have been feeling generous and surprised Stella when he replied, "No charge, you do tonight and tomorrow with Stella and we will call it quits. I will even go as far as giving Stella the lunchtime shift off and I will stand in here."

Stella went to get a glass. "I think I need a brandy, a very large one."

The news that Dave was back in town for a few days soon spread and he went along to see Maud and her sister Enid. He visited old friends at the Wellington Pier where he had worked for many years and he was also given a tour of *Ted's Bar* at *The Golden Sands*. He visited Jim's grave and laid some flowers and he was fortunate enough to bump in to Lilly Brockett who was also visiting the crematory. Lilly told him about her new home, what was happening at Brokencliff and that she had a beau whose name she could never remember, but she thought he was sweet on her.

Friday 18 June

The audience were beginning to take their seats and usherettes were busily selling programmes. Several locals were in the audience including Freda, Muriel and Lucinda, although the latter was sitting in a different row, away from the other pair, who she was pleased to see were not accompanied by their husbands.

Rita came out of the stage door and walked along the side of the theatre with Jenny at her side. "Let's hope this goes off as planned," she said. "Lauren Du Barrie, what a nightmare! Why on earth did I book her! Did you hear her warbling this afternoon when we passed by the dressing room? I have heard better noises from cats when they are on heat."

Jenny grabbed her friend's arm. "Rita, it will all be fine, you'll see. It's sold out tonight. Come on, let's go and take our seats."

Rita smiled and followed Jenny into the theatre

SUMMERTIME MAGIC
Let the Sunshine In
The JB Showtime Dancers introduce
LAUREN DU BARRIE
"I've got a Song for You"
The MAGIC FINGERS of
Jonny Adams
Hernando's Hideaway
The JB Showtime Dancers
Make Mine Music
LAUREN DU BARRIE
"Norfolk's Best Kept Secret"
The incredibly funny
TOMMY TRENT
Rocking and a Rolling
The Fabulous
Rick O'Shea and the Ramblers
Interval
Magic Moments
The JB Showtime Dancers introduce
The Spell Binding Magic of
The OSWALDS
Back for a Laugh - Tommy Trent
Miss Penny's Puppets
With a trick up his sleeve – Jonny Adams
The JB Showtime Dancers introduce
LAUREN DU BARRIE
It's a Pity to say Goodnight, The Entire Company

In *Ted's Variety Bar* following the show it was generally agreed that this year's show was a success, despite the fact that Lauren Du Barrie confused the orchestra by wearing a different colour frock for every part of the show in which she appeared. The new JB Showtime dancers with the added bonus of four male dancers brought a roar of approval from the ladies in the audience as it was the first time male dancers had been seen in Great Yarmouth. Jonny Adams who had been coached by the late Ted Ricer had really come into his own with an entirely new act that even baffled The Oswalds, whose own style of magic had the audience gasping. Comedian Tommy Trent showed that he was a worthy successor to Ted and didn't let up on the jokes which came thick and fast. Miss Penny's Puppets provided a comedic mime using popular music with puppets becoming the artistes of the sixties including a puppet that looked remarkably like Lulu and sang *Shout* with a backing group of mice and when Lauren saw it she exclaimed that there was the reason she had been asked to remove *Shout* from her own repertoire. But the real show stopper of the evening was Rick O'Shea and the Ramblers with their selection of rock'n'roll favourites and superb impersonations. The ladies and young girls in the audience could barely contain themselves and it was obvious to everyone that Rick and his boys would need to leave nightly under cover for fear of being caught up with adoring screaming fans. As Rick was heard to exclaim during the summer season, "There's not a dry seat in the house."

Rita sneaked out for some air and stood at the end of the pier looking out to sea. She wondered what Ted would have made of the show; she had taken a few chances here but they seemed to have paid off. She knew that Ted would be so proud of young Jonny and also his old mate Tommy who Rita had promised to look out for and was already lining up a show for him in Blackpool at the end of the season when the illuminations would bring in new audiences.

She smiled to herself and pulled her stole around her shoulders and then in the distance for a split second she thought she had spotted a bright star twinkling in the heavens. She felt a cold shiver go down her spine as she turned and walked back into the bar.

"Well Rita," said Don Stevens handing her a drink. "You have pulled it off again."

"I am not so sure, me old lover. I am a bit concerned about Lauren."

Elsie put her arm round Rita. "Come on Rita, don't be so hard on yourself, when you look back on some of the other shows we have been involved in... who could forget the June Ashby fiasco? What a season that turned out to be, but the show went on. Last year we had a great success with Derinda Daniels and now look at her! She is touring with Ricky Drew."

"Elsie is right," said Don looking around him. "I wouldn't worry about Lauren too much, she is a seasoned pro but maybe not really variety theatre stock. But the audience seemed to like her and, besides, you have Rick O'Shea on the bill and two fantastic magic acts and I never thought I would admit this but those male dancers do add something extra to the show. The work that Jill and Doreen have done with them is fantastic. That *Hernando's Hideaway* sequence was pure genius."

Over in a corner of the bar Muriel was seated with Freda who, as usual, was wearing a creation that had certainly seen better days. All through the show Muriel had tried to cover her nose as the smell of mothballs and a strange scent had been circulating the row. She took a gulp of her gin-and-tonic and broached the subject.

"Freda do tell, are you wearing a different perfume tonight?"

Freda smiled; she was already on her fourth freebie drink courtesy of a barman who appeared to have taken a shine to her. "It's a new fragrance, *Cat's Whisper*, recommended by the man on the market."

"Are you sure it wasn't meant to deter cats Freda, is it really a perfume?"

Freda reached into her handbag and produced a bottle clearly labelled *Cat's Whisper*, "the feline fragrance for a night on the tiles".

Muriel took the bottle of scent and looked at it carefully. "Do not use on polished surfaces," it said in small print. "Keep away from heat." Muriel studied her friend carefully. "Have you sprayed any of this on your neck?"

Freda nodded. "And behind my ears."

"Freda, I hate to tell you this but your neck is looking rather red, I think you ought to go and wash it off. This stuff could be dangerous."

Lucinda had been moving around the bar chatting to familiar faces, and was congratulated by many on her appointment as the chairman of GAGGA. Lucinda was particularly thrilled to get Rick O'Shea's autograph on her programme. She nodded at Rita and spied Muriel and Freda who seemed to be deep in conversation. Just behind her the loud voice of Lauren Du Barrie could be heard.

"Darling I said to my companion Millie here, playing this theatre has always been a dream of mine. I, of course, come from an operatic background but it is so lovely to be able to sing songs that I only ever hear on the wireless. Millie dear, run along and get me another bourbon, it's the throat don't you know, I have to keep it lubricated."

Lucinda smiled and moved away making a beeline for Rita who was now alone and who she was longing to have a chat with. Rita and her late husband Ted had been paying guests of hers for a couple of seasons and Lucinda had carried a torch for Rita's husband. Tragically he had died at Lucinda's guest house and from that sad day Lucinda and Rita had formed a friendship which had surprised both of them.

Matthew Taylor had been listening in on several conversations as he worked the room carrying a platter of sandwiches, leaving his stagehands to man the entrance and fire exits. He had heard someone mention *Henry's Bar*, which had been a favourite haunt of the late Jim Donnell and his friend Dave Grant. Dave had since moved to Blackpool with his beau, Dan. Although he had been in town a few weeks now, he had not had the opportunity to really get his bearings. It certainly was hands-on work and it didn't stop once the show was up-and-running.

He stopped and made the acquaintance of Jonny Adams. "That is a great act you have there," he said, smiling warmly at Jonny.

Jonny who had been quite shy when he started out in the business the previous year had come into his own and it was mainly thanks to the late Ted Ricer that he had almost cured his stammer. "Thanks very much, this is my second season here at this theatre."

"Yes so I have heard," said Matthew "One of the staff mentioned it. Do you know the area very well?"

"Quite well," replied Jonny taking a sip of his lemonade.

"Would you know whereabouts *Henry's Bar* is?"

"Oh yes, it isn't too far from here, if you have a pen and paper I can write it down for you."

Matthew put down the tray of food and felt in his jacket pocket. "Coming right up Jonny, thanks very much."

"That new stage hand seems to taking quite an interest in young Jonny," said Elsie as she turned to speak with Jenny who had just joined the gathering.

"I don't really know too much about him to be honest," said Jenny accepting the offer of a drink. "He isn't someone I have had much to do with, not like in the days when old Jim ran the place back there."

Elsie nodded. "Yes I think we are all in agreement that there will never be anyone quite like Jim. I have to say I didn't take to that Roger last season and I was mightily relieved to hear that he had moved on; he had a manner about him that I didn't like."

"Is there any truth in the rumour that Don is planning on quitting the business?"

Elsie laughed. "The times I have heard that over the years. It is true to say that since he has handed some of his acts over to Rita there isn't so much to keep him in the office. He really prefers being on the road and dropping in on all the venues. The day Don gives the business up I shall let my hair grow out and let everyone see just how white it really is."

"Funny how theatre gets into your blood," said Jenny. "Even when I handed over the dancing school, I really couldn't just let it go, that is why I am so grateful to Rita. Her suggestion about us joining forces at the office is one I have never regretted. It is good to see that Jill and Doreen have injected new blood into the dance troupe and the boys really are a bonus. I heard members of the audience talking about the new line-up during the interval; they really have caused quite a sensation."

Freda had just finished off her tenth sausage roll, she had crumbs down the front of her dress and Muriel despaired at her companion.

"Have you met that Glenda Duncannon yet?," asked Muriel. "She has taken over that boarding house on Wellesley Road. Apparently she moved down from Clacton."

Freda wiped some crumbs from her mouth with the back of her hand and took a slurp of her drink. "I think I heard she was divorced. Her husband ran off with a woman from the local chippie, Agnes O'Brien her name was, has four kids, a cocker spaniel and a tortoise."

"Who on earth told you that?," said Muriel raising her eyebrows. "It's the first I have heard about it."

"Nettie Windsor told me," said Freda adjusting her bosom which seemed to be sagging thanks to the worn elastic in her bra. "And you know, Nettie, she is always one who is up on the gossip."

"I never had much to do with Nettie. I don't really see myself moving in her circles," said Muriel with a sniff.

"They did say that her old man was a bit of a cycle path, got ten years, he's in Blunderston."

"I think you mean psychopath," said Muriel

"Fancy," said Freda. "Anyway you'll be seeing a lot more of Nettie soon I hear she has signed up to join GAGGA."

"Oh my word," said Muriel "please tell me you are kidding Freda Boggis."

Freda shook her head. "It is my belief that Shirley Llewellyn has been rounding up new members so that they challenge the new committee."

Freda huffed. "You know Shirley Llewellyn and her scheming ways, she changes her mind more times than I change my underwear."

Muriel coughed and replied quietly. "Really, as little as that."

Saturday 19 June

"A pint of lager mate, please".

Dave looked up and smiled. "Coming right up mate."

"You wouldn't be Dave Grant by any chance would you?"

Dave grinned. "The very same and who might you be?"

"Matthew, Matthew Taylor, I am the new stage manager at *The Sands*."

Dave held out his hand. "I am pleased to meet you. I know all about working back stage, I used to be at the *Welling Pier*."

"You were a friend of Jim, is that right?"

Dave began to wipe the counter. "You are well informed. Jim and I are, were, the best of mates."

"I heard what happened, must have been a shock."

Dave put down his cloth. "Yes it was a big shock."

Stella came through from the back. "Ken wants you. I can take over from here."

"Nice to have met you Matthew, I hope you get on okay. I am sure they will after you at *The Sands*."

Matthew grinned. "And you must be the famous Stella I have heard so much about. Matthew Taylor…"

"I don't know about famous, but yes that's me, Stella. So how are you enjoying it so far, here in Great Yarmouth?"

"It takes a bit of getting used to after the Smoke, but I like it. Do many of the company from *The Sands* come in here?"

Stella eyed Matthew; there was something about him she couldn't fathom. "No not often, they usually go to a pub on the market place, but I expect now *Ted's Bar* has been launched they will gather there more often than not."

Matthew nodded. "Yeah, that makes sense. That Dave seems a nice bloke."

"Salt of the earth is Dave," replied Stella. "Now my old love unless you have any more questions I must get tidied up, we close in ten minutes."

Dave had been given thought to the predicament of Ken being unable to find a suitable barman. He remembered his old friend Jamie and wondered if he was in the market for a job. Jamie often went off to different resorts during the summer and settled for a job in a supermarket during the winter months back in the town. Jamie's mother had been ill and he had heard that Jamie had stayed in Great Yarmouth following her death. He mentioned his idea to Ken and found that Ken was all ears, he needed someone that Stella could get along with who was reliable and if he came with Dave's recommendation than what could be better?

Shortly after the pub had closed its doors on the lunchtime trade Dave took his chance and rang the doorbell of number 41.

Jamie was pleased to see his old mate and showed him photographs of his latest girlfriend, Masie and told him about his mother's last days.

At the suggestion of a job at Henry's Bar, Jamie was all ears and he said that Masie was looking for part-time work to supplement her studies at college. She had been working in a gift shop along Regent Road, but had not found the work or the staff to her liking and had only stayed a couple of weeks.

Introductions were made and Ken agreed that Masie could train beside Stella one or two evenings a week and that with Jamie's references from holiday camps and hotels in various resorts around the country, he started immediately. Stella couldn't have been more pleased with the outcome and thanked Dave by giving him a small gift for him and Dan; it was a silver-framed photograph of Dave and Jim taken on *The Golden Sands Pier*.

The following morning and with the hope that Dave and Dan would visit towards the end of the season to try to catch the last performance at *The Sands* Stella waved him off and recalled the words Jim had said, "Dave, my mate, he is worth his weight in gold, that one," and that was one statement Stella agreed with wholeheartedly.

Tuesday 22 June

"Penge, bring the Bentley round to the front of the house. I would like to take a trip into Great Yarmouth."

Penge half bowed and left the lounge.

Sir Henry looked up from his shooting magazine. "What's that, Old Girl, going into town are you?"

Lady Samantha looked at her husband. "I thought I might go and do some shopping in *Palmers* and take a look at The *Golden Sands*. I haven't been over there in a very long time."

Sir Henry snorted. "I expect you will find it very much the same. Full of candy floss and hot dogs, dreadful things, why people eat them is beyond me. A nice bit of rump is what I like."

Getting up from her chair Lady Samantha tapped her husband on the shoulder. "That is maybe why people eat hot dogs, my dear. Perhaps they cannot afford expensive joints of meat and if business doesn't pick up here, we won't be able to either."

"I say. Steady on Old Girl. Things can't be that bad…"

Lady Samantha raised her eyes to the ceiling; really her husband sometimes never grasped the real facts. "I am going to allow the car park to be used by theatre goers and coach parties to the theatre here. It will bring in some much-needed revenue and also with the deal I have proposed it will also bring more visitors to the house."

Sir Henry dropped his magazine in his lap. "I say, when did you arrange all of this?"

"While you have been out on your shooting parties and heaven-knows what else, I have been trying to readdress the problems we have here at the Hall. It is high time, Henry, that you started pulling your weight around here; the place is falling down around our ears."

Sir Henry looked alarmed. "Sammie, old thing, why didn't you say something?"

"Because, Henry dear, you would have done what you have always done, buried your head in the sand and hope the whole thing would sort itself out."

"That's a bit strong, why, I am always suggesting things."

"Name them!"

"Well there was the erm... And the thingamabob and... well, damn it all, Sammie, a man needs his recreation."

Lady Samantha headed toward the door. "Yes Henry, of course you do. See you later."

"Morning Enid, see you've had a bit of a rush on, if those empty shelves are anything to go," said Petunia Danger as she entered the shop.

Enid looked up from her pricing gun. "Oh hello Petunia, I haven't had time to restock the shelves. Now that Maud is caught up at the theatre in Brokencliff, I have no one to give me a hand. Barbara used to do the odd day, but with Maud out of the box office and that new girl Dixie, she doesn't have the time."

Petunia selected some postcards of Great Yarmouth. "One of my regulars has asked me to send her some cards before she arrives in a couple of weeks' time. She likes to write them before she gets here and then post them."

Enid laughed. "Funny arrangement, I thought the whole idea was writing a postcard while you were on holiday, not before."

"She does it every year. Mind you, she does get caught out if the weather isn't too good and the recipient gets to hear about it."

"It takes all sorts," said Enid taking the cards and finding a paper bag to put them in.

"How much do I owe you?"

"I wish I knew," said Enid earnestly. "This decimal currency is driving me up the wall. I have price lists with pounds shillings and pence on them, then I have to convert that to the new money; it's a headache. Maud has told me time and time again what to do, but I am still not sure. If truth be known that's why half the shelves are empty; I don't know how to price the stock."

Petunia looked at Enid and felt sorry for her. "Look, I have a free afternoon; if you like I will come back and give you a hand, I am not doing evening meals this week, only B&B."

Enid sighed with relief. "Oh, would you Petunia? That really is very good of you, I will pay you of course."

"Don't be daft," said Petunia. "That's what friends are for, but I will let you treat me to a cup of tea and a cake."

Enid handed the postcards to Petunia with a grateful smile. "Look have these on me. I will organise a couple of cakes for later on. You really are a life-saver, Petunia and no mistake."

"And to think, she eats yoghurt," Enid thought as she watched Petunia leave the shop.

Chapter Nine: *The Show on the Clifftop*

Rita Ricer and Jenny Benjamin present for a limited season at

The Little Playhouse – Brokencliff-on-Sea

Opening Friday 23rd July at *8pm* and

thereafter **nightly at 7.30** (except Sundays)

(Strictly limited season until Saturday 4th September 1971)

The Sweethearts of Song

PEARL & SIDNEY ARBOUR

in

"Showtime on the Clifftop"

with

Ventriloquist

Jimmy Joe and Tiny Tom

Hughie Dixon "Having a Laugh"	The Clifftop Gaiety Girls	Ukulele Una A Song and a Smile
Produced in association with Alfred Barton Directed by Rita Ricer	**Maestro of Music** Phil Yovell at the Baby Grand	**Choreography** by Doreen Turner and Jill Sanderson in association with Jenny Benjamin

By arrangement with Don Stephens

Special Guest Star

"MYSTIC BRIAN"

and his Turtle Doves

Bookable in Advance from the Theatre Box Office

55p & 45p

T he posters were on hoardings in Great Yarmouth, Lowestoft and as far away as Norwich. Business for the small venue was looking good on paper and requests for tickets had been flooding in. Owlerton Hall was also seeing a turnaround with several coach parties, who would also be going to see the variety show, booked.

Until such times as a permanent box office assistant could be found, Maud had reluctantly agreed to run things at the *Little Playhouse*. Maud was not so happy with the size of the box office area, with barely room to swing a cat, let alone house a chair to sit on. The books of tickets were crammed onto a shelving unit that had seen better days. There was little to be done but grin and bear it. Maud toiled with the idea of insisting that Dixie took over the box office, but then as the girl was new she was probably better placed with Barbara back at *The Sands*. But being so far from what was her permanent place of work, she could not keep a close eye on things, something she had mastered over years of experience. Now if Jim were still around, he would have found a solution to the problem and Maud would be in her rightful place at *The Sands*. Maud racked her brain several times to come up with an idea or a person she knew could be trusted to run this small box office, even considering her own sister Enid, which she quickly dismissed, Enid was having her own problems with the new currency as she well knew.

The idea of selling tickets from the box office at *The Golden Sands* had been too complicated, but Maud was quite happy to hold tickets for customers who would pay on arrival. A quick call from Barbara or Dixie meant that Maud would mark tickets for collection and hoped that the customers in question did turn up. It meant that no money for the *Little Playhouse* changed hands at *The Golden Sands* box office. However a brisk business was in operation from Owlerton Hall with a volunteer taking bookings from visitors to the *Hall* and going down to the box office to buy the show tickets. It was a plan that was working particularly well. It was only on the odd rainy evening that Maud found tickets were not being collected and paid for because the weather had put some off travelling from Great Yarmouth; this meant that the theatre wasn't as full as it might have been.

Accommodation for the small company had been sourced locally with some being housed in a property they let out for the season. Others had opted for a room at the *Beach Croft* at a greatly reduced rate which would surely keep Alfred and Jean Barton's staff on their toes.

Pearl and Sidney Arbour were staying in the hotel much to the annoyance of the neighbouring guests. Not a day passed when the two couldn't be heard arguing about something or other. But when they both descended the staircase or came out the lift on their way to the theatre, they were both wreathed in smiles and holding hands like love-sick teenagers.

This scenario continued when they went on stage and looked adoring into each other's eyes as they sang their songs of undying love much to the enjoyment of their audiences.

"They say they fight like cat and dog," many an audience member had been overheard saying.

"You would never know it to look at them, would you? The way she hangs onto his every word..."

Back in their small dressing room, other members of the company could hear Pearl shouting at Sidney. "You have moved my mirror again, how many times have I told you to leave my things alone, you useless looking article! My mother warned me off getting entangled with men like you and she was right; I should have listened to her."

And under his breath Sidney muttered, "If only you had listened to her my sweet..."

Mystic Brian was housed up in one of Joe Dean's caravans which meant his beloved doves Caroline, Enid and Lottie could enjoy the fresh air on fine days by being outside in their cage. As usual the birds played up during some performances and the audience were subject to having doves circling above their heads, reminiscent of scenes from a Hitchcock film. Rita made sure that Brian wasn't up to his old tricks of downing a few bevvies before he went on stage. But of course Rita could not always be there and Jenny, who often stepped in, missed the signs that Brian was slightly under the influence until he was heard hiccupping on the stage.

Also sharing the dressing room was Jimmy Joe and his vent. doll Tiny Tom. Jimmy was of the old school and had been brought up on Musical Hall variety as his parents had performed a unicycle and juggling act. Jimmy's wife Clara travelled round the country with her husband and was often seen hanging around the theatre foyer if she couldn't get a complimentary from Maud, who didn't see the necessity of a woman watching her husband on stage every night; Maud thought it was unhealthy.

Una and her Ukulele was something of a novelty. Audiences described her as a female George Formby, though Una did not sing any of his songs. Quite a petite woman, Una had energy that a woman half her age would have liked. Staying in one of the small cottages in Brokencliff, she was neatly dressed when she arrived at the theatre in her smart red jacket and black skirt with a red beret fastened to her red hair. Wearing little make-up until she went on stage, she attracted the attention of others who thought her dress sense a little daring. When she emerged from her dressing room which she shared with the Gaiety Girls, her red hair had been replaced by a blonde bouffant wig with a red and yellow feather plume, fishnet stockings, a sequinned leotard and high stiletto heels adorning her feet. She sang in a strong clear voice, plucked her ukulele for all it was worth as she tap-danced across the stage and had the audience tapping their feet with her. She always left the stage with shouts for "more" ringing in her ears.

Hughie Dixon shared the dressing room with Mystic Brian and the two found they had a lot in common with Hughie being a bit of a pigeon fancier, so being in the same room as the doves he was in his element. Hughie talked fondly of his wife back in Bolton and his three grown-up children. Hughie had played many clubs up and down the country and seemed to follow the late Ted Ricer around, though he had never met the man. Brian would reminisce about Ted and become quite emotional and Hughie, by the very descriptive narrative Brian gave, felt as if Ted were actually there in the room.

Phil Yovell was an accomplished pianist and was well-known around Norfolk. He had often played in the *Maurice Beeney Orchestra* when Maurice's regular pianist was unwell. Phil was an accompanist for acts in local clubs and often called upon as a rehearsal pianist for local theatre groups. A well-spoken and genteel man who had married well. His wife had since died leaving him the small house they shared together in Belton. There had been no children and apart from a brother and two siblings on his wife's side of the family, led a quiet life, which was the way he liked it.

Sitting out front on various nights, Rita, Elsie or Jenny would keep an eye on the way the show was shaping up. There was no doubt about it that the small company offered good value for money and that despite their off-stage persona, Pearl and Sidney knew how to please an audience. Their *Indian Love Call* was a thing of master timing with Pearl approaching the stage from the back of the auditorium. They did a top-hat-and-cane routine, singing and dancing to *By the Light of the Silvery Moon*, performed love duets from *West Side Story*, *Kismet* and *The King and I*. When Alfred Barton dropped in on the show, as was his wont, he was happy to hear the audience having a good time and he tapped his trouser pockets in time to the music. Business was good and it was with thanks to Rita, Jenny and his new-found association with all at Owlerton Hall.

Saturday 24 July

In Great Yarmouth Lucinda went to her front door and there stood her two regulars George and Dinah Sergeant; she stood to one side and welcomed them in.

"It is lovely to see you both," she said, following them into the lounge.

"I said to George," said Dinah, sitting herself down. "It will be lovely to go back to Great Yarmouth and have a few days sunshine, didn't I George?"

"You did Dinah," said George settling into an armchair after their long drive.

"We are looking forward to seeing some shows," said Dinah. "I see that Rita Ricer is doing the show at *The Sands* again this year."

"Yes," said Lucinda. "And she is also presenting a variety show over at Brokencliff."

"Did you hear that George?," said Dinah rubbing her hands together at the thought. "We went to a play over that way once, didn't we George. It was some kind of thriller, quite good weren't it George?"

George duly nodded, knowing full-well that competing with his wife when she was talking was useless.

"Rita will have her work cut out," said Dinah. "Is she staying with you again this year?"

Lucinda shook her head. "Sadly no, but she has bought a house over in Gorleston and has some offices in Northgate Street in town. She seems to be settling down nicely since her dear husband Ted passed on."

"That was a sorry business, "said George finding his voice. "He was a good comedian and a lovely man all round."

The two ladies nodded in agreement.

"We've been reading about you, haven't we George," said Dinah. "We heard you are the new chairman of that society you all belong to."

"GAGGA," offered Lucinda with a smile.

"Beg pardon?"

"GAGGA, it's the Great Yarmouth and Gorleston Guesthouse Association," said Muriel.

"Oh yes I see," said Dinah "Did you hear that George, Lucinda is GAGGA!"

Once Lucinda had settled the pair she went to look at what the postman had left. She picked up her shopping basket and headed off to Mrs Jary to buy some extra provisions. Freda and Muriel were there talking about the cost of everything as Mrs Jary acknowledged Lucinda.

"A quarter of ham, a pound of your best cheddar and a pound of butter please, Mrs Jary," said Lucinda with a smile "And if you have any Eccles cakes, I will take six of those as well."

Mrs Jary smiled and set about putting the order together.

Muriel turned to Lucinda. "Lady Chairman, have you any dates in mind for our next meeting?"

"Indeed I have," said Lucinda. "Perhaps you and I could discuss them over a coffee one morning.

Freda added her own thoughts to the conversation while scratching an itchy bosom. "I am still surprised that Shirley stood down as chairman, there are many that say she will worm her way back, especially with all the new members she has encouraged to join."

Lucinda huffed. "Well, we will see about that. I have a good mind to pay Shirley a visit."

"Sorry to disappoint you," said Muriel "But I heard she has gone away for two weeks."

"How ridiculous!" exclaimed Lucinda, feeling her blood beginning to boil. "We are at the beginning of the season; who on earth is managing her guest house while she is away?"

"No one," said Muriel happy that she knew something that Lucinda clearly didn't. "She has closed the house down and gone for a holiday; I believe Bournemouth was mentioned."

"And where did you hear that from?"

"Petunia Danger mentioned the other day when I bumped into her in Woollies; she was buying some pick and mix. I was after some barley sugar for Barry; he is very partial to barley sugars."

"I always put your Barry down as more of a liquorice allsorts kind of man," said Freda, wishing she could get home and have a good scratch. "My Dick likes allsorts."

Muriel nodded. "Yes, I have heard."

Mrs Jary handed over her purchases and Lucinda paid her with a grateful smile. "Thank you Mrs Jary. Goodbye ladies." And with that Lucinda left the shop.

"Well something is eating her," said Freda turning her attention to a Battenberg.

Muriel smiled. "I wonder what it can be?"

Sunday 25 July

"I said to you, George, that we had a lovely afternoon out."

"You did, Dinah," said George, cutting into a rasher of bacon.

"That model village is a beauty to behold," said Dinah, looking up at Lucinda who was bringing another pot of tea and extra toast. "If all the streets were as tidy as in that Merrivale Village, the world would be a nicer place, isn't that right George. Mind you, that ice cream was a bit of a rip-off weren't it George? I said to the man at the stall, you are getting a bit mean with your whippy cornets. I expect it must be this new money. It's a beggar to work out sometimes. I said to you George, didn't I George, that we are being ripped off all over. They should have left things as they were, messing about with addings. Anyway, while I think it, George and I have decided we would like to book a fortnight, end of August through September, if you have any vacancies?"

"I will check the book for you, won't be a minute."

"I have to say George, Mrs Haines has really pulled out all the stops here, hasn't she? Them there bedrooms look a treat, you would think we were staying at *The Carlton*."

"I do have vacancies for those two weeks Saturday twenty-first of August until Saturday fourth of September and you can have the same room you are in now. I had a cancellation," said Lucinda acknowledging some other guests that were late down for breakfast.

"That would be champion Mrs Haines. I say George, that would be champion."

* * *

Bessie Reeve answered the front door. "Hello Lucinda, what brings you to these parts? Don't very often see you over in Gorleston."

Lucinda followed Bessie through to the kitchen and accepted the offer of a cup of tea.

"Bessie, I wondered if you had thought any more about joining GAGGA. I know you have had some wonderful things done to this old place and you really should become part of the landladies' association; it has so many benefits."

Bessie looked at Lucinda with a smile. "I am hardly in the same league as you all. I only agreed to do B&B because of my son Patrick who is in the Navy, as you know. It really is more a holiday home-from-home for the parents of the boys at sea. I don't take in regular paying guests and some of the rooms are still without modern décor but, according to Patrick, that doesn't seem to matter."

Lucinda stirred her tea. "But Bessie, you would have the support of all the other landladies and there are the social events we run, not to mention the discounts we get from our suppliers."

"It is very kind of you to think of me, Lucinda and I will think it over."

Lucinda drank her tea. "It would be so lovely to have you on board. You know some of the other ladies."

"One or two," said Bessie. "I went to school with Muriel."

"Ah yes, dear Muriel," said Lucinda with an unconvincing air of caring. "Muriel serves on the board with me. You did know that Shirley Llewellyn has practically given up her business, at least that is what I have heard on the grapevine."

Bessie poured another tea for them both. "I never take much heed to the grapevine," she said. "One hears so many little stories and most of them unfounded."

Just then Molly and Nellie arrived, bringing the conversation to a close.

"Thanks for the tea Bessie, so think over my proposal. Good day ladies," and Lucinda picked up her bag and headed out of the front door.

"And what did Lucinda Haines want?" said Nellie, putting some shopping bags on the kitchen table." I got that bullock's heart you wanted."

"Wants me to join GAGGA," said Bessie, getting up to make her friends a fresh pot of tea."

Molly sneered. "You want to stay away from that coven of witches."

"Molly, I hope you're confessing to Father O'Dougal on Sunday," said Nellie with a laugh.

"Well that's just what they are. Witches, you should hear some of the stories about that lot, it would make your hair curl."

"Do tell," said Nellie "it would save me a fortune from the *House of Doris*."

"Well," said Molly taking off her coat. "Where shall I start?"

Monday 26 July

Matthew was getting quite used to his job at *The Sands* and surprisingly he found himself enjoying it. The back-stage boys did as they were told and he had struck up a rapport with Bob Scott, Beverley and the once-foreboding Mona Buckle. He was getting used to her funny ways and when Mona said it was time for elevenses, he downed tools and joined her.

Personally Mona wasn't too struck on the new back-stage manager; he was certainly nothing like Jim or even Roger who followed him. With her job working out at *Rita's Angels*, Mona was reasonably happy with her lot.

"Tell me more about Jim," said Matthew as Mona sat down in the green room, where the two often had their break.

"He was a lovely man," said Mona. "You could tell that from his aura, and if I know anything at all, I do know about people's auras. It's a gift, you know, Mr Taylor; some have it, some don't. I have been blessed with the gift."

"He was certainly well thought-of from what I have heard."

Mona's eye watered as she placed her hands firmly on her knees. "He was a grafter, was Mr Donnell, he never shirked. It was a sad day when he died, but his presence can still be felt about this old building, oh yes it can, make no mistake. Sometimes when I am collecting my Brasso from the stores, I can feel his spirit around me. It was a happy day for Mona Buckle when I began working for him."

"Does my aura tell you anything, Mrs Buckle?," Matthew asked, helping himself to a Bourbon.

Mona looked Matthew in the eye. "I can see things, Mr Taylor. You have been troubled in the past and you carry those troubles with you."

Matthew felt slightly alarmed, sometimes being around Mona spooked him.

Mona sat back. "The spirits never lie, Mr Taylor. You are troubled and you need to seek some advice. Now I don't give advice Mr Taylor, it isn't my way, but there are those that can. I will say no more." And with her eye watering, Mona stood up. "Now I must get on with my work Mr Taylor, the devil makes work for idle hands."

As he watched Mona leave the green room, Matthew felt slightly worried by Mona's words. Could she really see all of that in him?

He finished his biscuit and went to out of the stage door giving Jack a wave. "Just off to the box office, back later."

"Righto," said Jack, looking through that day's post. Another envelope for Rick he noted, doused in perfume and he didn't need to read the contents to know who that was from. His attention was interrupted by the clanking of Mona's mop and bucket as she edged it along the floor. When she reached his window, Mona leaned heavily on the mop looking toward the stage door.

"Mr Taylor is a caution," she said turning to face a startled Jack. "Oh yes, the spirits never lie. He is up to something I'll be bound. He needs watching he does."

Matthew tapped on the box office door and Dixie greeted him with a smile.

"No Barbara?," he asked, stepping inside.

"Gone to get some change from Bev," said Dixie eyeing Matthew up, and not for the first time. "We've been busy today with advance bookings."

"It is a good show, you ought to go in and see it sometime."

"I've no one to go with," said Dixie coyly

"Thought a good-looking girl like you would have had men running after her."

"Not me," said Dixie.

"You are not from these parts are you?"

"Like you then, aren't I. Bit of a gypsy me. I like to go to different places, see things, and meet people. I get bored if I'm always tied to the same area. Bit like you so I've heard, you travel around a bit don't you?"

Matthew grinned and put his hands in his jean pockets. "Depends on where the work is and the kind of company I find when I get there."

Dixie lowered her eyes. "So have you found any company here in Great Yarmouth?"

"None to speak of, I have been keeping myself to myself lately, you know how it is, new job, got to keep your eye on the ball."

"But you seem to have mastered it now; you should have a little fun."

"Yeah, maybe I should."

Chapter Ten: *Due to Indisposition of...*

Friday 13 August

"**M**rs Barton," said Angie struggling with her left false eyelash. "We've had more complaints about Mr and Mrs Arbour. Shouting at the tops of their voices again last night after the show according to Mr and Mrs James in room seventeen."

Jean Barton put down the linen she was carrying on the reception desk. "I will mention it to Alfred, any idea where he might be?"

"Last I saw of him he was heading out of the front door towards the cliffs."

"Off to that blessed theatre no doubt," replied Jean with a heavy sigh. "If he spent less time there and more time looking after the business here, we might actually get somewhere. Don't worry Angie I will have a word with the Arbours myself and there is no time like the present. Ask Janine to collect his linen and take it to room ten, the Robertsons checked out early this morning. A right Friday the thirteenth this is turning out to be."

"She wasn't happy, you should have seen her," said Angie checking her nails as Janine picked up the linen. "Like a bear with a sore head."

Janine sneered "She's always like that lately, I run the other way when I see her coming, even Chef says he has noticed a change in her attitude, I am going to see if the *Cliff* is taking on any staff, don't know how much more of madam I can take."

Jean knocked and Sidney opened the door. "Mrs Barton good morning, and what a lovely morning. I was just saying to my wife we should go for a walk along the sand."

"Would you mind if I came in?," said Jean "I would like to have a word with you both."

Sidney stood to one side "Please come in. My sweet, Mrs Barton has come to see us."

Pearl emerged from the bathroom wearing a floral robe, a headscarf and dark glasses. "Mrs Barton, to what do we owe the pleasure? Please have a seat."

"I will stand if you don't mind," said Jean. "It is quite a delicate matter really, but we are getting complaints from other guests about raised voices from this very room, guests say they can hear you arguing late at night and first thing in the morning."

Pearl walked toward the bay window and turned. "Ridiculous, I have never heard such tommyrot."

Sidney blushed. "There must be some mistake Mrs Barton. Pearl and I were…"

"Rehearsing a play," said Pearl walking toward Jean. "We are thinking of doing a tour after the season here."

"That's right my sweet, we are rehearsing a play."

Jean was not to be fooled and stood her ground, prepared to tackle the problem she knew her husband wouldn't. "This is not the first time we have had complaints about you both from other guests and I am sorry but I must ask you both to vacate your rooms by the end of the week."

"But Mrs Barton," said Sidney trying to take control of things and getting flustered.

"Leave it to me Sidney," said Pearl removing her dark glasses. "In the fif… forty years my husband and I have been in the business we have never been asked to leave anywhere. What does your husband have to say on this matter?" Pearl was beginning to raise her voice.

"My sweet, don't take on so. I am sure Mrs Barton was only…"

"I will speak to my husband later," said Jean firmly. "I hope I have made myself clear."

"Very clear indeed Mrs Barton," Pearl replied angrily. "And while you are at it you can tell your husband that Pearl and Sidney Arbour will not be continuing in his show tonight or any other night, we quit. Sidney start packing NOW!"

"Yes my sweet."

"I shall inform my husband of your decision," said Jean "I am sure he will be sorry to lose you both."

Pearl laughed. "And he will also see the takings plummet without us at the helm; we were the reason audiences were coming to Brokencliff. I will have you know we are an institution!"

Jean headed towards the door and turned with a smile. "And if your past behaviour is anything to go by, you should both be in one."

"Sidney my tablets, get me my tablets NOW!"

Jean went down to reception "Mr and Mrs Arbour are leaving today," she said to a much surprised Angie. "Prepare their bill ready immediately. If you want me I shall be with Alfred at the theatre."

Maud was surprised to see Jean Barton enter the foyer. "Good morning Jean, everything alright I hope."

Jean smiled at Maud, who she had great respect for, Maud was one of the old school, hardworking and reliable, and it was a pity that there weren't more like her.

"Is Alfred in there?"

Maud nodded. "Yes he is looking at a problem with the lighting."

"Jean, what brings you here, is everything okay?"

Jean looked at her husband who was at the top of a stepladder adjusting a spotlight at the side of the stage.

"Put it this way Alfred. You will need a new top of the bill, Pearl and Sidney Arbour have just quit."

Alfred wobbled as he came down the ladder. "You had better explain; they can't just quit, they are under contract."

Jean told Alfred what had happened. "You have known about these complaints for weeks Alfred and like you always do, you bury your head in the sand."

"But Jean you could have asked them to lower their voices you didn't have to evict them."

"Alfred I am tired of your excuses. If you spent less time twiddling with bits and pieces in this goddamn awful theatre, you might see what was under your nose. That hotel doesn't run itself and I am sick of the bloody place day in, day out and no support from you. The whole place needs redecorating; it's just a bloody shrine to your late parents, God rest their souls."

Jean sat herself down and for the first time Alfred noticed her frustration.

"I'm sorry Jean, what can I say?"

"Oh sort your bloody lighting out for goodness sake. I am going back to see if I can make a dent in the mess I found in the linen room. Janine is next to useless when it comes to organisation; it's time we got rid of her and that bloody receptionist. No one else would employ them that's for certain, but good old Alfred he will employ anyone." Jean stormed up the aisle and out through the theatre doors as Maud watched in disbelief. Something was definitely up. Alfred came into the foyer.

"Maud, please prepare yourself for a bit of a shock, our top of the bill have just quit, so my lovely wife has just informed me. Can you give Rita a call at her office for me and tell her I am on my way over to see her?"

Rita listened to Alfred as he told her what has occurred earlier. Rita leaned heavily on her desk. "So we are now without the top of the bill! didn't you try to stop them leaving?"

"It was too late, they left very hurriedly according to Angie at reception; they paid their bill and went."

"They are in breach of contract of course," said Rita "but the immediate problem I have is who to put on in their place. I can't take anyone from *The Sands* and to be honest I couldn't even if I wanted to. I need someone who will appeal to the older audience, nostalgia that kind of thing. That was what was so good about Pearl and Sidney."

Just then Jenny popped her head round the door. "Sorry to interrupt but a couple of people has just turned up who I think you might like to see."

Rita looked puzzled. "Sorry about this Alfred. Jenny, can it wait, I need to sort out the immediate problem at Brokencliff."

The door opened wider. "Well maybe we can help," said a voice that Rita recognised all too well.

"Derinda Daniels, Ricky Drew what the heck are you both doing here?"

"We're on our honeymoon," said Ricky and a little dog woofed his approval.

"Jenny, call *Look East*, see if we can get a spot on there tonight, get in touch with BBC radio and the EDP office, we may just get something in the evening news tonight."

Jenny smiled. "Elsie and I are on it right away."

Introductions were made, Alfred shook hands with Derinda and Ricky and received a wet trouser leg from Bingo, but he was so pleased to meet the pair that he said nothing.

"Now if Mona Buckle were here she would say that the spirits had sent you," said Rita with a laugh. "She works here as well as at *The Sands*. So honeymoon, when did this all happen?"

"We will fill you in later," said Ricky. "All I need to know is, do you have a piano at the theatre in Brokencliff and will you let Derinda and I finish the season there for you?"

"Yes, yes and yes," said Rita "but I thought you two were working abroad?"

"And we were," said Derinda. "But we weren't too happy with some of the venues and then Ricky asked me to marry him, so the first thing I did was ask my daughter Jeanie what she thought and she loved the idea, so we did it and decided to head back to Norfolk. We dropped by *The Sands* hoping to catch you and Barbara told us that you were having a problem with the show at Brokencliff and we immediately came on here to see if we could help."

Rita could barely believe her luck. "There are still three weeks of the Brokencliff show to run; we are closing it on fourth of September, are you sure you are able to do them?"

Ricky nodded. "We can do them Rita you have no worries about that," and right on cue Bingo barked his own stamp of approval on the matter and ran around the office.

Derinda and Ricky checked in at the *Beach Croft Hotel* courtesy of Alfred and made their way to the theatre. Phil Yovell was more than happy to share his baby grand with Ricky, who he had seen perform many times before. Keeping in the theme of the golden oldies, Derinda had asked one of her old band members to bring down some suitable scores and within two hours had managed to put together a repertoire that would appeal to those older audience members who had originally booked to see Pearl and Sidney. Mystic Brian was delighted to make their acquaintances again after sharing the bill with them at a midnight matinee performance in honour of Ted Ricer the year before at *The Golden Sands*.

The company assembled at the request of Jenny Benjamin who had decided to take care of things and it became apparent that they were all glad to see the back of the bickering couple.

"Now let's just run through a couple of things," said Jenny getting into her stride. "The running order will remain the same and Derinda and Ricky will fill the spot left vacant by Pearl and Sidney. Rita has asked me to express her thanks to you for coming in here at short notice and, of course, our very grateful thanks go to these two here. Now there will shortly be a lot of activity around Brokencliff as we are expecting a film unit from *Look East* to arrive, so all of you make sure you get noticed. This is an opportunity for you all as we are also expecting some local reporters to come along."

There were murmurs of excitement among the company.

"Perhaps we should get started," said Ricky. "Once we have introduced ourselves properly to all of you. Derinda perhaps you could organise some tea?"

Bingo, who had been hiding under a front row seat, woofed. "Oh and some water for Bingo too please."

A camera crew duly arrived to interview Derinda Daniels and Ricky Drew. A BBC radio interview was also broadcast much to the delight of the locals. Never had Brokencliff received so much media attention. It was also an opportunity for Lady Samantha and local caravan park owner Joe Deans to advertise their businesses. Lady Samantha stood at the entrance to Owlerton Hall in her best refinery and pearls and, speaking to a reporter, declared that Brokencliff-on-Sea was somewhere everyone should visit at least once.

The hotel also got some free publicity with Alfred and Rita speaking in the lounge about the good fortune that had come out of the blue. Jean watched the broadcast later that evening on a black-and-white TV set that was housed in the linen room as she began sorting some sheets. "If that husband of mine fell in a bucket of manure he would come out smelling of roses," she muttered under her breath.

In a hotel room in Lowestoft, Pearl and Sidney Arbour were licking their wounds and, on seeing the *Look East* programme with a smiling Derinda Daniels and Ricky Drew, Pearl retired to the bathroom in a huff and took a long hot bath. Sidney poured himself a large scotch and wondered how they were ever going to work again.

The audience that turned up on that Friday evening were in for an unexpected treat when the announcement was made that due to the indisposition of Pearl and Sidney Arbour, the management were delighted to welcome in their place Derinda Daniels and Ricky Drew. Word soon spread that *Showtime on the Clifftop* was the show to see and it was only a couple of days later that the 'House Full' boards appeared outside the small venue for the first time that season.

Rita could not believe her good fortune and said to Elsie over a much-needed brew, "All we need is June Ashby turning up and we will have the full set."

Elsie couldn't help but reply. "Anything but that Rita, I don't think my nerves could stand it," and they both laughed loudly.

Chapter Eleven: *The Talk of the Town*

Saturday 14 August

M uriel had just come out of the *House of Doris* and walked across Lowestoft Road to where Freda was waiting for her in the bus shelter. Freda had been visiting a friend on Marine Parade and the two had travelled over to Gorleston on the bus.

"It looks very nice," said Freda looking at her friend's new hairstyle.

"Coming from you, Freda Boggis I will take that as a compliment," replied Muriel sitting down and looking at her watch. "There should be a bus in about ten minutes; if you like we can do some shopping on the market before going back home, I need to get some extra vegetables in, as I've quite a full house this week."

"Fancy," said Freda rustling a sweet bag and offering Muriel a bonbon. "I was just reading all this fuss about that show at Brokencliff. All over the news last night it was. Apparently that Pearl and Sidney Arbour were not the loving couple they made out to be. If you ask me, spending too much time with your other half always leads to problems, but just imagine having to sing love songs to each other night after night, when all you really want to do is tell them what you really think of them."

"A bit like you and your Dick then," said Muriel.

"There is nothing wrong with my relationship with my husband. Admittedly he can be a bit lazy at times, but he always comes home at nights."

"And therein lies your problem Freda Boggis, I have always said you would be better off without him."

Freda chomped on her bourbon and gave the matter some thought. "You have a point Muriel, but in the end who else would have him? I mean I could have the pick of the crop when it comes to men. I had a couple of offers only last week."

"Really!," said Muriel "What kind of offers? You never said anything."

"Well for a start that bloke that runs the stall on the market that I sometimes buy household things from asked me if I would like to go out for a drive one afternoon and he would show me his cottage over near Stalham. I told him, Jimmy I am a happily married woman, but I have to say I was quite chuffed."

"Is Jimmy the one with the toupée that turns up at the end when the breeze catches it?"

"Oh I've often wondered about that. But whatever you think Muriel, he is a very nice man."

"So what was the other offer you had, Freda?"

"That night I was waiting for the bus from the *Palace* bingo and the streetlights weren't working and this man came up to me and asked if I was looking for business. I have to say I wasn't quite sure what he meant; I told him I had a business of my own and he offered me ten quid."

"Please tell me you didn't accept it," said Muriel feeling quite alarmed.

"Of course I didn't," said Freda brushing some icing sugar off her dress. "I told him I wanted twenty or nothing was doing."

And then Freda burst out laughing. "Oh your face Muriel, it was a picture. As if I would accept money from a strange man, now Jimmy on the other hand…"

Muriel nudged her friend and couldn't help but smile.

"Doris was quite busy this morning," said Muriel "a couple of ladies I have never seen in there before, they must be new to the area."

Freda chewed on her bonbon and took another from the bag.

"Your teeth will fall out," said Muriel. "You eat far too many sweets."

Freda huffed and carried on regardless.

"Are you wearing any perfume today?," asked Muriel sniffing the air.

"I am as a matter of fact," said Freda. "It's called…"

"No don't tell me," said Muriel remembering *Cat's Whisper*. "I don't want to know. Put this way it isn't by *Elizabeth Arden*. A tip for you Freda, I was told that the best way to use perfume was to spray it in the air and walk toward it."

"Fancy," said Freda chomping on her sweet.

"However, my advice to you is when you spray your perfume run in the other direction," Muriel said with feeling.

Freda looked at her friend and huffed again.

"Look," said Muriel jabbing Freda in the side. "Who is that, I wonder, coming out of *Doris's?*"

Freda looked across the road. "Her? That's Bob and Janet Roller's daughter."

"I don't think I know them."

Freda folded her arms. "Janet was a Brown off Church Road, her father was a cobbler by profession and her mother worked as a home help for years."

"No I don't think I ever knew them," said Muriel checking her wristwatch again, hoping the bus would hurry up. "So is the daughter married?"

"No I don't think so," said Freda who intended to find out the minute she got home by making a few phone calls.

"What's her name then?"

"Carmen," replied Freda. "I think Janet is fond of opera."

Muriel flashed a quick glance at Freda, "You are telling me that they called their daughter Carmen! Carmen Roller!"

Freda nodded. "If I had been blessed with a daughter I would have called her Carmen, I think that's a lovely name."

Muriel shook her head in disbelief. "But not if your surname was Roller."

Just then the bus arrived and the two ladies boarded. Freda wedged herself into the window seat and popped a couple of bonbons in her mouth. Muriel balanced herself next to her and prayed that the bus driver wasn't going to drive too fast.

* * *

Reverend George greeted Joe Dean with a smile. "Hello Joe, I hear things are looking up on the business front."

Joe was pleased to see his old friend. "Well since all that publicity around the show, my caravans are booked solid until the end of September."

"It's a shame the show ends the first week in September," said Reverend George rubbing his forehead from the heat of the sun.

"You never know, now that Derinda Daniels is on board they may extend it, I did hear some talk in the *Fisherman's* the other night."

"And it is so great that Lady Samantha has been able to let people have use of her car park, which must have made things easier for everyone."

"But you haven't heard the best news," said Joe inviting Reverend George into his office. "British Rail is going to sell the land that the old station stood on."

"No, when did you hear this?"

"I have a mate who works for the railway and an agreed sale with the Eastern Counties Bus Company will mean that

Brokencliff will have its own regular bus service. There is to be a parking area, which can only benefit our small community even more. But here is the big news, Reverend. I have been given planning permission to change my caravan park into a mobile home park. You know, those stationery homes you see over at Burgh Castle and the like. They will be fully equipped and have their own supply of water and gas heating. Of course that won't happen for a couple of years and I will need to raise some capital first but to me it's Christmas come early."

"Indeed it is Joe; I couldn't be more pleased for you."

"I am keeping it quiet for the time being," said Joe. "you know how people hate change around these parts and I don't want a falling out."

"Understandable," Reverend George. "Now I must say goodbye, I am on my way to visit Lilly Brockett."

Lilly welcomed the Reverend and invited him in. "The thing is I am not too sure about getting married again, especially at my age, though I have to say I am flattered to have been asked."

"You are talking about the gentleman who tends your garden?"

"Oh yes of course, he does trim my bush out front beautifully and keeps the lawn cut and the flower beds looking lovely. I never had a garden at my old house and I have never been a one with growing things so he is a Godsend, if you'll forgive me saying so."

"So he is quite serious about wanting to marry you?"

"Oh my goodness, yes, he has given me bunches of flowers from his own garden, and his stalks of rhubarb are something to behold. Yes he has asked me a couple of times. Now when was it, last week when he came to pick me up from my class in Lowestoft, as he parked up he said to me, ;Lilly Brockett would you do me the honour of being my wife?'"

"And what did you say?"

"Bill, Gary, Malcolm, whatever his name is, I said I will give it my due care and retention and let you know."

"Sorry, what did you say his name was again Lilly?"

"I wrote it down once, I am dreadful with names."

"But Lilly you should know the name of the man you might one day marry."

Lilly looked puzzled. "Do you think so? I suppose you're right, I'll ask him again when he drops me off some plums tomorrow. Oh he has some lovely plums."

Reverend George took out his notebook. "I can help, I have his name here, remember he is my gardener too."

Tuesday 17 August

"And not that I am one for gossip Muriel, as you know," said Freda. "But word is out that Lilly Brockett has accepted a proposal of marriage from her gardener.

"Really," said Muriel, deciding on whether to buy some more rashers of bacon or a couple of pounds of sausages."

Mrs Jary looked up as Lucinda came through the shop door. "Half of your best ham and two tins of plum tomatoes please and if you have any of that nice cheddar you sold me last week, I will take a pound of that as well. Ladies."

"Oh hello Lucinda," said Muriel grateful of the distraction. "Freda was just telling me about Lilly's proposal of marriage."

"Well if anyone would know, Freda would," said Lucinda. "You are after all the fount of all knowledge when it comes to gossip."

"How very kind of you to say so Lucinda."

"I don't think Lucinda was paying you a compliment," said Muriel whispering quietly to her friend.

But Freda was taking no notice, it wasn't often she received a compliment. "I shall find out the finer details and let you know, Lucinda."

"Thank you dear, you are most kind."

Mrs Jary handed Lucinda her groceries. "I will put that on your bill."

"Don't forget the meeting next week," said Lucinda waving a goodbye. "It is being held at the Town Hall."

Muriel nodded. "Don't worry, Lady Chairman, we will be there."

Thursday 19 August

As Rick came through the stage door, Jack called out to him, "Letter for you, Rick."

Rick removed his dark glasses. "For me? Who on earth would be writing to me at the theatre?"

"Probably a fan wanting a signed photograph," Jack replied handing the mauve-coloured envelope to Rick. "It smells of perfume too."

Rick sniffed the envelope, he recognised the scent from somewhere, and he had smelt it before. He tore open the envelope just as some of the boys in his group were coming through the door. They waved at Jack, patted Rick on the shoulder and went off to the dressing room to get ready for the first house.

Rick read the note and sighed. "Oh good heavens, it's that Llewellyn woman. I knew I recognised that perfume. She hangs around me like a limpet. Twice last week I had to wait until everyone had left the theatre and sneak out with the backstage crew. She wants to take me for a meal after the show tonight."

"Sounds as if you've got a real fan there," said Jack.

"Whatever can I do to shake her off?," said Rick, wiping his brow. "I am used to the young girls screaming at us during the show and one or two of them asking for autographs, but Shirley Llewellyn is something else altogether. I have seen her in the audience quite a few times; she must know this show backwards."

Jack smiled. "Many a time I have witnessed these crushes. You should have been here a few years back when we had Billy Fury, now that caused a real problem. We had to disguise him to get him safely out of the theatre every night."

"Thanks Jack," said Rick. "You have given me an idea; I will have to disguise myself so I won't be spotted leaving the theatre."

"So how do you intend letting the lady know you won't be joining her for dinner tonight after the show?"

Rick laughed. "We have a stretcher in the green room that the St John Ambulance uses if there is a person taken ill. I'll bribe the two men to carry me out on it and feign sickness."

Jack laughed out loud. "Well that solves tonight, but I bet there will be others."

Rick waved as he headed towards the dressing rooms. "I'll cross that bridge when I come to it."

Lauren Du Barrie was pacing up and down outside her dressing room practising her scales as Rick passed.

"Good evening Lauren. A nice evening for it, box office says we are full, second house."

Lauren smiled. "My dear of course we have a full house, with such star quality, how could we not have?"

"First house doesn't look great though."

"It's the second house that counts; I always look upon the first house as a rehearsal."

Rick smiled to himself, by the sound of Lauren's warbling she needed all the practice she could get.

Millie had prepared some hot lemon a
you really are on the ball tonight," said Laur
gratefully. "It's the voice you know, I think I .
outdoors too long today, I am having problems, .
catch in my vocals. Oh for the days of *La Sca*
Coliseum. What colour should I wear for first house,
want to over-stretch myself, I need to be on top of my ᴜ
for the second, that darling boy Rick tells me we are ᴜ
Word must have got out that I am here for the season. Nᴜ
doubt coach parties are on their way down the Acle Straight as
we speak, I expect they will have a restaurant booked before
the show, that nice *Avenida* is the place to be seen. Did you
know Millie that *Avenida* means avenue in Spanish? Oh my
dear Millie I am so excited, I shall have to have a sit down.
Now what colour frock shall it be, the blue?"

Millie had heard it all before. Looking at Lauren and
remembering years of watching her perform, she knew in her
heart there was one colour frock that would never see the light
of day on the stage of *The Golden Sands*, not unless by some
miracle, Lauren really did practice her scales properly and hit
that top note. Millie prepared a blue gown and went off to
inform Vic.

Vic Allen and his boys were setting out their music in the
orchestra pit and Vic hoped they would get advance warning
on the colour of Lauren's costume as at some shows she
couldn't seem to remember which one she was wearing and
surprised them all by singing lower than the colour suggested.

Millie approached Vic and informed him that Lauren
would be wearing blue for the first house and possibly the
second; Vic gave Millie a knowing wink and she smiled to
herself.

Mona was coming along the theatre aisle, doing one last
check that everything was as it should be. Millie waved to her,

ad Mona, never one for such pleasantries, actually found herself waving back.

"Is everything okay, Mrs Buckle?" said Matthew as he came through the auditorium.

Mona huffed, her eye watered and she turned to face Matthew. "Mr Taylor, you have my word that everything is as it should be."

"Have you seen the show yet?"

"I have seen bits and pieces of it," said Mona. "I have watched them all in rehearsal but, Mr Taylor, I really do not have the time to sit in a theatre for two hours, I have things to do. The spirits guide me where I am needed." Mona looked at her watch. "And right now the spirits are telling me that I need to get my coat, head home and put something in front of my Bertie, otherwise he will starve."

Matthew nodded at Mona and continued toward his goal, *Ted's Bar*; it was the first time he recalled Mona ever mentioning her husband.

At the box office Barbara was handing a ticket to Shirley Llewellyn. "How many times is it now?" she asked handing the pre-booked ticket over.

"I have lost count," said Shirley with a girlish giggle. "But it is such a good show. Has Rick arrived yet?"

Barbara had heard the rumours and stopped herself from breaking into a grin. "Most of the artistes are here a good three-quarters-of-an-hour before the show, but you are seeing the second house."

Shirley put the ticket in her handbag. "I have a little something to drop off at the stage door."

Barbara could not resist coming out of the box office to watch Shirley head down the pier carrying a *Palmers* carrier bag. "Ten to a penny she has bought him a shirt," she said to Dixie who came out to see what all the fuss was about.

"Or maybe it's some underwear," she said nudging Barbara.

"Well there is no getting away from the fact that she is a fine looking women, but a little bit on the old side for Rick I would hazard a guess."

"Some men like older women," said Dixie going back through the box office door.

Barbara smiled to herself, but not Rick she thought, especially if all the tales she had heard were true; he had more girls around the country that sailors had ports.

"Are you doing anything on you day off on Sunday, Dixie?" she asked.

"Yeah, I am as a matter of fact. Matthew is taking me over to Oulton Broad."

"You two getting serious then?" Barbara asked. "He has been sniffing around a lot lately."

Dixie grinned. "He's okay for a laugh, he is good company. We'll see how things go."

"Treat 'em mean, keep 'em keen! That was my motto when I was your age."

"Yeah, mine too."

Shirley Llewellyn took a stroll along the pier and watched as the queue for the first house was beginning to form. The sun was still shining and there was plenty of activity on the sands below where youngsters were throwing balls to each other and one or two braver ones were paddling in the cold waters of the North Sea.

Going through the stage door she handed Jack the package. "Could you see that Rick O'Shea gets this dear?"

"Of course," said Jack. "Is there a message?"

Shirley gave a girlish giggle. "No thank you, I hope to be able to see Rick after the show. I am front row centre tonight. I just love watching him on stage."

Jack put the *Palmers* carrier bag to one side. "There's no doubt that Rick and the Ramblers are quite an attraction and have caused something of a sensation, the likes of which we haven't seen for some time."

Shirley waved her hand. "Thank you again, I am most grateful. I must dash; I am meeting a friend for a sherry before the show."

Jack grinned as watched Shirley leave; Rick certainly had made one big impression there.

Sunday 22 August

"Nice car," said Dixie winding down the window.

"Borrowed it off a mate," Matthew replied turning down the music on the cassette player. "Thought we might have a walk along the broads and get some lunch in a pub I know."

"That sounds good to me."

Matthew parked the car and as the two walked along by the Broads a flock of geese was waddling across the grass. Several cruisers were moored and others were setting out to enjoy what promised to be a day of sunshine.

"How are you enjoying the work in the box office?" asked Matthew taking Dixie's hand.

"It's okay, it brings in some money. I have done this kind of work before, selling tickets. Barbara is okay, but I am pleased that Maud isn't around so much."

"Maud has been there a long time from what I gather. Everyone knows her."

"And don't I know it," said Dixie through gritted teeth. "Every local that comes to buy tickets insists that if Maud were there she would offer them better seats. I have had to ask Barbara to step in a couple of times. After all, if the seats are taken you can't offer them."

"Perhaps Maud held some back for locals."

"Well if she did she didn't tell me about them."

They continued their walk in silence and then looking at his watch, Matthew took Dixie along to the *George Borrow* hotel where they served lunches and bar snacks.

Settling down near the window, Dixie accepted the offer of a Babycham and Matthew was satisfied with half a bitter shandy.

Over a Sunday roast they discussed other places they had worked and people they had met. Matthew was quite astute when it came to others, realised that Dixie wasn't telling him the whole story.

He brought her another Babycham and had a bitter lemon.

"So these other places you've worked, was it a seasonal thing?"

Dixie sipped her drink and lit a cigarette, her first that day. "I like moving about, not so easy in the winter months, but I do okay I usually land on my feet."

"You must find accommodation a bit of a problem, I know I did when I moved down here, the rents vary so much."

"I usually manage to find someone to share with," said Dixie, taking a long drag on her Benson and Hedges. "This room I have taken down here I saw advertised in *Middleton's* window, until then I was sleeping under the pier at night."

Matthew sighed. "Well I have never had to do that."

"Well you get used to it."

"You've never mentioned any family, so you have brothers and sisters?"

"One brother, he's inside for grievous bodily, got in with the wrong crowd back in Manchester."

"I'm sorry to hear that. You from Manchester then?"

Dixie stubbed out her cigarette in the ashtray. "Nope, not me. I could murder a coffee."

"Come on then, let's go for another walk and we can get a coffee down near the Broads, it's a bit stuffy in here."

On the drive back to Great Yarmouth, Matthew suggested to Dixie that she went back to his for some tea and cake.

"Cake is it?," said Dixie with a laugh.

"I always enjoy a cake," said Matthew. "I picked one up from *Fine Fare* yesterday."

"I went to *Palmers* coffee shop the other day," said Dixie. "I was feeling a bit flush, I had a sandwich, a pot of coffee and a cream cake; it was lovely."

Matthew awoke the next morning and heard the sound of Dixie filling the kettle. He pulled on some shorts and went to join her. "Sleep okay?"

"Yes thanks," said Dixie "I've put some bread under the grill, fancy a bit of toast? Keep an eye on it while I nip down the hall to the bathroom."

"Best put my robe on," said Matthew taking it from the back of the door. "You don't want to bump into any this lot here without a stitch on, they might get the wrong idea."

Matthew filled the teapot and went to straighten up the bed. He picked up Dixie's clothes from the floor and as placed them on the settee, a wad of money fell out of Dixie's jean pocket. He picked it up and estimated there was at least forty or fifty pounds in fivers. He quickly put the money back in the pocket and went to retrieve the bread under the grill.

Dixie came back into the room and sat herself down at the small table. "I will have to get a move on, Barbara is expecting me at ten this morning."

Matthew handed Dixie some buttered toast and a mug of tea. "You've plenty of time yet. I can give you a lift if you like; I told John I would have his motor back to him by eleven."

Dixie bit into her toast. "Best not, I might just make a quick dash back to mine and change. Don't want anyone getting ideas about us do we?," And then she remembered what she had said to Barbara, well she could always play that down and say nothing happened.

"You got any brothers or sisters?"

Matthew sat down. "I had a sister, but she is dead now."

"Sorry I didn't mean to pry," said Dixie. "That's really tough, man, to lose a sister. My brother drives me up the wall, but I wouldn't want him dead."

"I didn't want my sister dead," said Matthew. "But circumstances as they were at the time caused it."

Dixie looked at Matthew with concern, but didn't ask anything further.

Chapter Twelve: *To Be or Not to Be?*

Monday 23 August

Mona was just putting the finishing touches to Rita's desk with some polish and what she and many others termed as "elbow grease", when Rita walked in unexpectedly.

"You are very early, Mrs Ricer," said Mona. "You must have got a lot on today."

Rita smiled at Mona. "Yes, sorry Mrs Buckle, there are some papers I need to go through before the others get here. I won't disturb you."

"I can tell you have a lot of your mind Mrs Ricer, the spirits never lie you know, I can feel it all around me."

Rita opened the desk drawer, took a folder from it and sat down near the window.

"What you need is a nice cup of tea," said Mona limping her way to the door.

"That's very kind of you Mrs Buckle."

Mona began to hum the *Old Rugged Cross* as she made her way to the kitchen.

Rita looked at the contacts that Pearl and Sidney Arbour had signed and then re-read the small print. Rita had been very angry when the pair had walked out on the show and intended to see that justice was done. As it was, the theatre needed to be full every night to enable them to pay for the services of Derinda and Ricky although the two had not fully discussed their terms with her, but she knew they would not come cheap.

She heard the office door open next door and guessed rightly that Jenny had also decided to come in early. Within a few minutes Jenny had popped her head round the door. "I know what you are up to, can I come in?"

Rita smiled at her old friend. "Mona is just making a cup of tea and with any luck she might offer you one too."

"I thought I heard her singing as I came up the stairs, she never tires of the *Old Rugged Cross*, does she?"

"I don't know for certain, but I would say she went to church in her youth and maybe she still does, you know as well as I do Mona doesn't give much away. Now I have been going over the Arbour's contract and we are quite within our rights to sue them."

"Do you really think it would be worth it?," asked Jenny pulling up a chair near the window.

"Yes I do," said Rita. "After all, they left us in the lurch."

"Well not really, Derinda and Ricky turned up."

"And what were the chances of that happening? We were lucky I know, but think of the consequences we would have been faced with if they hadn't; the punters would have been demanding their money back and several other artistes would have been left without work, thanks to those two."

Mona entered carrying a tray with two cups of tea and a plate of Bourbons. "I heard voices," she said. "I have made you one too Miss Benjamin."

Jenny smiled. "Good morning Mrs Buckle that is very kind of you."

"I couldn't help but hear what you were saying about that theatrical couple, not that it's any of my business of course, but I can tell you this, the spirits say you take them to court. I can see it and the spirits never lie, Mrs Ricer."

Mona then waddled out of the office and gently closed the door behind her.

"Well that settles it," said Jenny. "We sue them." And as she said it, she thought she saw a sign of mirth in Rita's expression.

* * *

"I am sorry old love, the show is completely sold out," said Maud to a couple of holidaymakers who had appeared at the box office.

"That's such a shame; when me and Harry heard that that nice Miss Daniels was here we came down on the off-chance. We did try to go and see her last year, but at the big theatre in Yarmouth, but my Harry was laid up queer, weren't you love?"

Harry nodded.

"We only live on the other side of Norwich and so we thought a few days of sea air would do us both good, especially Harry, he doesn't get about as much as he used to, do you love?"

Harry shook his head.

"Harry used to work on the lightships years ago and then he moved onto the trawlers, but that was his downfall, wasn't it Harry?"

Harry responded.

"Harry never had what you would call sea legs, though his brother Ray had been in the Navy and his father afore him. Harry was more of your dry-land kind of man, weren't you Harry?"

Harry agreed.

"Harry had this dreadful accident with a fishing net, got his feet caught up see and he went over the side like a rocket; it was lucky that they managed to get him back on the trawler after half an hour of him missing. Came in with a catch of cod, didn't you Harry?"

Harry nodded again.

"Well it's been nice passing the time of day with you and I am sorry you haven't got any tickets left but perhaps we will drop by again at the end of the week if that's alright with you.

I am Gwen Talbot and this is my husband Harry, if you do get anything in, will you keep them by for us? We'd be ever so grateful, wouldn't we, Harry?"

Harry smiled.

"Well come on then Harry, we mustn't keep this nice lady from her work. Bye then, it's been lovely talking to you."

Maud watched as the couple made their way from the theatre foyer to the pavement beyond. "Come on Harry, I will buy you an ice cream. You'd like that, wouldn't you Harry?"

Maud could only conclude that Harry had nodded in agreement.

* * *

"This hotel could do with a bit of loving care," said Derinda taking an outfit from the wardrobe. "The rooms are lovely, but so old-fashioned."

Ricky nodded. "But the bed is comfortable and that sea view is to die for, you agree don't you Bingo?"

Bingo was standing on his hind legs at the bay window and woofed, he could see the gulls circling above and couldn't wait to get outside and chase them along the seafront.

"Do you fancy going in to Great Yarmouth for lunch," Derinda asked "I could do with getting some more Pretty Polly tights from *Palmers*."

"We can do," said Ricky who was adjusting his wig, something that had become quite a talking point the previous season when Derinda discovered his secret by accident after Bingo had dropped the wig on the floor of the dressing room.

"What does Bingo think?" said Derinda "Great Yarmouth or Brokencliff for the day?"

Bingo ran towards her and looked up in the way only Bingo knew how and woofed once. "Great Yarmouth it is then. Ricky, grab the car keys and let's go."

Walking along Marine Parade with Bingo trotting along at their side, Derinda and Ricky began to discuss plans for the future. They had talked about going to live in Derinda's Norwich home or moving up North somewhere and the possibility of setting down roots abroad.

They were both in demand work-wise since unexpected developments had bought them closer together the previous year. While Bingo made hay and chased a couple of gulls, Derinda and Ricky played a leisurely round of crazy golf.

They headed down Regent Road and wended their way through the crowds of holidaymakers and onto the market place, where the smell of freshly cooked chips hit their nostrils. Without saying anything they were both soon enjoying some and watching the activity about the town.

"Coffee in *Palmers*," said Derinda. "It has to be *Palmers*, they do the best and then afterwards I can buy some tights. Did you want to get anything?"

Ricky took Derinda's hand and they walked toward the store happily.

"I said to you at the time, Muriel, there was something going on there when they was here last year."

Muriel turned to her friend. "Yes Freda, I believe you did. Now for goodness sake are you buying carrots and potatoes or are we going to *Matthes* for a cup of rosy?"

Thursday 26 August

"Bob have you got a minute? I need you check these returns from the box office."

"Yes of course Beverley. What appears to be the problem?"

Beverley sat down on the opposite side of the desk and handed Bob the cash sheets and receipts. "I don't think it's my imagination but the ticket stubs don't tally with the takings and vice versa. Normally Maud would have done this and as she is over at Brokencliff we are one box office person down on what we had planned. Barbara has been holding on to the paperwork in the safe and only came with it all to me this morning. She banks weekly as you know, unless you or I do it. I really cannot make head or tail of it."

Bob looked over the sheets Beverley's mental arithmetic was second to none compared to his own. "Look, best leave these with me, Beverley and I will study them later on."

"But why can't you do it now Bob?"

"Because I have to be at *Lacon's* in half an hour for a meeting about renewing our contact to carry their beer here," Bob replied picking up his car keys and putting the papers in his desk drawer.

"Well, that's news to me Bob Scott," said Beverley getting back up again. "It isn't in the diary and you have a rep coming from *Walls* this afternoon."

"Can you deal with *Walls* and I'll deal with *Lacon's*?" said Bob heading towards the door

"You know I can't stand that creep from *Walls*; he has hands like an octopus. If my Ian ever got to hear about his antics he would have his guts for garters."

Beverley followed Bob out of into the theatre foyer. "Bob whatever you do, as soon as you get back, for goodness sake look at those sheets. I am telling you there is something very wrong. I have one of my hunches."

Bob knew all about Beverley's hunches and to give her her due, she was rarely wrong. "Okay Beverley I hear you, as soon as I get back."

"And don't come back smelling of *Affinity*."

"Trouble at mill?"

"Oh hello Matthew I didn't see you there. Nothing you need worry about."

Matthew watched as Beverley returned to her office and he headed out of the main doors and on to the pier. He had overheard most of the conversation and he remembered the money he had seen that morning Dixie had been in his room.

He strolled down the pier and knocked on the box office door, Dixie opened it.

"Hello Dixie, is Barbara about?"

"No, you've just missed her. She's gone to purchase some tea which a certain person, no names mentioned, failed to deliver from stores this week."

"Blast, I knew I had something to do," said Matthew. "Really sorry, I will bring some more down later. I was wondering if you fancied having a bit of fun on Saturday night. Thought we might go to the *Tower Night Club* and you could come back to mine."

"Or you could come back to mine for a change," said Dixie. "I actually have my own bathroom since the girl down the hall moved out and a nice little kitchenette to boot."

"Really, sounds tempting, must be costing a bit more?"

"A couple of quid, but that's all, so what do you say?"

"It's a date."

Dixie closed the door and smiled.

Beverley looked up at the clock, Bob still wasn't back. She toyed with the idea of retrieving the box office receipts from his desk drawer and going over them again. She looked at her in-tray and decided to plough on with things that needed her attention.

"Is Bob around?," asked Rita who had decided to make an impromptu visit.

"Oh hello Rita, no I'm sorry he is over at *Lacon's*, he really should have been back by now, but you know how long these meetings can go on for sometimes. Is there anything I can help you with?"

Rita sat down. "I have been going through some ideas about the theatre and I wondered how feasible it might be to put on an end-of-season show here. As you are aware, Blackpool has its illuminations season and now I have Derinda and Ricky back for a while, I thought it might be something we could look at."

Beverley glanced at the calendar. "It is a lovely idea Rita and I am sure Bob would welcome it, but it is a bit late in the season to start advertising another show. Besides we don't have the attraction of Blackpool lights. The theatre isn't heated and once the easterly wind takes hold, audiences would not be too keen on making their way down the pier."

"Yes I have to admit Beverley, I had thought along the same lines, but it is always good to get another point of view."

"If you were dealing with the *Regal ABC* then you might have a chance, but once things start closing along the seafront, there isn't much in the way to tempt holidaymakers."

"Of course these are the things I would normally have talked over with Ted." She paused for a moment and continued. "Jenny is currently keeping things ticking over at Brokencliff, Elsie has been a Godsend. I have no idea how Don manages without her. I never knew I would be so busy with this agency."

Beverley smiled. "But you have made such a success of it. Don Stevens was the one that we always turned to when we needed a pre-season or off-season attraction, now the first person we think of is you at *Rita's Angels*. Even when Don has been approached he has said, 'I will speak to Rita'. Bob was somewhat miffed when the *Delfont* organisation pulled the plug on *The Sands*, but he is more than happy with what you and Don have managed to achieve."

"That's kind of you to say so. When I became involved during the June Ashby saga a couple of years back, I never imagined where that might lead me. As you will remember I even resurrected my old act as Moira Clarence for a while. I miss old Ted, but actually living and working here has made the memories sweeter. That bar is something Ted would have loved."

Beverley got up from behind the desk. "I don't think you and I have ever had a proper conversation. Let's have a drink."

"A cup of tea would be lovely."

"Oh sod that," said Beverley, grabbing the office keys. "Let's go and have a bevvy down in *Ted's Bar*; it's quiet of a lunchtime and I am sure I can get one of the boys to rustle up some sandwiches on the house."

"This place always looks different in daylight," said Rita sitting down in one of the leather armchairs. "Somehow it comes alive at night, especially when all of the posters are lit."

Beverley handed Rita a gin-and-tonic and sat down to enjoy half of *Encore*. "I have ordered ham-and-tomato and cheese-and-pickle if that's okay. We may get a couple of sausage rolls thrown in. It is time we started thinking about offering more in the way of bar snacks. I am going to push for it for next season."

"Perfect," said Rita taking a sip of her drink and kicking off her shoes which had been killing her all day. It really was nice to sit down and relax. "You're married aren't you?"

"Yes, Ian and I have been together a while now. He is picking me up after work tonight we are going to *The Star* for a meal."

"I like *The Star*," said Rita. "And I am also quite fond of *Henry's* where young Dan used to work, though not for a meal you understand. Stella is quite a card, puts in the mind of a young Ruby."

"Ruby at *Diver's*," said Beverley. "She is an institution, everyone loves Ruby. Stella is a lovely lady, she hasn't had a great life if all be told, but she gets on with things and without her at the helm I am sure that *Henry's* would have folded years ago. Ian and I have known Ken for years and although he is a nice bloke, he is a bit work-shy at times."

They both sat quietly, enjoying the relaxing ambience and were both quite surprised by their lunch when it turned up. They had been provided with a platter of assorted sandwiches, pork pie and salad.

"Have you any ideas what you might bring to *The Sands* next summer?" said Beverley enjoying the feast.

"You are saying that as if you know I have got the gig."

"I think it is safe to say that the discussions we have had with *Don Stevens* confirm that. I think Don is hoping to retire."

"Yes, he has hinted at that, but I bet he keeps going if only in a small way. Once this business gets under your skin, it is hard to shake it off. It would be lovely to put on a musical here, I have chatted about it with Jenny. It is such a lovely theatre and the stage and fly-tower are a great advantage."

"Aren't musicals expensive to stage?"

"That depends on what you choose and of course what you would be able to licence. There is an abundance of talent in Norfolk, so putting together the right cast wouldn't be a problem, choosing the right vehicle might be."

"The Operatic Society did *The King and I* a few years ago at the *ABC*," said Beverley "it was wonderful. Jack Bacon was the King and they had brought in a professional to play Mrs Anna; Dorothy Brown I think her name was."

"And that was an amateur production," said Rita "I remember someone mentioning it. This would have to be a professional production, a different kettle of fish, but I have always fancied trying my hand at one. I will have to see what is out there. Of course it is only an idea, nothing concrete. If we are looking at the season of 1972 then I suppose we are looking at another twice-nightly variety summer show."

Beverley finished her drink. "So just suppose you were able to stage *The King and I*, who would you want to play Mrs Anna?"

"My immediate answer would have been June Ashby, the real one, but she has moved over to films and the like in Australia. She would be the perfect English Rose. With a bit of coaching I think Derinda Daniels would fit the bill."

"And the King of Siam?"

Rita laughed. "If the old bugger had lived I would like to have seen Ted in the part, but seriously how do you follow the likes of Yul Brynner?"

Beverley nodded. "I see the problem."

* * *

Bessie Reeve went to the front door looking hot and flustered. "Come through Lucinda," she said standing to one side and wiping her hands on her apron. "I am in the middle of some cooking."

"It smells lovely. I thought you were only doing B&B."

"Patrick asked me if I could make an exception for the family I have staying here at the moment. They have never had a holiday and her husband has been seriously injured and so won't be able to come home to see them all. They are from Birmingham. Nice family, two boys, a girl and a dog. She is a very nice woman and has her children well trained and mannered."

"As it should be," said Lucinda glancing around the kitchen. "Are you still working for the Bartons?"

"Only if they are short staffed, this has to come first. I don't want to let the boy down. I am very proud of him. I would offer you some tea, but as you can see my hands are rather full at the minute."

"No matter," said Lucinda. "I really popped in to see if you had given any more thought to joining us all at GAGGA.

I will be drawing up plans with the committee in the next few days to look at venues for our annual Christmas bash. It is such a lovely affair, one my predecessor Shirley Llewellyn did very well and one I wish to carry on. The ladies do look forward to it."

Bessie busied herself rolling out some short-crust pastry to finish off the steak and kidney pies she had decided on. "I really don't know what good I would be at GAGGA. As I've said before, this arrangement is very different to that of the other landladies."

"But my dear Bessie, think of the support you would have from the others, and besides, our little socials and meetings are usually something of a triumph."

"She is even beginning to sound like the Llewellyn woman," Bessie thought. "No I don't think so Lucinda and besides I have Molly and Nellie who give me a hand with things. I am well suited thank you all the same."

Lucinda stood up. "Well if you change your mind, you know my door is always open. Those pies look delicious, you must give me your recipe sometime."

"One of my late mother's," said Bessie wiping her hands once more and showing Lucinda to the door. "Thanks again for dropping by."

As she closed the door she let out a big sigh. Molly came out of the lounge with Nellie behind her. "You managed her really well. I'll pop the kettle on. I'll say one thing for her she doesn't give up easily."

Saturday 28 August

It was quite busy when Dixie and Matthew arrived at the *Tower Night Club*. A comedian was working the cabaret floor as they went to the bar to order some drinks.

"We can order scampi or chicken, and chips in a basket," said Dixie "I didn't have much before I came out. Didn't leave the box office until eight thirty!"

"Didn't Barbara lock up? She usually does."

Dixie handed over some money to the barman. "She wanted to get off early, her cousin is down for the weekend and she said they were all going out for a meal."

Matthew took his pint of beer and ushered Dixie toward the back of the club where they could sit down at a table and order some food.

"Did she cash up before she left then?"

"No she left me to do that. I didn't mind. She hadn't done the banking either, all the takings from yesterday still in the safe."

"Did you let Bob or Beverley know?"

"Nah, no need, it will keep till Monday."

They ordered scampi and chips and watched the singer who followed the comedian. She was very good and Matthew recalled having heard her name from way back. "That's Nancy Whiskey," he said "Used to sing with a skiffle group, Chet someone or other. Bet she sings *Freight Train*."

"Never heard of her," said Dixie

"My uncle was always playing their records."

As Nancy's set came to a close she came back for a final bow and, right on cue, sang the famous *Freight Train*.

"See, I told you," said Matthew. "Come on, I'll get us another drink in and then we can have a dance."

"Fancy yourself as a bit of a mover do you?" laughed Dixie, following him to the bar.

The following morning they both woke up with hangovers and neither seemed too keen to get out of bed.

"Come on Dixie, be a darling and make me a cup of tea, my mouth is like the bottom of a birdcage."

Dixie rolled over the top of him. "Just as well I need to go to the bathroom, or else you'd be making it."

When Dixie had left the room, Matthew got out of the bed and had a look round. He checked Dixie's jean pocket and there, as before, was a wad of money. Hearing her coming down the hallway he went into the kitchenette and looked for the teabags, taking down a caddy from the shelf, but inside he found another wad of notes. He quickly replaced it and called out, "Dixie, where do you keep the teabags?"

Dixie came into the room yawning. "There in a box there look, marked Brooke Bond."

They shared some breakfast and Matthew got dressed to leave. He pulled out his wallet and checked it. "Blast, I forgot to put the other ten quid in here to get some petrol; promised John I would return the car with a full tank. Don't suppose you can lend me a few quid?"

Dixie went over to her jeans and produced a five pound note. "Will that see you through? You can give it back tomorrow."

Matthew kissed Dixie on the cheek. "Thanks Dixie, I owe you one. Enjoyed last night, we will have to do again sometime."

Chapter Thirteen: *Planning for the Future*

Monday 30 August

J ean Barton ran down the stairs to the reception desk. "Angie, have you seen Daisy and Linda this morning? They are late. The kitchen doesn't clean itself."

Angie looked up from the morning newspaper which was meant for the couple in room fourteen. "I think there was trouble with the buses Mrs Barton, I had to get my neighbour to give me a lift."

"Have you seen my husband this morning? He seems to have done a disappearing act as well."

"He said he was going over to *Tidy Stores* to get a magazine."

"He has gone over there for a cup of tea and a biscuit, no doubt, just like he used to do when his aunt was still alive. Philippa Tidy and I are going to have a falling out very soon. He spends more time out of this place than he does in it. Oh, there you are, you two, get changed quickly and get that kitchen sorted out, Chef is doing his nut in there."

Daisy and Linda smiled a sheepish good morning and headed off in the direction of the kitchen.

"And for goodness sake Angie, get this reception desk tidied up and stop reading newspapers, there will be no print left on them by the time a guest gets to read them."

* * *

Matthew was making his way down Regent Road and noticed Dixie heading towards him. "Morning Dixie, you're an early bird this morning. Shouldn't you be going the other way? You are going to the theatre, I take it."

Dixie stopped and kissed Matthew on the cheek. "I had just started to go down the road when I remembered I hadn't picked my bag up. I will have to go back and retrieve it."

"I can come along with you if you like," said Matthew. "I am early myself this morning so I have time to spare."

"No, you're okay Matthew, you get yourself off. I think I will have to change these shoes as well, they are killing me. I can pick up some cakes on the way back, Barbara does like a vanilla slice, what do you fancy?"

"Well if you let me come back with now, I could show you."

Dixie punched Matthew lightly on the shoulder "Hey you, none of that, besides it's too early in the morning and we've both got a day's work to do."

Matthew grinned. "It wasn't too early the other morning."

"I'll see you later," said Dixie and hurried off.

Matthew walked slowly down the road, whistling to himself.

Beverley arrived at Golden Sands and hurried down the pier to her office. The milk was still standing outside the main doors and she tutted. No doubt Bob was going to be late again. She unlocked the door and went inside; she could hear the voice of Mona Buckle singing and her bucket and mop clanking down the theatre aisle.

Unlocking her office door she placed her bag down on the desk, placed the milk in the fridge and went along to Bob's office to see if he had sneaked in the stage door entrance along with Mona.

She pulled the blinds and opened the window; it often got stuffy and the room needed a good airing.

She heard the key turn in the main door and Bob came bounding in whistling. "Good morning Beverley, good weekend?"

"As weekends go," she replied, she was feeling particularly Mondayish. She and Ian had a great day out with some friends and Monday morning had come round all too soon. "How about you Bob?"

"So so, I am glad we don't have a Sunday show running, the thought of coming in here yesterday would not have been a welcome one. Is the kettle on?"

"Give me a chance," said Beverley, heading back out of the door. "I have only just got here myself. Oh and by the way, I hope you have looked at those sheets by now, it has been playing on my mind since Friday."

Bob sank down into his chair and unlocked the desk drawer. There they still were, the dreaded figures. He took the sheets out and lay them down in front of him.

The telephone rang. "Hello. Bob Scott, how can I help you? Oh hello George, no not at all, look I will ask Beverley to check the diary and give you a call back. It was a great match, didn't know they had it in them."

Beverley walked in, carrying a cup of tea as Bob continued to chat. Making a space, Bob picked up the sheets and put them back in his drawer. "No George, really it is no trouble, leave it with me mate. Say hello to Keith and Daniel when you see them, and of course your lady wife, how is she keeping these days? Oh good, glad to hear they got to the bottom of it. All the best George, bye for now."

He redialled. "Beverley, can you get back to George Darby with a date please? Need to go over the paint job for the end of the season."

"Don't forget the figures," came back the reply "I saw you put them back in the drawer."

"Yes Beverley, on to it."

Jenny pulled up a chair. "I like the idea, of course I do, but a musical at *The Sands*?"

"I just think it will be something new for the area," said Rita. "We are surrounded by variety shows. We have just lost *The Little Theatre* and the one at Brokencliff is no longer staging plays so there is nowhere for anyone to see anything different."

"It couldn't be twice nightly and you would have to fill the theatre every night; the overheads would be enormous."

"Maybe we can get some research done and see what kind of figures we come up with. I think it would be worth exploring even if it comes to nothing."

"I had a word with one or two of them about extending the season at Brokencliff, but most of the acts are booked in somewhere else. I also got the feeling that Derinda and Ricky wanted to get on with their own plans for settling down properly, so I don't think they would be on board either."

Rita smiled. "Well that's probably for the best, the show can close on the fourth as advertised and Maud can move back to the box office at *The Sands*, I hear that Barbara has been finding things a little tricky without her, even though she has had the help of Dixie."

"I think old Maud has found it a bit claustrophobic over there. I know for a fact that Enid has been missing her about the shop. I went in there the other day and poor love was still struggling with decimal currency. She even had one of the landladies in there a couple of times giving her a hand."

Rita stood up and moved to the window. The sky was not looking too promising and heavy rain was forecast. "Alfred is giving the company a party on the Saturday evening after the show in the hotel, we are expected to attend."

"Well that will be something to look forward to. I might be tempted to buy a new dress."

How very different Jenny Benjamin was now to the one Rita had met those years before; it was what Rita termed as progress.

* * *

Lady Samantha rang her bell and waited for Penge to appear in the morning room. The sun seemed struggling to make any kind of effort and she felt in need of cheering up. Sir Harold had left shortly after breakfast to go and visit some friends over near Lound.

No doubt Her Ladyship thought he would return a little worse for wear, especially as he had not taken his car and insisted that he was well able to use the bus. Bookings for house tours were healthy and the army of volunteers that had helped keep Owlerton Hall going were certainly being kept on their toes. The revenue that was coming in from the coach companies to use the car park had also helped boost revenue and Lady Samantha was very happy that she had taken the necessary steps and presented her idea to Alfred Barton. She looked again at the letter he had sent her which included two tickets to the final performance of *The Little Playhouse* summer show. She smiled to herself that she would be seeing Derinda Daniels and Ricky Drew and not Pearl and Sidney Arbour whose antics preceded them. Just who she would get to accompany her on Saturday evening, she had no idea, knowing that Sir Harold would not be keen.

"You rang, Your Ladyship."

"Penge, I wonder if a little trip out might be the thing. I rather enjoyed Great Yarmouth the other day and I thought I might also try and get a ticket for the closing of the show at *The Sands*. Do you know the date it closes?"

Penge coughed and bowed slightly. "Indeed I do, Your Ladyship Saturday the 18th of September."

"Is the Bentley tank full?"

"I dealt with that yesterday Milady and at the same time I took Sir Henry's Rolls in for a service."

Lady Samantha sighed, here she was trying to keep costs down and Henry was throwing the money away quicker than it came in.

"Are all the volunteers in today?"

"Indeed they are Milady and we have a long queue forming, the weather is bringing them in by the coach load. Cook has said she will have to call on the services of Mrs Reeve to help with the baking."

"Of course, of course, if Mrs Reeve can spare a couple of hours away from her own little business, I am happy to pay her the going rate."

Penge coughed. "Cook has already called her and she is sending her friends Molly and Nellie over ahead of schedule, it will be all hands on deck."

"After due consideration I think that perhaps one should stay here and meet and greet some of the visitors, I know that some of them like to see aristocracy in the flesh."

"A very good idea Your Ladyship, I am sure the visitors would appreciate that."

"Thank you Penge, now if I could trouble Cook for a coffee and a toasted teacake, I will finish up here, change my attire and be on parade."

Penge nodded and left the room.

* * *

Beverley knocked on Bob's door and walked in. Bob was engrossed in the ticket returns.

"Well I am glad to see you are finally looking them over," said Beverley putting some letters in the tray for him to sign."

"Have you spoken to Barbara about these?," asked Bob looking up.

"As soon as she gets in I will," said Beverley. "She is running late, had relations over the weekend." Bob laughed. "I meant she had some of her relations down to visit over the weekend. Honestly, your mind! Now, do you want a brew? I am making one for myself and I picked up a couple of buns from Matthes on the way in."

Bob smiled. "Thanks Beverley that would be great. You could have a word with Dixie."

Beverley picked up Bob's receiver, tapped in three digits and handed it back to him. "You speak to her, I'll make the tea."

When she returned, she found Bob looking worried. "No answer, so who is running the box office this morning, it should be open by now. This would never have happened if Maud had been here."

"Don't worry," said Beverley putting down the tray "I can go and take care of things until one of them arrives, they can't both have had relations over the weekend."

No sooner had Beverley gained entry to the box office, pulled up the blinds and settled herself behind the window, than Barbara walked in. "Oh I am so sorry about that Beverley, not like me at all. Isn't Dixie here yet? she does have her own sets of keys."

Beverley hopped off the stool. "She must be running late as well, Bob is furious, says it never would have happened if Maud had been here."

Barbara blushed. "And he is right of course. We have been pretty stretched in here at times, having an extra pair of hands was supposed to take some of the pressure off and then Maud got sent over to Brokencliff."

Beverley nodded in agreement. "It hasn't been the best solution I grant you and Bob is grateful that you agreed to doing longer hours with Maud gone; I am sure there will be a little something extra in your pay packet at the end of the season."

"Talking of money, Friday's takings are still in the safe along with Saturday's; we were so busy on Friday I didn't have time to go to the bank."

"No problem," said Beverley. "I can take it back to the office now and get it sorted."

"Oh that would be a great help," said Barbara putting her bag down and acknowledging a customer at the window. "Be with you in a minute love, won't be a tick."

Barbara took the keys from the tin on the shelf, turned the dial with the combination memorised over a number of years and turned the key, pulling open the safe door.

"Oh my God!" she exclaimed. "It's empty, the safe is empty! I think you had better call the police Beverley and quickly, we've been robbed."

The Evening News, Great Yarmouth

Dixie Galloway aka Linda Marchant is wanted by police in connection with a robbery at *The Golden Sands Theatre*, Great Yarmouth. Linda who has gone under various aliases over a number of years is a professional confidence trickster. She is also wanted in connection with a series of seaside robberies over the last couple of seasons. Police believe she may be operating as part of an organised group.

Bob Scott, the manager of *The Golden Sands Theatre* said that Dixie had come with glowing references from previous employers, now thought to be forged. Mr Scott admitted that telephone endorsements had not been followed as was usual. Matthew Taylor, the back stage manager of *The Sands* who had been walking out with Dixie said she was fun to be around, but he did become suspicious when he discovered that she carried large amounts of cash. He said that he had intended to bring this to the attention of his manager Bob Scott but had been caught up in a delivery for *Ted's Variety Bar* on his arrival at *The Sands* this morning. He stated he had last seen Dixie heading home to collect her bag; the couple had spoken briefly. Mr Taylor is not under suspicion. The amount taken from the theatre has not been disclosed, but it is expected to run into several hundred as the theatre had been busy with advance bookings as the season comes to a close. Mr Scott said it would be business as usual, though several members of the staff had been upset about what had happened and had gone home for the rest of the day. The box office will re-open tomorrow.

Maud read the headlines and was not impressed. She had received a call from Beverley earlier to tell her what had happened.

"This would not have happened if I had been there," she said to Beverley. "I said all along them should have found someone else to man *The Playhouse*. I cannot wait to get back to *The Sands* next week, it's like being in a tomb here; this box office is too small for the likes of me."

And Beverley wholeheartedly agreed with her.

Rita and Jenny arrived at *The Sands* to ensure that everything was okay back stage. One of the boys seemed particularly bothered by the news. It was Matthew who seemed the most upset. "I should have said something earlier," he said to Rita. "I knew something wasn't quite right."

"Don't take on so, me old lover," said Rita "It's not your fault, we have all been fooled at one time or another in our lives. You should have been here in '69, now there was something to blow your mind. You must have read about it in the papers, it was the pre-season attraction of June Ashby."

Matthew shuddered at the mention of the name. "Yes I think I read about it, there was a murder involved."

"That's only half of it, me old lover, now let's get you to the green room and you can have a nice cup of tea with me, I am fair parched. Even on a miserable day like today, a cup of tea always cheers me up."

"Darling, such dreadful news," said the voice of Lauren Du Barrie. "One wonders why these people do such things."

"The money?" said Millie handing Lauren her lemon and honey.

"But darling, one can make an honest living if one puts one's heart and soul into it."

Tommy Trent laughed. "But some people don't always lead a straight life, look at those Kray twins."

"I hardly think they are in the same league," said Rita handing Matthew a cup of tea from a pot that Millie had made for everyone.

"We could all be murdered in our beds," said Lauren waving her hand theatrically in the air. "Is it any wonder my poor voice suffers with the anxiety of it all?"

"Well, it saves the audience suffering," said Tommy and made a hasty exit.

Jonny Adams came into the green room clutching the *Evening News*. "Fancy this happening here, it doesn't seem right. I spoke to Dixie a number of times, she seemed very nice."

"That's just it my boy," Lauren continued. "You get involved with these mobster's molls and you never know where it will end."

Rick O'Shea rolled his eye. "And what movie have you been watching lately, *Bonnie and Clyde*?"

"You can laugh my man, but believe me, when you have travelled the world as I have and seen the things that I have seen... The way they treat donkeys in Spain and the dreadful burial plots in Egypt, they had no idea about giving their women folk a good send off. Oh yes, you would be of the same opinion."

"You'll be telling us next that you are related to Judith Chalmers," said Rick enjoying the banter.

"As a matter of fact," said Lauren, "Judith and I go way back. She is a great fan you know, she has seen me perform at the Coliseum."

Rick put down his cup and saucer. "Yes, even the Romans needed entertainment."

Vic Allen popped his head round the door just as Lauren was about to respond; Rita was doing her best not to laugh. "There are some red roses for you at the stage door Rick, Jack asked me to tell you."

"Oh not again," Rick groaned. "That bloody woman will not leave me alone."

"I am surprised," said Lauren making her exit, "that any woman worth their salt would want you."

"And that's me told," said Rick.

"You asked for that," said Rita. "So who is the lady may I ask?"

"I thought everyone knew," Jonny piped up. "It's that landlady, Shirley Llewellyn, she's being chasing Rick for months."

Now it was Rita's turn to look surprised, it was unlike Jonny to be so frank.

Rick grinned. "It is bound to make the headlines anytime soon, I think she wants my hand in marriage."

Tommy burst out laughing as he came back into the room. "Looking at those tight trousers you wear on stage me old mate, I don't think it's your hand she is interested in."

"More tea anyone?" said the timid voice of Millie hovering with the teapot.

Chapter Fourteen: *Curtains!*

Saturday 4 September

"It is a beautiful morning, that's for sure," said Joe Dean, paying for a paper and some milk.

Phil smiled. "Are you going to the closing night?"

"I do have a couple of tickets, but I've no one to go with. Alfred gave me some complimentary."

"Why don't you ask Reverend George? He likes the theatre and to my mind he doesn't get out much in the evenings."

"I wouldn't have thought it was his cup of tea and, to be honest, if it wasn't for the fact that Derinda Daniels was in the show, I wouldn't be going at all."

"I saw it when it first opened," said Phil, handing over his change. "It is very good. I have seen Derinda and Ricky before when they were in Great Yarmouth last year, you'll enjoy them. She is very good and his piano playing is brilliant, puts me in mind of Russ Conway."

"The guy with the missing finger," said Joe. "I remember him being on the telly in the Billy Cotton Band Show."

"Oh that brings back some memories. Kathie Kay, she was a lovely singer, don't hear much of her now. It's all Cilla Black and Lulu."

Joe headed out the door. "See you later Phil, I might take your suggestion and see what old Revvy is up to."

Joe headed along the parade and turned towards the caravan park just as Deanne was emerging from the front door of the Fisherman's. "Morning Joe, you are looking particularly dapper this morning."

Joe laughed. "Well if a demi jacket and a pair of old Levi's can be called dapper, then I'm your man."

"Are you popping in tonight for a quick one?"

"I might do after the show; I am going to go and check out Miss Daniels," he said with a wink and headed on his way.

"I think you will find she is a married woman."

Deanne adjusted her blouse buttons and set off for a walk before the lunchtime opening. What was she thinking? She was a married woman too, but it wouldn't stop her looking!

"Well that is very kind of you," said Reverend George. "A little bit of light entertainment might be just the thing. I have a couple of Christenings tomorrow afternoon, plus the usual morning and evensong. Yes Joe, count me in, I will treat you to a pint or two in the *Fisherman's* afterwards." He replaced the receiver and looked over his sermon for the following morning's service again.

His doorbell rang and he found Lilly Brockett smiling at him. "I hope I am not disturbing you, but thingamajig and I may have got a date in mind."

"Come in Lilly, come in please, I am in the study, just going for my sermon for tomorrow, the fishes and the loaves."

Lilly beamed. "I used to love Bible class at school, it was all so lovely. Mind you Reverend, I have never understood how Noah got all of those animals into that Ark, it must have been very crowded. I went to Cromer Zoo a few weekends ago with thingamabob and if half of those were on the Ark, you would have been a bit pushed for space."

"The Lord moves in mysterious ways, Lilly. Now what's this about a date? I'll just get my diary. It is looking pretty good for any Saturday in October."

"Oh no, that wouldn't do," said Lilly "I've a book launch coming up and I have to be ready for that. We were thinking more of next year, perhaps May or June. It doesn't have to be a Saturday. I don't think it really matters when you get to our age, a few friends and a couple of drinks, a sausage on a stick thrown in; nothing too fancy."

Reverend George allowed himself a quiet chuckle. "Well, if that is the case I think all you need do is decide on a day of the week and I can do it, I will pencil in a couple of Saturdays for you just in case."

"I was thinking about who to invite, you see I would like my friend Muriel to be there, but if I invite her I have to invite Freda Boggis and she can let the side down a bit, especially when it comes to an outfit. Then of course there is Rita and Jenny to consider. Of course the trouble with people who are getting on in years is they might all be dead before the day; I tell you it's a muddle to know what to do for the best. I have books coming out of my ears and articles to write for a couple of magazines."

"And will thingamabob, sorry, I mean your intended be inviting anyone? Friends, family perhaps."

"Oh I dare say," said Lilly "I've told him to make a list."

"And have you remembered the name of your intended?"

"The gardener?" said Lilly in a thoughtful mode. "Now, let me see, I think it is Bob, William, I will have to check. I keep meaning to write it down."

"So what do you call him when you he takes you for driving lessons or out for the day?"

"Oh I just call him 'Gardener'. It's less muddled that way."

* * *

Henry's Bar was experiencing quite a lunchtime rush. Stella was serving customers as quickly as she could with Jamie now an expert at keeping things flowing behind the bar, they made a great team. Jamie's girlfriend Masie came in part-time most evenings and the occasional weekend shift, meaning that Stella was once again getting a regular day and a half off. Even old Ken had started pulling his weight, knowing that with competition strong he had to ensure that regulars and holidaymakers alike were kept happy.

Stella had received a letter from Dave and Dan; together with their friends Josie and Madge they would be coming down to Great Yarmouth for a few days and would catch the closing night at *The Sands*. Dave had arranged for them all to rent a large caravan on Vauxhall Caravan Park. It would give them all the freedom they enjoyed to come and go as they pleased.

Dan had also invited Stella to go and enjoy a few days at their home in Lytham St. Anne's and she had already arranged some time off with Ken so that she could travel back with them in September; she was really looking forward to a change of scene.

Matthew came into the bar and ordered a pint of *Encore*. "Hello Stella, you have quite a crowd in here today."

Stella smiled. "We have been non-stop today that's for sure, what with the races and the special events going on."

"You must have heard about the robbery."

"My goodness yes," said Stella. "That was a turn-up for the books. Have the police caught her yet?"

"Not to my knowledge," said Matthew. "It was a bit of a worry to say the least, I had been walking out with Dixie for a bit. I had no idea who she really was."

"But the papers said you noticed she seemed to have plenty of money?"

"Well yes," said Matthew. "But not knowing that much about her, who was I to say where the money had come from? But I did get suspicious the last time we went out and I was going straight to the management to tell them of that. It came to light before I had the chance."

"You never know the half of it when you take on staff," said Stella, "though we have been pretty lucky all in all here."

"Are you coming along to see the final show at *The Sands?*"

"As a matter of fact, I am," said Stella. "Dave and his mates are going to be in town for the eighteenth; we have seats booked."

"That's interesting, I wouldn't have thought they could have got away, surely Blackpool must be really busy in September?"

"Well that's just it," said Stella. "They have the illuminations that stretch their season through to November, so they can afford to get in a break. I can't tell you how lovely it will be see Dan again, and Dave of course. Dan and I became firm friends and I really enjoyed working with him, he was a great laugh. Excuse me love, there is a couple over there that need serving. Yes darling, what would you like?"

Matthew moved away from the bar and sat himself down in a vacant seat near the window. So, Dave Grant was heading down here for the closing of the show at *The Sands*, things were just getting better and better.

* * *

Enid was at the end of her tether. The sooner the government realised that changing the old system of pounds, shillings and pence to this new lark so much the better. She had dealt with confused customers all season and it didn't help that she was failing to grasp it herself.

"Enid, you are looking all of a doodah."

Enid turned round to see Lilly smiling at her. "Oh hello stranger, what brings you into town? I thought you'd be hard at it, writing one of your stories."

Lilly smiled. "I have decided to give myself a rest this afternoon. I have been quite busy this morning trying to arrange things with Reverend George."

"Who is he, when he's at home?"

"My local vicar over at Brokencliff-on-Sea. My gardener friend and me are getting married next year and I have been trying to sort out a date."

"Lilly Brockett, you are full of surprises in your old age. Does Maud know?"

"I can't remember if I mentioned it to her or not, anyway I think it's going to be in June, though it might be May; I don't think we will have it on a Saturday, leave that day free for the young ones. So keep June free, you are on my guest list."

Enid smiled to herself, same old Lilly. "What kind of dress will you wear? Will you go for traditional or perhaps a nice suit?"

"Well, you see, that's just it," said Lilly. "When I was first married we couldn't afford a new wedding dress so I had one from a second-hand shop; it didn't look too bad and once it had been taken in slightly and a veil added, it did the job. But this will be second time round and I don't think I should be seen wearing a frock with a train, it would look silly on me."

"And what does your intended think?"

Lilly screwed up her eyes. "No idea, I don't think we have ever talked about it."

"Then perhaps you should," said Enid. "It might be a start."

"I was thinking of asking Bessie Reeve to make me something, she is very good with a needle and thread and she does do dress making sometimes, but now she is taking in people she may not have the time."

"Have a chat with her, there is plenty of time between now and June did you say?"

"Or May," said Lilly. "Anyway, I really came in for a little gift for a reader friend of mine, she likes knick-knacks."

Enid looked around her. "Well you have certainly come to the right place. I will help you choose something if you like."

Lilly nodded. "That would be most agreeable Enid, thank you."

* * *

That evening Lady Samantha got into the back of the Bentley.

"Good evening Mrs Haines, I am so pleased you were able to join me. Penge drive slowly on to the theatre please."

"I am delighted having been asked," said Lucinda. "It is most kind of your ladyship."

"Not at all my dear, I am glad of the company, besides I have been hearing what sterling work you have been doing with the association. I know one or two of the landladies you know, I went to university with a couple of the older ones, who have now retired. I doubt you would know them, but they know of you and keep me updated on all that is going on. I hear you are looking for a venue to hold your Christmas outing, it was *The Star* last year and *The Cliff* the year before, am I right?"

"You are well informed," said Lucinda racking her brains to think who among the landladies could be so well connected.

"We are in the process of renovating parts of Owlerton Hall, in particular the large room which, in its day, was used for banquets and social events. I would be delighted for you to hold your event at the Hall at a very reasonable price."

"That is most kind of you Lady Hunter. If you could let my committee have your tariff I will certainly consider your generous offer."

Lady Samantha opened her clasp handbag and handed Lucinda a folded leaflet. "You will find the details there, Mrs Haines and for the remainder of the evening you must address me as Samantha."

Lucinda smiled to herself; if only Shirley Llewellyn could see her now. "And you must call me Lucinda, Samantha."

Alfred stood at the back at the back of the auditorium and was pleased there only a few empty seats that would be filled shortly by invited guests. Lady Samantha and her guest was seated fourth row centre, he could see Joe and the Reverend a few rows behind and the heads of several others he knew. Elsie, Rita and Jenny arrived and took their seats, accepting a complimentary programme.

Maud came and stood beside him. "Well Alfred, here it is, the final night. At least no one ran off with the takings."

"Thanks for all your help Maud. I know you have been missing *The Sands*, but without you here I don't think I could have coped."

"That's very kind of you to say so Alfred."

"Shall we take our seats Maud?" Alfred said, handing her a box of *Weekend*.

"I should be delighted to Alfred."

Jean Barton crept into the auditorium and listened to the overture being played by Phil Yovell. She gazed around the theatre and as the lights dimmed she left through the velvet curtains and out on to the parade. She breathed in deeply and took in the sights of the sea beyond that had been so familiar to her over the years. She turned on her heels and headed back towards the hotel feeling a great weight lifting from her shoulders.

The curtain fell to thunderous applause from the audience and Rita Ricer went up onto the stage to say a few words of thanks. She asked Alfred to join her and received cheers with audience members shouting out, 'Well done'.

The company and invited guests assembled in the lounge of the hotel where a buffet had been prepared and drinks were served by waiters especially bought in by Alfred.

"You have done what you set out to do," said the Reverend. "You have saved the theatre. If what I saw tonight is anything to go by, your future summer seasons are secure."

Alfred nodded his thanks. "I couldn't have done this without the expert help of Rita Ricer."

"Ah yes, the lovely Rita, you know the old saying Alfred, behind every successful man is a woman, which reminds me where is the lovely Jean tonight? I didn't see her at the theatre."

"She is upstairs changing I expect," said Alfred. "The hotel has been quite busy. I will go up and see where she has got to."

"I enjoyed the show immensely," said Lady Samantha. "It has made me even more determined to get a ticket for the last night at *The Sands*."

Lucinda smiled. "I might be able to help you out there Samantha. I purchased two tickets some time ago, perhaps you would allow me to return the favour and invite you as my guest."

"That would be most splendid Lucinda, most splendid indeed."

On an Eastern Counties bus, Freda and Muriel were seated on the top deck.

"Well, I thought my eyes were telling porkies," said Freda, adjusting the front of her flowered frock which appeared to have a life of its own. "There she was, as bold as brass, Lucinda Haines."

Muriel, who was somewhat dumbstruck, could only nod.

"Lucinda Haines, of all people, with Lady Samantha from Owlerton Hall and did you see them get into that car? All to go about two feet down the road to some gathering at that hotel. Did we get invited? Did you as a committee member get invited? "

The bus stopped to let some more passengers get on.

"We were never even offered a programme, how much did we pay for these? And they've still got the photographs of the Arbours inside and they weren't even in the show.

There was a long silence.

"And then there was Maud with that Alfred Barton, swank as you like and where was his wife? I would like to know."

The bus came to an abrupt halt to allow an ambulance to pass by.

"And that gown Lucinda was wearing must have cost a fortune."

"Any more fares please?"

Freda put a bonbon in her mouth and began chewing.

"And those diamonds on that necklace that Lady Samantha was wearing, I mean they have got to be real, you couldn't buy them in *Martyn's Gift Shop*."

"Gorleston Railway Bridge, any more fares please."

"I wonder if she had her hair done at *House of Doris*, her neck didn't look red to me."

The bus stopped to allow passengers to get off and on. "Next stop Gorleston Library, any more fares please?"

Freda helped herself to another bonbon.

"And just when I thought I had seen it all, that bloke from the caravan park and the vicar. I'm broad-minded, I listen to *The Archers*, but what were those two doing together? It didn't seem right to me."

"The *White Horse* next stop, any more fares please? Let's be having you."

"Excuse me love, have you got a light? Only me lighter's out of gas."

Freda fumbled in her bag. "I don't smoke, but I do happen to have a box of matches with me."

"Thanks love."

"He seemed quite pleasant, for a youth. I wasn't too crazy about his tattoo but he spoke very nice."

"Halfway House. Is there anyone for the Halfway House?"

Freda sighed heavily. "I could have murdered a nice sherry."

As they passed *Jewson's Wood Yard* a ship could be heard sounding its horn.

"Southtown Station, Two Bears."

"But Lucinda Haines I ask you Muriel, whatever next?"

"Freda…"

"Yes Muriel."

"Are you wearing *Cat's Whisper* again?"

"Yes Muriel Evans, I am, as a matter of fact."

"Oh good," Muriel replied "I thought that man's dog at the front had farted."

Derinda and Ricky circled the room and spoke to the invited guests. Mystic Brian had a few of them laughing as he reminisced about some of the seasons he had played around the country and the talk naturally turned to the late Ted Ricer and how much his presence was missed in the area.

Rita smiled when she overheard the conversations concerning her late husband and Jenny was at her side to make sure she didn't find it all too overwhelming.

"Well you have certainly pulled a few rabbits out of the hat with this little show," said Don Stevens, who had arrived earlier that day and stood beside his wife Elsie. "I think I might hand over next summer season at *The Sands* to you lock, stock and barrel. I have been hearing about some of your plans, Elsie says you would like to stage a musical."

Elsie took a small sip of gin and tonic. "Don Stevens, me old lover, you love nothing better than flattering women. You remind me of my Ted, I'm surprised Elsie doesn't keep you on a leash."

Elsie laughed. "You know as well as I do Rita, that trying to tame Don would be pure folly. "

"And I don't think you are quite serious when you say you want to take a step back from the business, it's in your blood."

"You see Elsie, Rita knows me better than I know myself."

"That has never been in any doubt," said his wife with a wry smile. "I do wonder though, whether this little theatre here might be another regular feature in your plans Rita, you really have made the best of a bad job."

"You were very lucky with Derinda and co turning up as they did," said Don. "I have to say they work very well together on stage."

"And they do make a lovely couple," said Elsie

"Excuse me, are you Rita Ricer?"

Rita turned and came face-to-face with a tall gentleman, dressed very smartly, greying at the temples with a youthful smile that beguiled his years.

"Yes I am Rita Ricer. I am sorry, I don't think we have met before."

"I am really sorry to barge in on your conversation, I am Malcolm Farrow, I have recently taken over as the entertainment manager of *The Sparrows' Nest* in Lowestoft."

"Allow me to introduce you to Don Stevens," said Rita "and this is his wife Elsie."

Malcolm acknowledged their presence with a handshake and a nod. "I have heard of you Mr Stevens of course."

"You see my dear, people do know who you are," said Elsie with a laugh. "You haven't been forgotten."

"I think I saw you mentioned in *The Stage* a few weeks ago. I had heard on the grapevine that *The Sparrows' Nest* was going through a few changes."

"Indeed yes, I am looking at how we can improve what is currently being offered at the theatre, hence my seeking out the delightful Mrs Ricer."

Elsie gave Rita a quick smile. "I am going to organise some more drinks, Don you can give me a hand. Malcolm can I get you anything, Rita another gin and tonic?"

"I will pass, thank you," said Malcolm. "But if you would allow me, I would like to buy Rita a drink."

Don and Elsie made their escape. "What do you think is going on there?," asked Don, following Elsie and avoiding the offer of a sherry from a passing waiter.

"Well I am sure we will find out later," said Elsie, "if we leave them to it. Did you see the way he looked at her?"

"Can't say I did Elsie, why?"

"Typical man, he was looking at her in that I-have-got-designs-on-you sort of way. Come on, you must have felt the electricity."

"The trouble with you Elsie is you watch too many of those soppy films."

Elsie sighed "And you wouldn't notice anything unless it had pound signs before it, come on let's fight our way to the bar and leave cupid to fire his arrow."

"I must congratulate you on a wonderful performance," said Lady Samantha addressing a surprised Una. "Did you teach yourself to play the ukulele?"

"It was at my father's knee to be sure".

"Were your family musical?"

"My father played the spoons and my mother used to sing sometimes on a Saturday evening in a public house down our street."

"Fascinating," said Lady Samantha with a warm smile. "One has always yearned to have another string to one's bow; my husband used to play the clarinet when we first met."

"He could have been another Acker Bilk then."

"I'm sorry, Acker who?"

"He was in the pop charts with *Stranger on the Shore*."

"Really!" said Lady Samantha. "How fascinating indeed. Are you performing somewhere else next week? I understand that a lot of artists move on to other shows."

Una thought for a moment. "Well I have an engagement in Sterling next, but that's not for about three weeks and I have a panto lined up in Grimsby at Christmas, I am going to play one of the fiddlers to Old King Cole."

"You play the fiddle as well? You really are very talented, my dear," said Lady Samantha, sipping her sweet sherry.

"Excuse me Samantha," said Lucinda, coming to the rescue and in a voice loud enough to let everyone know she was on first name terms. "There is someone over there who would like to meet you."

Lady Samantha touched Una's arm. "If you'll excuse me, my dear… It has been lovely chatting with you and good luck with your next little show."

"Perhaps I could send you some tickets for Grimsby," said Una. "And you could come and see me."

Touched by Una's charm and obvious enthusiasm Lady Samantha smiled warmly. "Well that would be quite delightful I shall look forward to it and of course I shall pay for the tickets. Grimsby you say, I don't think I have ever been to Grimsby." From her handbag Lady Samantha handed Una one of her cards. "My dear, if you are still here tomorrow afternoon pop along to Owlerton Hall and have some tea and cake, I should be very pleased to see you, and bring some of the other players if you so wish."

A few moments later Lady Samantha was heard to say, "Lucinda dear, can you explain to me later, what exactly are pop charts?"

Elsie made her way back towards Rita and Jenny leaving Don at the bar chatting to Hughie Dixon. There was no sign of Peter Farrow.

"Okay, what's the gossip?" said Elsie. "What did handsome want?"

"I am beginning to see another side to you, Elsie Stevens," said Jenny.

"That's too many years spent in a stuffy London office," said Elsie. "I feel I have a bit more freedom when I am down here. Come on, fill me in."

Rita took the gin and tonic from Elsie. "Basically he was offering the agency more work. He would like me to take a look at *The Sparrows' Nest* and see if I can offer something in the way of variety for next summer."

"So when he is taking you out for dinner? I saw the look he gave you."

"He is going to call me to arrange a meeting," said Rita.

"Somewhere nice I hope, with candles."

"Sorry me old lover, he wants to meet me and Jenny at the office, it's business."

But Elsie wasn't so sure that that was all on offer.

Alfred opened the door of the apartment, the lights were on and he could hear the radio playing softly. "Jean darling, are you coming down to meet the guests, Lady Samantha has graced us with her presence, there is quite a party going on down there. Jean, my love, where are you?"

He wandered into the lounge area and turned off the radio and walked through to the bedroom. The room looked just as it always did, the bed was made, it was tidy and he could see the ships on the horizon from the turreted window. He turned and looked at the dressing table, there was the brush and the looking glass with their pearly handles. The pots of cold cream lined up and the boxes of tissues beside them. He saw the envelope propped up against the musical box and walked closer, his hand hovered over the envelope and he caught sight of himself in the dressing table mirror. A single tear escaped down his cheek, he knew without opening it what the content of that envelope would tell him.

Chapter Fifteen: *Turning Tides*

Monday 13 September

"**A**ll I can say on the matter Barbara is thank goodness she has been caught. According to the papers, she was stealing from all and sundry in her few weeks here. How did she gain entry to these places? Says here she was doing a shopkeeper a favour and looking after things for him while he took a break. I have to say I wasn't too keen on her when she first arrived."

Barbara handed over some tickets to a customer and said she hoped they would enjoy the show.

"Of course it is lucky they have been able to recoup all of the cash she took from here. Apparently she had it stashed in a bag in a locker somewhere."

"I did wonder about Matthew's involvement with her," said Barbara. "He is a strange character, she didn't seem his type."

"I haven't been able to fathom him out," said Maud. "Though according to the powers-that-be, he does his work and keeps his nose clean."

"They will never find another one like old Jim, that's for sure."

"On the subject of Jim I bumped in to young Debbie the other day and everything seems to be working out for them both, Peter seems quite settled here in Great Yarmouth now."

"Oh yes, I forgot to tell you, Stella and I were having a chat the other day and she told me young Dave and Dan were coming down, sometime this week, I think she said, and bringing those two friends of theirs Josie and Madge."

"It will be lovely to see old Dave again," said Maud. "What a nice man he is and that Dan... I tell you that Christmas we spent at Jim's was hilarious. Enid was on top form as usual, one too many sherbets and she was on the floor. Oh we did have fun that day. Any idea where they are staying?"

"Vauxhall Caravan Park," said Barbara offering Maud a pear drop.

"No I won't, love if you don't mind, it will spoil my lunch. Hand me over that knitting Barbara I've a bed jacket to finish for old Mrs Tate, she is hospital again."

"Not her leg?"

"Flared up like a balloon according to her daughter, poor old love, she won't be going to another tea dance anytime soon."

Beverley was taking a leisurely walk around the town centre racking her brains to think of some suitable end-of-season gifts that Bob liked to give staff. At least she wouldn't have Dixie to consider, though she did like the idea of getting a pair of cufflinks from the police station.

She spotted Matthew on the market and looked at her watch. It was unusual for him to be anywhere other than the pier during a weekday. She headed towards *Arnolds* to have a scout around the accessories section; she knew that Barbara and Maud would appreciate a headscarf.

Looking through the selection on offer she picked a rose pattern for Maud and a plain gold for Barbara.

She heard someone call her name and saw Stella walking towards her. "Hi Bev, not often I see you about town."

"I am doing a bit of gift shopping for Bob."

"What is it with these men?" said Stella. "I have to do the same for his master's voice back at Henry's. He wants to give our part-time worker a small gift for when she leaves at the end of the month and returns to full-time study. I hardly know the girl, besides she would probably be better off with a few quid in her pocket."

"I suggested tokens to Bob but he was having none of it. I've had to place an order with *Lacon's* to supply the stage hands with a selection of beers apiece, Jack is partial to a bottle of whiskey or rum, but Mona Buckle is my headache. I mean what do you buy a woman who goes everywhere with a galvanised bucket and mop?"

Stella laughed. "A packet of Flash might be an idea perhaps!"

"Don't tempt me, what time have you to be back at Henry's?"

"Not for another hour or so yet, why do you ask?"

"Come on then let's go and grab a cake and coffee in *Palmers*, I fancy treating myself."

Beverley paid for her purchases and the pair headed off in the direction of *Palmers*.

"There's Matthew again," said Beverley. "I saw him a little while ago, it's funny him being up here at this time of day."

"He is becoming something of a regular in *Henry's*," said Stella. "strange that, because most of the stagehands drink in the *Growler*. He is always asking questions about Jim and Dave, I suppose he is just making conversation, but why would he be interested in them? He didn't know Jim and he certainly doesn't know Dave apart from saying hello to him when he was down earlier in the season."

"He is a good worker," said Beverley, "but I don't really know what to make of him, maybe it's because he isn't from around these parts."

"Is Bob planning on keeping him on?"

"As far as I know, that's unless Matthew has other plans. All of the staff are usually told when they come back for the following season. Matthew's post is a sort of all-year-round one, though he won't have much to do in the winter. When Jim was with us, he would check in on the theatre every so often. Bob and I are still working in the offices, but it is nice that someone else takes care of the nitty gritty. It is also a good time to give the place a touch of fresh paint. Bob is considering trying to keep *Ted's Variety Bar* open during the winter, but who would fancy walking along the pier and around the side of the theatre to gain access with the North Sea crashing over the side?"

"I suppose they could always man a lifeboat for casualties."

The seafront was busy with late holidaymakers making the most of the warm weather, the crazy golf course was doing a good business, and the amusement arcades were full with people trying their luck to win back some money to spend.

The cries of 'bingo' and 'house' could be heard as another player won a ticket to keep until they had enough to choose a prize to match their winnings.

The snails in Joyland were wending their way along the rails and surprising their riders with the sharp dips that made them feel they were on a larger rollercoaster.

Deckchairs lined the golden sands as mums and dads made sand castles and fetched buckets of water from the sea to fill their moats. Beach cricket was a great favourite among the older children with granddad keeping score and grandma looking on. Coloured windbreakers shielded those who wanted to keep out of the breeze and make the most of the sun's rays to gain a tan on their pasty skins. Ladies with their heads decked in sunhats or women's magazines were aplenty while their spouses sported a nice line in a straw trilby or a knotted handkerchief.

Grotto Castle was pulling in the people, the baboon in the cage at the front of the attraction always made people want to explore more and see what was inside. The air was filled with fresh horse manure, hot dogs and candy floss and the number of people wearing kiss-me-quick hats was at a record high. Here along the Golden Mile there was something for every age to enjoy.

The pedal cars were keeping youngsters happy as their parents looked on. The boating lake was full with many a dad paddling or rowing his son or daughter around and around.

The galloping horses at the Pleasure Beach were going around as the laughing sailor guffawed in his glass case at the front of *Fun House*. Whoops and screams could be heard from those brave enough to venture onto the Waltzers, the Sky Jets or the Scenic Railway. Stall holders were taking money from men keen to display their shooting skills believing in their heads they were in a cowboy film, youngsters were fishing for ducks hoping that the number on the bottom would award them with a big prize, others were tearing lucky tickets at the Teddy Bear's Picnic Stall in the hope of landing a large teddy to take home with them. If you had money to spare and the will to enjoy yourself, there was no greater place on earth than an English seaside resort.

Rita, Jenny and Elsie were taking some time away from the office to enjoy the sea air and using the opportunity to discuss how they could progress with ideas and plans for the following summer season. Elsie was now firmly of the idea that she would prefer to spend her summers in Great Yarmouth than in a stuffy office in Regent Street. Don who now had a new employee in place was intending to spend more time on the road looking at venues and artistes and was happy for his wife to do as she pleased.

"I am considering buying a little house down here," said Elsie. "It would be nice to have my own base and somewhere for Don to come when he needs a rest and a change of scenery."

"Is there an ounce of truth that Don may give up the business?," Jenny asked remembering her own decisions when she stood back from her dancing school.

Elsie laughed out loud. "You know as well as I do Jenny, that Don without his show business connections would go stir crazy. Of course he is getting older, but this business doesn't allow for retirement, you only have to look at the greats, the Delfonts, Grades and even some of the not-so-well-known. Once this business gets under your skin, it claims you as its own. Even my own association over the years has reeled me in. I have to confess that for all its problems and challenges I love this life, though you must both promise me that you will never say a word to Don or he'll be taking advantage."

Rita smiled, remembering her Ted. "Isn't that what men are supposed to do?"

"Rita Ricer, wash your mouth out with soap, I have never let any man take advantage of me," said Jenny with a slight comedic tone. "Though saying that, I will have to tell you girls about the night that an Italian tenor thought he was on to something."

"I think we should have a night out ladies and let all our sordid secrets surface," said Rita. "We must get a date sorted for the end-of-season when things have quietened down."

The three ladies enjoyed an ice cream and found themselves a bench in the shade outside the model village.

"Taking on *The Sparrow's Nest* might be quite a challenge," said Jenny. "Holidaymakers in Lowestoft are not the same as here, for a start there is less for them to do, although of course a lot of them come in from Oulton Broad and the shows there attract a lot of the locals."

"And the shows are only once nightly," added Elsie. "*The Nest* is quite a nice little theatre but not really on par with *The Sands*."

Rita finished her cornet. "Then there is Brokencliff, from what Alfred was saying to me the other evening he really would like to continue with our arrangement."

"You've heard his wife has left him of course," said Elsie.

"Where did you hear that from? He has said nothing to me."

"I heard one of the staff talking about it when Don and I went over there for lunch yesterday."

"Poor Alfred," said Rita. "Mind you, as I said to Jenny when we went there initially, that hotel is caught in a bit of a time warp and how any woman in her right mind hasn't taken a wallpaper scrapper to it is beyond me."

"Well, maybe now the wife has gone he will buck his ideas up and do something about it," said Jenny with feeling. "And sort out some of those staff as well, especially that ghastly receptionist."

"The one with the eyelashes," said Elsie. "Don pointed her out, she really shouldn't be representing a hotel, goodness knows what the guests make of her."

"Right, enough gossip," said Rita. "We need to put our heads together and come up with a plan."

"Oh by the way," said Elsie "Don says if we want to take lunch at *The Star* he will pick up the tab."

"Well we had better get some ideas sorted first, I feel like a leisurely lunch today," said Rita. "I am sure they can manage back at the office without us for one afternoon."

Bob put his head round the box office window. "How are we looking for the final performance, Maud?"

"Well it's not sold out yet," said Maud putting her knitting to one side. "We do have several seats blocked out for invited guests, the mayor and local dignitaries."

Bob whistled. "I better get Bev to confirm who is and who isn't coming. Can you put ten aside for me please, I have invited some of the firm that did such a good job on *Ted's Variety Bar*."

Barbara was looking at the seating plan "Row J centre is the best spot for ten together," she said. "We appear to be holding quite a few seats for the local landladies."

Maud huffed. "That should be stopped; they get complimentary tickets for the opening night, and they really should not be allowed more for the closing night."

"Yes, you're right Maud," said Barbara. "We could be selling those seats."

Bob nodded in agreement. "You are both right of course. I will have a word with Beverley later and see why we are still doing this. Thanks ladies, see you both later."

"I do wonder if that man can ever make a decision by himself," said Barbara handing Maud back her knitting. "Bev practically runs that office."

Maud did one of her sighs. "Without Beverley at his side, Bob Scott would be running around like a headless chicken. Do you remember that season when the ceiling caved in in the theatre foyer?"

"I do, poor old Bob was all fingers and thumbs. Brilliant when it comes to figures and paperwork, useless at anything practical; he reminds me my old man. Show him the running form of a racehorse and he is spot on; ask him to take a look at a job that needs doing and he is totally lost. I am so pleased I have my own electric drill, it has been a Godsend."

Maud began clicking her needles trying to picture Barbara with an electric drill, it didn't bear thinking about.

Rick O'Shea was not having a good day. He was very concerned about the constant attention from Shirley Llewellyn. Nearly every night when he arrived at the theatre, Jack had a card, flowers or a small gift for him that had been left at the stage door. He had caved in twice during the season and agreed to meet the lady, once for a drink and on the other occasion a meal. Some nights he dreaded doing his act as there within a few feet of where he was performing, Shirley's face would be beaming back at him. It was enough to put a man off women for life. The boys in the band were taking the mickey out of him and he knew he had to do something to shake off the unwanted attention.

"I will have to invent a fiancée or a wife," he said to the boys.

"Just tell her straight that you are not interested, we have all had admirers before, give her the big heave-ho and move on," said Stevie who was rolling a cigarette and making a mess of it.

"Why don't you get one of the dancers to walk out with you and pretend to be your girlfriend?," suggested another.

"Let's face it," said Stevie "Rick's got more chance of getting a date with one of the male dancers. I've seen the way one of them looks at him."

"You lot are no bloody help at all," said Rick finishing a mug of coffee that had gone cold and pulling a face.

"Look, we only have until the end of the week and then we will be moving up North, she won't be able to follow you there."

"I am not so sure," said Rick with a very worried expression. "She said in her last note she was prepared to follow me to the ends of the earth, she even mentioned selling up her business to be with me."

"The woman is deluded," said Stevie. "Are you sure she isn't taking drugs? Sounds like that Polly all over again, you remember her, as mad as the day was long."

"But she is a well-renowned business woman, I don't think she would dabble in drugs. No, she is far too much of a lady," said Rick. "Oh shit, I don't know what I am going to do."

"I've got an idea," said Stevie taking a long drag and puffing out a smoke ring. "Have a word with that magic act, get them to have a word with this woman and make out that you have been promised to their daughter, slip them a couple of quid and a box of chocolates and I bet they would do it for you. We all get on really well as a company backstage with the odd exception. Now, if that Mona wasn't married I bet she would do it for you."

"Now you are taking the piss," said Rick "but actually that idea about the Oswalds is a good one. He and I get on really well and his wife is such a lovely lady, they might just help me out."

"Well me old mucker, there is no time like the present, you will find the Oswalds rehearsing as they always do at this time in the afternoon at the theatre, though you would think they would know that act backwards the number of times they have to perform it in a week."

Salvador greeted Rick with a big smile. "What brings you along to the theatre of an afternoon? it can't be to hear Mona's latest rendition of the *Old Rugged Cross*."

Mona was cleaning the brass rail at the back of the auditorium.

Rick told Salvador about the problems he had been experiencing. "Oh yes, Carmen told me about the gifts and cards, I didn't realise it was getting out of hand."

"And the rest," said Rick. "Normally I can sort these things out for myself, but this has been going on a while now, not helped by the fact that we played one of the landlady get-together nights a while back; ever since them she has been chasing after me."

Carmen walked onto the stage with daughter Conchetta following. "So Rick you are having a bit of trouble with the ladies," she smiled. "We are just about to rehearse a new addition to our act for when we move on next week, stay and watch if you like."

"I am really sorry to ask you this but how would you feel about Conchetta and I pretending we had an understanding?"

Conchetta burst out laughing "Oh my goodness he sounds just like old gran, that's the kind of thing she says."

"I would make it worth your while."

Carmen bashed his on the arm. "Don't be so daft, of course we will help you out. Jack has been saying to me that you had been looking worried. I remember I had a bloke sending me flowers once when Salvador and I were courting. We were just starting out in the business then and worked cabaret floors, sometimes too near an audience for comfort. Well, Salvador soon put him right didn't you love?"

Salvador nodded. "I threatened to put him in one of our cabinets and make him disappear completely, you never seen a man move so fast. He was from Mexico if I remember rightly and he didn't speak too much English and I swear to God he thought my magic was real."

"When are you supposed to meet your admirer next?"

"Tonight in *Ted's Variety Bar* after the show."

"Then I suggest that you don't show up and leave the rest to us three, for the purposes of this exercise our Conchetta is going to be pregnant," said Carmen.

"Oh Mum! Thanks a bundle," said Conchetta rolling her eyes but laughing.

Rick let out a sigh of relief "Do you think it will work?"

"Look once that lady hears from two very concerned parents and from the girl in question who will be beside herself in tears, you will have nothing to worry about, trust me."

Wednesday 15 September

"Hello Ken, is Stella about?"

Ken turned round and smiled at Dan Forrester. "Hello me old mate, oh it's great to see you. I was told you were coming down. Where is Dave?"

"He's back at the caravan park sorting out some things with the girls."

"Stella's out the back," said Ken. "I'll give her a shout, what will you have to drink?"

"A nice pint of *Encore* would go down a treat," said Dan making himself comfortably on a bar stool. "It's great to be back in the old place. I see you have made one or two changes in here."

The two men looked at each other and said in unison "Stella!"

"Did someone call my name?" said Stella. "Oh, knock me down with a feather, it's our Dan." Stella ran out from behind the bar with a few tears in her eyes and hugged Dan. "Oh Dan, it really is so lovely to see you, how have you been keeping? How is Blackpool? Oh, there is so much I want to know."

Ken smiled. "Stella, you and Dan go over to the window table, I'll organise some drinks and some sandwiches. We have got a new supplier since you were here, Dan and I can recommend the pork pies."

Dan grinned at his old boss. "The sandwiches will be fine thanks Ken. We are all out for a meal later on, be great if you could both join us."

Ken poured a gin and tonic for Stella and another pint for Dan. "I can't take the evening off, but there is no reason why Stella can't, if she would like to."

"Thanks Ken, are you sure you'll be able to manage?"

"You go and catch up with your mates. We'll be fine here tonight, besides the other two are expected in."

"What's all this?" asked Dan, when Ken had gone out the back. "Has Ken undergone a personality change?"

"Do you know that since you left, he really has been pulling his weight and thanks to Dave we found a barman we can rely on, if you come in one night you'll see him for yourself, nice lad. I was getting a bit fed up after you left and I told Ken I was looking for another job, if truth be known, I was offered two other positions, one at *the Star* and the other at the *White Horse*. Anyway, I think old Ken realised that the days of taking advantage of my good nature were over and he knew that when you left he had lost a valuable member of staff. He still has his moments of course, but compared to what he was like, he is a bloody brilliant boss to work for and that is something I never thought I would hear myself saying. I even get a regular day-and-a-half off."

Dan took Stella's hand. "I am really so very pleased for you. I do miss the old days, but life up North isn't so bad. Dave and I have both got steady jobs, a nice home, good neighbours and some new friends, but I do miss the old ones I made here."

Stella smiled. "Thanks Dan that means a lot, now come on tell me about the job, I want to hear all the gossip."

"And so," said Muriel selecting a cucumber and a lettuce, "I have it on good authority that Shirley Llewellyn is selling up."

Freda couldn't make up her mind whether to take one or two pounds of tomatoes. She had found herself unexpectedly busy and had even put up the 'No Vacancies' sign. "Who have you been speaking to then?"

"I bumped into Fenella yesterday and apparently there has been something of an upset. Fenella was very coy about the whole thing, being Fenella, but from what I could gather it had something to do with a man."

Freda huffed. "Men are at the bottom of everything. Two pounds of tomatoes please, half a cucumber and two of your nice lettuces."

"I also think that she has never quite got over the committee business. I think she changed, she wasn't seen about a great deal, hasn't shown up for one of Lucinda's meetings and according to Petunia Danger who has been helping out Enid in the gift shop, she hadn't been taking in any guests at all, spent most of her time out and about at night."

Freda nodded at the stall holder. "Fancy."

Muriel looked up at the sky. "I think we are going to have rain any minute now by the look of those clouds up there. Come on, Freda let's make a dash to *Palmers* for a coffee and it's your turn to pay."

The town and seafront became awash with heavy rain. People were running for shelter and the arcades began to fill up. The number of people chancing their luck on winning at Bingo doubled. Tarpaulins were thrown over the kiddie rides and things came to something of a standstill. The tethered ponies stood still as the rain fell and anxious owners hoped the rain would pass over quickly so that they could make a few extra pounds with the season soon to come to an end. The shops in Regent Road began doing a brisk business selling souvenirs, postcards, sticks of rock and one shop sold out of Pac-a-Macs within an hour. The House of Wax had queues as holidaymakers escaped from the rain and other indoor activities normally shunned by the sun worshippers were doing a brisk business.

Others were scanning the showing of films at the cinemas and debating whether they would be out in time to get back for their evening meal.

Cafés saw a surge of business and Matthes ran out of their popular teacakes and scones. Whatever the weather at the seaside, someone always profited.

Over in Brokencliff, Alfred Barton was coming to terms with the fact that his wife Jean had left him. He knew now that he would have to get on top of things and not leave it to someone else, as he done in the past.

Taking some advice from a business colleague, he decided that the first thing that needed to be tackled was underperforming staff, followed by a complete refurbishment of the hotel to bring it up to the standards of others and to appoint two house managers who could take care of the daily running of the establishment, leaving him to deal with all the things that Jean had handled in the background. It was a difficult pill to swallow, but Alfred was determined to make the changes that he for so long neglected. He admitted that he had spent too much time looking after *The Little Playhouse* and maybe it was time for him to make some changes there too. The bookings for the hotel were quite healthy until the end of September, with a few days in October. Taking the bull by the horns he decided that to close the hotel while necessary changes were made would be his only option and he instructed the reception desk to accept no bookings beyond October.

With the services of a legal advisor at his side, Alfred would take the painful steps he knew he should have taken years ago.

Lady Samantha was conducting her own itinerary at Owlerton Hall, thanks to the income generated from letting out the car park and the revenue from coach parties that had visited the hall; she had looked over the finances and decided that some money must be spent to bring the Hall back to its former glory, starting with the large room that could be used for banquets and parties. Sir Harold wasn't so sure, but with some gentle persuasion he was soon on board with the proposals and was off telling all of his shooting party chums that Owlerton Hall was coming back from the brink.

Joe Dean was looking over the plans he was going to submit to the council concerning proposed changes to his own business. He discussed them over a pint in the *Fisherman's* with Reverend George who was always a good sounding board and always told Joe his honest opinion. They were both aware that Deanne Turner's ears were not too far away and as she pretended to busy herself at the end of the bar, they changed the subject as often as was necessary, much to her frustration.

Bessie Reeve was sitting down at her kitchen table and answering Patrick's letter. She was always pleased to receive a letter from her son, but had found if difficult to spare enough time to answer him. The families that came to stay with her had spread the word that they would receive a home-from-home welcome and the bookings had flown in. She gazed at the beginnings of a dress she had started for Lilly Brockett's big day, hanging within a plastic covering on the back of her pantry door.

She had told Lilly that it was high time she remembered that her gardener had a name and it was William Robertson and he lived in Lowestoft. He had no children, had been married to a girl called Ellen who had died a few years later after being diagnosed with a brain tumour. He was a year older than Lilly, owned his house, worked as a gardener mainly as a hobby, had served some years in the Army and had been a driving instructor until he decided to call it a day. Bessie had gathered this information with the help of her Molly and Nellie.

She finished the letter and enclosed a couple of cuttings from the *Great Yarmouth Mercury* she thought Patrick would be interested in, addressed the envelope and put a stamp on it ready for posting. She glanced at the clock, put her apron back on and went back to preparing some food for the guests who were arriving later and had requested a meal. She smiled happily to herself and began to sing along with a tune on the wireless, it was Ronnie Ronalde, one of her favourites.

Chapter Sixteen: *At the End of the Pier*

Saturday 18 September

I t was all hands on deck at *The Golden Sands Theatre*, Mona was making sure that everything looked clean and sparkly in the auditorium and that *Ted's Variety Bar* was sparkling. Matthew Taylor was checking everything backstage.

One of the boys stood in the wings on the opposite side of the stage and jabbed his mate in the side. "See that, every day without fail, he checks everything. Jim didn't do that, nor did that Roger bloke, though he was next to useless."

"He's just doing his job, leave him be."

"Not keen on him, the way he speaks to us sometimes, I'd like to see him fall off that pedestal he places himself on."

"Get on with your work and stop your mithering, you are never happy unless you have got something or someone to moan about."

Matthew walked across the stage looking up at the light gantry. He looked out at the auditorium and wondered what it would be like to have the adulation of an audience every night. The cheers and applause and for doing what? Things they enjoyed doing: singing, dancing, telling jokes - money for old rope. No one had ever applauded him on any of his achievements not even his late sister, she always had her own trumpet to blow. He missed her sometimes and thought about how things could have turned out differently, Gwen had been a strange one but he had loved her all the same.

"Hello Matthew, have you got a minute?" Bob Scott was coming from the back of the auditorium. "I wondered if you had thought over our offer of you staying on and keeping an eye on the place in the winter months. Unfortunately the pay isn't much, but a strong lad like you should find other work about the town, I could put in a good word for you."

Matthew walked down the side steps off the stage and stood by the orchestra pit as Bob approached him. "I have been thinking it over Mr Scott, but as yet I haven't made up my mind. I was thinking of returning to the smoke for the winter, can't say I fancy knocking about here when the weather turns nasty."

"Your official contract for the season is up on the second of October, with the clause, if you recall that we could extend it on a more permanent basis but not full-time, there just isn't the work here."

"So how did Jim and Roger get by then?"

"Jim was with us for years and he had another job in the winter at *Sparkles Nightclub*, but he came to check on the theatre and its buildings at least twice a week. Beverley and I will still be working in the offices and we are still looking at the option of keeping *Ted's Varity Bar* open, though no firm decision has been made yet."

"So what keeps you so busy in the winter months with no show on here?"

"Lots of people ask that question, I am retained by the company that owns *The Golden Sands* and Beverley and I do other administration work for them, does that answer your question?"

Matthew nodded. "Sorry, I didn't mean to sound rude, I was just curious."

"Look, let Beverley know what you decide, I will away for a few days at the end of the month."

The sounds of Mona clanking her galvanised bucket could be heard and Matthew looked at his watch, it was time for elevenses and Mona didn't like to be kept waiting.

Maud put down her knitting having completed the bed jacket and Barbara put a brew in front of her. "We still have a few seats for the first house tonight," she said. "The second house is completely full now."

"I hope he did as I suggested and released all those tickets we were holding for the so-called guests," said Maud, holding the bed jacket and showing Barbara her handy work.

"Oh yes," said Barbara. "He got Beverley to ring round and ask them, the message was the tickets could be collected and paid for at the box office up until last night. I sold the twenty seats we had been holding this morning before you came in, there was a bus load over from that *Brokencliff Hotel* asking. I offered first house, but they were adamant they wanted second."

"Enid was feeling a bit queer this morning," said Maud. "Otherwise I would have been here on time. Not like her to feel unwell. Anyway I have insisted that the shop remain closed today and she is to rest up, I don't want her being ill all winter. She is dreadful when she gets one of her chests."

"Stella is coming to the show tonight with Dan, Dave, Madge and Josie," said Barbara. "Ken has given Stella an extra night off. Mind you, she does work hard and she deserves a treat every now and then."

"Excuse me love, are there any seats for tonight?"

"Only the first house," said Maud. "I have some lovely ones in Row F."

"What do you think Fred, is row F okay with you?"

Fred nodded as he bit into a doughnut. "If we do the first house we can get over to Gorleston and catch the bingo."

"My thoughts too my love," said his wife. "We'll take those two seats love please. I've heard it's a good show, they say the Oswalds are out of this world."

Maud tore the tickets from the book and marked the seating plan with her large blue crayon. "They are fascinating to watch and you'll enjoy Jonny Adams too, he is a local lad."

"Oh that's nice, must be good for a local to get a turn in one of these shows. We were here a few years ago, thought we'd come back, didn't we Fred?"

"You can't beat the Great Yarmouth sea air," he said swallowing the last of his doughnut and smiling at Maud. "We went to Morecombe last year, didn't we pet? We always went to Brighton, but those pebbles do leave a mark when you sit on them for too long."

"That will be one pound and five new pence please," said Maud. "Enjoy the show."

The pair waved and went on their way.

"I wouldn't fancy Brighton every year," said Barbara. "I went there once, that was enough. Let's have a look at the *Daily Mirror* crossword."

"I'll get me reading glasses," said Maud fumbling in her bag. "I can never focus on that print."

Dressed in a stunning sequinned gown, Rita Ricer stood with Jenny Benjamin and Elsie Stevens and watched as the audience for the second house began to file in.

Maurice Beeney and a few of his boys from the orchestra had come along, one or two of the landladies with paid-up tickets and the local dignitaries. Lucinda caused quite a stir arriving with Lady Samantha and one or two of the landladies were seen to be craning their necks to get a better view. Lucinda took it all in her stride, waved to Muriel and Freda who were sat in one of the side sections with their husbands and generally enjoyed every moment of the attention, but did her best not to make it too obvious.

The trio made their way to their seats in the third row centre where Don Stevens was already sat talking to Alfred Barton and Malcolm Farrow.

Rita caught the eye of Dave and his party and waved, noticing that Lilly Brockett was sat a few rows further back with the intended.

Vic Allen and his orchestra made their way into the pit. As Vic raised his baton, the house lights began to dim and the final performance of *Summertime Magic* began.

The JB Showtime Dancers were in fine form with their opening number *Let the Sunshine In* and the gyrating hips of the male dancers had many female members of the audience reaching for a handkerchief.

Lauren Du Barrie walked on to the stage in a emerald gown and sang *I've Got a Song for You* which, even judging by Rita's own singing standards, was a marked improvement on previous performances she had witnessed.

Jonny Adams appeared from a cloud of dry ice and stunned the audience with his deft hands of magic, receiving oohs and arhhs from a very receptive audience, Jonny had come a long way since he first trod the boards at *The Golden Sands*.

The ingenious choreography made *Hernando's Hideaway* from the *Pyjama Game* a crowd pleaser. The set and lighting were in keeping with the musical it had come from.

Lauren Du Barrie appeared again with a selection of songs under the heading of *Make Mine Music*, sporting a yellow frock which managed to hide the rather cumbersome figure beneath it.

Comedian Tommy Trent had the audience laughing and, not for the first time, audiences were reminded of the late Ted Ricer.

Then it was the turn of the Dancers again, dressed as Teddy Boys and Rockers to introduce the act that had become the show stopper of the season: Rick O'Shea and the Ramblers. Young and old tapped and swayed along to the music and even Lady Samantha rattled her jewellery getting into the moment.

The second half opened with the JB Showtime Dancers in black with white face masks as The Oswalds had the audience gasping with their magic act. The high speed act left little room for error and the trio delivered it with aplomb.

Back briefly Tommy Trent delivered a few well-chosen jokes that led to the appearance of Miss Penny's Puppets, a delightful act that captured the spirit of an art that audiences around the world adored.

Jonny Adams was back with three mind-blowing tricks before the Dancers dressed in tops-and-tails introduced the star of the show, Lauren Du Barrie.

Millie stood watching from the wings as Lauren descended a silver staircase from the back of the set dressed for the very first time in red. Vic Allen tapped his stand in order to get the attention of the orchestra and mouthed, "It's red," to them all.

Lauren sang her way through her set moving with the grace of a woman twenty years her junior. Then she stood centre stage as the microphone rose from the stage floor to deliver her closing song. Rita gripped her hands together and Vic Allen braced himself. Millie looked on anxiously from the wings and felt the comforting hand of Jonny Adams on her shoulder.

The audience were aware that a change in the style of singing was taking place as a backdrop lowered behind Lauren. With the voice of an angel, as described on the posters, she delivered the song, she had sung at every performance but this time she did with panache.

You'll Never Walk Alone started off low and beautifully and Lauren relived the time when she had appeared in the stage musical *Carousel* years before and this was her 'eleven o'clock' number. For the first time that summer season, Lauren began to feel the emotion she had felt before and her spine tingled as she reached the end of the song, her voice without a swoop or wobble hit the top C which rang throughout the theatre.

There was a silence as Lauren stood in the spotlight her arms outstretched and then like a storm quietly brewing the applause from the audience got louder and louder.

Millie felt a tear escape down her cheek and she began to clap too. Several of the company who had been preparing for the finale where standing in the wings and they too applauded.

Lauren took a deep bow, followed by another and another and as the curtain slowly fell in front of her, she felt very happy. Millie rushed to her side to escort her from the stage and to dress her for the finale walk down.

"I hope you have some honey and lemon at the ready Millie dear, it's the voice you know."

The JB Showtime Dancers entered from left and right and went into a glittering routine in their top hat and tails. Bowing, they parted either side of the staircase as each act in turn came down to take their final bows.

When Lauren Du Barrie appeared at the top of the staircase, several audience members got to their feet and cheered. Visibly moved, Lauren was taken by the arm on one side by Jonny and on the other Tommy.

The curtain fell for the final time as Vic and the orchestra played off with a selection of tunes from the show, especially compiled for the occasion.

Sunday 19 September

The day was going to be a busy one as the large transit lorries came to take away the sets. Matthew and the boys were on site to see that everything was ready to load and oversee the gantry lights being taken down and stored.

Jack sat at the stage door and watched as some of the artistes who were too tired the night before came to pack away their costumes and props. The Oswalds strapped up their magic cabinets and prepared them to be wheeled down the pier to their waiting truck which advertised their act on the side.

Dan and Dave were taking an early morning walk with Madge and Josie along Marine Parade and stopped to watch some of the activity.

"That brings back some memories," said Dave as they stood on the opposite side of the road. "The show hoardings will be the last thing to come down. I remember one year Jim forgot all about it until the Delfont organisation got on the telephone demanding to know where Dickie Henderson and company were."

"Come on," said Josie. "Let's walk up to the Pleasure Beach and then grab some breakfast on the way back in one of the cafés."

"It was great to have Stella with us last night," said Dan. "I hope she is ready to leave with us. We can take her to that new club."

"You and your clubs," said Madge. "It's all I can do to get this one away from the telly on a Saturday night now, with her favourite Cilla on."

"Ere watch it lady," said Josie with a giggle. "I work bloody hard all week and the last thing I want to do on a Saturday night is go to a club, especially around our way, now Blackpool is a different beast altogether."

"I think that's means she hoping for an invite to come and spend the weekend with you boys," said Madge.

"Well, that can be arranged," said Dave. "We will sort something out and let you know when is best."

The four continued their walk in relative silence enjoying looking around them and watching the early-bird holidaymakers who were out and about before going back to their guest houses for breakfast.

Later that day they all went in to *Henry's Bar* for a lunchtime drink and to say their goodbyes to Ken.

Stella waved them out the door. "See you all later, I am all packed," and went back to drying some glasses. It had been just like old times.

Ken came through bringing Stella a cup of coffee. "Thought you might need one of these, now go and sit yourself down and put your feet up for a while, we seem to be very quiet in here this morning, no point two of us standing about."

* * *

Maud was feeling a bit restless and Enid was doing her stock-take in the shop, so she picked up her light mac and handbag and went and caught the bus over to Brokencliff to see Lilly.

"I hoped I would catch you at home, sorry to arrive unannounced but I am all fingers and thumbs today."

Lilly welcomed her guest and they went through to the lounge. "I really did enjoy the show last night and William was quite taken with that magic act, the Olanzos was it?"

"No Lilly the Olanzos were her last year, you must remember they sang while spinning plates. The Oswalds are the magic act, and yes they are very good aren't they, Spanish I believe and a very nice family. Young Jonny Adams has come along in leaps and bounds and that Tommy Trent had my sides aching."

"I am sorry William and I couldn't stop for the party afterwards," said Lilly, "but William is helping out his local church this morning and I had some writing I needed to get on with."

"And here I am disturbing you, I am so sorry."

"Oh don't be Maud, I have been up since five and I have stopped for the day now. Sometimes you reach a point where you think, 'Well, I don't know what will happen next'."

They chatted about the old days when Lilly worked at the hospital and also at *The Sands* during the season and the time flew by. At one o clock, Maud said goodbye to her friend and decided she would see what lunch was on offer at the Barton residence. Alfred was near the reception desk when she walked in and after a few pleasantries she invited Alfred to join her for lunch. They talked about the season and what he hoped to achieve with the theatre and then he mentioned Matthew Taylor.

"And what did you make of him?" said Maud finishing a main course.

"He seemed a pleasant kind of bloke," said Alfred. "I understand he is looking for some work to tie him over the winter months and I was wondering whether I might be able to use him here. I am planning to make some changes and I will need to take on some staff and he seemed to me to be the perfect kind of handyman to have about the place."

Maud nodded. "Well, there is no harm in asking him."

"I am planning to close the hotel for four months from November and get this place back into shape. Jean went on about it for years and it is only since she walked out on me that I realised just how much I had neglected the place, putting all of my energy into the theatre, which I hasten to add is something of a passion of mine."

"That much was evident when I was working for you," said Maud, refusing the offer of a dessert from the sweet trolley and asking for a coffee. "I wish you well, Alfred and I am sure that if you ever need a spare pair of hands I can see my way to helping out."

"Thanks Maud, I really appreciate that," said Alfred. "A brandy with your coffee, I insist and I shall arrange a car to take you back to Great Yarmouth so let's just relax and enjoy the peace and quiet while we can."

Don Stevens called in on Bob Scott.

"Hello Don and what brings you here on a Sunday morning? Come to see that none of the sets are left behind?"

Don sat down. "Goodness no, that's what the likes of Matthew are for. No Bob, I have been thinking over some arrangements for next year. I think that Rita made a bloody good job with this show and I would like to carry on with that arrangement."

Bob nodded his approval. "As you know Goldberg Holdings, who own the pier, leave me to my own devices and I am very grateful to you for being able to step in when the Delfont organisation decided to pull the plug on *The Sands* last year. No one at Goldberg has the slightest interest in theatre as such. Many of their other investments are with freight. *The Sands* was something they purchased for a song back in the late fifties when this was owned by the local council who wanted shot of the responsibility and needed the money."

"I keep dropping hints to my wife that I will hang up my hat, but I love variety and now Elsie seems quite keen for us to find a small cottage or house here so that she can spend more time away from London."

Bob smiled. "Yes, I rather got the feeling that Mrs Stevens was enjoying working with Rita and Jenny after the trouble you both had in 1969."

"It's okay, Bob you can say the name out loud. It was a stupid oversight on my part, but it did prove one thing: that I love my wife more than anything or anybody, including this business, but of course I would never let on to her."

There was a silence only broken by the ticking of the clock above Bob's desk.

"Sorry Bob, I am holding you up and I know you are off on holiday soon. I wanted to ask you if it would be possible for me to use *Ted's Variety Bar* to carry out some business early next month. I would like to meet with some acts and as a few of those I am interested in are quite local, I would sooner it be here than London. I was going to ask Rita if I could use her office but they are pretty tight in there and the thought of using a room at a hotel doesn't fill me with excitement."

"Not to mention the cost," said Bob. "They can charge what they like, especially out of season when they need the revenue. Let's have a look in the diary. How would Monday the fourth of October suit you?"

Don consulted his pocket diary. "That would be good actually as it would give me time to invite the acts along. What would access be like?"

"Beverley will be working here as normal and I think Mrs Buckle will be here tidying things up. Not too sure about Matthew at the moment. Jack could be on hand if I asked him to be. It would be best for your guests to come through the stage door and then into the bar via backstage, rather than using the entrance from the pier. We plan to close *Ted's* at the end of next week. I still haven't decided whether it will be viable to open it in the winter months."

"That sounds fine Bob, thank you very much. I can put the wheels in motion." He stood up and shook hands with Bob. "If I don't see you before, have a great holiday."

Wednesday 22 September

"Right, let's get you sorted out once and for all," said Maud. "Give me the pricing gun and the conversion chart. You just make sure that all your invoices are up-to-date and ready for the audit stock-take. I have said this to you before, Enid, you have to get to grips with decimal currency, it isn't going to go away."

Enid handed Maud the gun. "It doesn't make any sense. I went to the *House of Doris* last week and she wanted to charge me one pound and fifty new pence for a wash, cut and perm, it only used to be twelve and six."

Maud gave a big deep sigh as only she could, looked at the pricing gun and for a split second wished it was real and loaded with bullets.

Monday 4 October

The easterly wind was at its worst and the warmer days of summer had disappeared. Putting her best foot forward Maud set out to *The Golden Sands* where she had promised Beverley a helping hand with the box office returns and accounts for the season now that Bob Scott had left for his annual holiday.

She let herself into the theatre with her pass key and could hear the dulcet tones of Mona Buckle who was busy cleaning everything in sight before leaving her post for the winter. She bumped into Matthew Taylor who was counting the stores and checking off what they were short of.

"I see Matthew has stayed on then," said Maud taking off her mac and hanging it up.

"Only for a couple of days," said Beverley. "He doesn't want to stay on, he left Bob a note last Saturday, says he want to return to London. Great Yarmouth, he says, is too quiet for him."

"Oh, that's a shame because Alfred Barton was going to offer him some work at the hotel over the winter months with accommodation thrown in."

Beverley shrugged her shoulders. "Well if he has been offered he hasn't mentioned it. He likes to keep himself to himself, that one, although when all is said and done he has kept on top of things here."

The rain could be heard beating down outside, the office windows became steamed up inside and it was a job to see any daylight through them. Maud and Beverley worked harmoniously together, Beverley providing a packed lunch for them both and at odd times they could hear a Hoover or Mona singing a refrain from one hymn or another.

Don Stevens had been auditioning acts in the *Variety Bar* during the morning and was getting ready to call it day having a clear idea who he would suggest to Rita as a possible line-up for next season. He sorted through some papers and placed them in his briefcase. He sat back and relaxed, it had been a long day and his eyes felt heavy, that last drink Matthew had given him had been strong.

Backstage Matthew was moving the remaining boxes of rigging to the storage cupboards. He looked at his watch and crept into the *Variety Bar*. He removed the glass from the table in front of Don and, after washing it, replaced it on the shelf below.

He closed the door behind him and went and sat in the front row of the theatre where he opened his lunchbox taking out a sausage roll and a bag of crisps.

"Now look what you have done," said Mona limping along the aisle. "You've got crumbs everywhere; I shall have to get my crevice tool out again and give that a good Hoovering."

Matthew put his hands up "Sorry Mrs Buckle I didn't mean to make more work for you."

Mona looked at Matthew "Are you alright Mr Taylor, you don't look your usual self, is something troubling you?"

Matthew shook his head. "No not really, but thanks for asking."

"I can see things Mr Taylor, I have the gift."

Matthew sat quietly and looked down at the floor.

"You have a great sadness in your face Mr Taylor, I have seen it before and something is troubling you today. It is none of my business of course, but if you want to talk I am happy to listen."

Matthew's shoulders began to shake and at first Mona thought he was laughing at her, but it soon became apparent that he wasn't laughing, he was crying. He took a photograph from his wallet and handed it to Mona.

"Is this a relation, she looks a lot like you?"

Matthew nodded. "It's my late sister Gwen, Gwen Taylor."

Mona studied the photograph. "I have seen this lady before. I never forget a face. Where do I known her from?"

Matthew sat very still and said nothing, wiping his eyes on his handkerchief.

"I know where I have seen your sister before," said Mona. "She was in the papers a couple of years ago, something to do with this theatre am I right?"

Matthew nodded. "It's because of her connection with this theatre and Don Stevens that she is dead now."

"I will go and make you a cup of tea," said Mona handing back the photograph. "I think you need a cup of tea. Then we can have a chat."

"At least the rain has stopped," said Maud. "I think the sun is trying to break through. My goodness, will you look at the time it's almost three-thirty."

"We really ought to call it a day," said Beverley "We have really made great strides today, if you are free tomorrow Maud, perhaps we can finish up then."

"Of course, of course," said Maud

"Usual rates and a packed lunch thrown in," said Beverley. "I wonder if Mona is done yet. I haven't heard her come along the corridor; she usually pops her head in when she has finished."

Beverley picked up her car keys. "Come on Maud, I can give you a lift. I want to pop in to *Palmers* and pick up a birthday present for Ian, there's a couple of nice shirts I had my eye on, we are off to a wedding in a couple of weeks' time, so I can kill two birds with one stone."

Maud followed Beverley to the main door. "Blast it's stuck," said Beverley. "It won't open."

"Try your key, maybe Mona locked it when she left."

Beverley turned the key and tried to pull it open but something was preventing her from doing so. "Maud this door, it won't open, I think it has been chained or something from the outside. Oh don't say Matthew has forgotten we are here and gone off for the day. Come on, we will have to go through the theatre and out the stage door, if not we can get through the *Variety Bar*."

They made their way into the auditorium. "What on earth is that smell?" said Maud sniffing the air. "It smells like petrol to me."

"Oh my God," cried Beverley. "Look, there are flames coming from the bar area, we are on fire! Quick, let me phone the fire brigade."

Beverley dashed back to the office and tried to get an outside line. "I don't believe this, the phone line is dead."

"We'll have to try and get out some other way," said Maud taking command of the situation. "Let's try the office window."

"No bloody good," said Beverley they have bars across the top and bottom for security reasons, what the hell are we going to do?"

"Rita you had better grab your coat and come with me quickly," said Jenny with Elsie at her side who was looking scared.

Rita looked up from her desk. "Whatever is the matter? You two look as if you have seen a ghost."

"It's *The Golden Sands*," said Jenny with a tremor in her voice. "It's on fire. We have just heard it on the BBC radio programme; fire engines are on their way now."

"Oh my word," said Rita, following the others down the staircase. "Maud was working there with Beverley today and I think Mona said something about it being the last day she was needed. Someone had better get in touch with their husbands."

Elsie turned pale. "And Don was supposed to come here when he had finished his business at the theatre."

The shocking scene that greeted them was like something they had only seen in films. Flames were leaping in the air at the end of the pier and the fire brigade were doing their best to bring things under control. The sounds of an approaching ambulance and police sirens filled the air. An explosion made the gathering crowd gasp in horror and people were heard muttering that the beer canisters in *Ted's Variety Bar* were probably the cause.

The cries from fireman could be heard calling the names of those missing. Through the chaos one fireman was seen carrying what looked like a metal bucket by a news reporter using binoculars.

Elsie trembled as Jenny put a comforting arm around her shoulder. "everything will be alright, you'll see Elsie."

A figure wrapped in a blanket was seen being escorted to an ambulance by a fireman and a voice shouted, "Jack me old mate, are you okay?"

Rita turned to see the anxious face of a man who was struggling to get through the crowd and recognised him from a snapshot she had seen. Rita grabbed hold of his arm. "It's Ian, isn't it?"

The man nodded, fear etched across his face. "Beverley my wife, she's in there somewhere."

"Hold on me old lover, they are doing all they can. Best stay here with us for the time being."

A very calm lone figure at the back of *The Golden Sands Theatre* stood at the end of the pier looking out to the seascape beyond. Climbing onto the railings the man sat gripping the sides of the barrier and stared at the turbulent waves which were rising and falling as the wind became stronger. Turning to look back, he smiled. As the voice of a fireman called out, his hands lost their grip of the wet railings and he fell forward into the crashing waves of an angry North Sea below.

A Word from the Author and Acknowledgements

With the exception of the references to the stars of the day, The Beverley Sisters, Ted Rogers, Dora Bryan, Frank Ifield etc. all other characters in this story are fictitious and do not represent any person either living or dead.

Rick O'Shea and the Ramblers appear by kind permission of David McDermott.

At the time of going to print - The Britannia Pier Theatre continues to present one-night attractions during summer months. St Georges Theatre has a varied programme of concerts and plays that will delight audiences. The Gorleston Pavilion is the heart of entertainment with shows, pantomimes, visiting theatre companies and variety acts throughout the year. The Hippodrome Circus continues circus tradition with a varied bill throughout the year with Peter Jay and son Jack overseeing productions.

Palmers Department Store in the Market Place remains Great Yarmouth's prestigious store where quality is affirmed and a restaurant that is bound to please the hungry shopper.

Lacons

Lacons Brewery, famous for its Falcon emblem, landed back in Great Yarmouth last year after a 45-year hiatus with the launch of three new permanent beers – ENCORE, LEGACY and AFFINTY. I would like to thank the brewery for giving me permission to use the new beers in *my novels*, and take this opportunity to wish them every continued success.

My Thanks to

My many faithful readers, especially Steve and his family (you know who you are) for their continued loyalty and support who make my job all the more rewarding.

The emails I receive, the comments to my website and via on line media, I always enjoy reading and listen very carefully to what you tell me.

None of this would be possible if I didn't have such a great team working behind the scenes at my publishers in Peterborough: Simon, Pauline, Marika and Curtis.

I must make a special mention to Shane for additional ideas and to Cousin George for his gentle nudges along the way.

A Note to my Readers

Authors, proof readers and editors are human and while every endeavour has been made to ensure that text and punctuation are correct at the time of going to print, please forgive any slight error.

I sincerely hope you will enjoy this third outing in my Tales from Great Yarmouth series and if you do please tell your friends and ask them to purchase a copy for themselves or as a gift.

And coming in 2016 my new novel - "BACKSTAGE" - please check my website for details.